W9-BNU-595

TURTLE MOON

ALSO BY ALICE HOFFMAN

Property of
The Drowning Season
Angel Landing
White Horses
Fortune's Daughter
Illumination Night
At Risk
Seventh Heaven

Alice Hoffman

TURTLE MOON

G. P. PUTNAM'S SONS   NEW YORK

This is a work of fiction. The events described are
imaginary, and the characters are fictitious and
not intended to represent specific living persons.

Copyright © 1992 by Alice Hoffman
All rights reserved. This book, or parts thereof,
may not be reproduced in any form without permission.
Published by G. P. Putnam's Sons,
200 Madison Avenue, New York, NY 10016.
Published simultaneously in Canada

The text of this book is set in Caslon.

Library of Congress Cataloging-in-Publication Data

Hoffman, Alice.
Turtle Moon / Alice Hoffman.
p.   cm.
ISBN 0-399-13720-3
I. Title.
PS3558.03447T87   1992   91-37222 CIP
813'.54—dc20

Designed by MaryJane DiMassi
Printed in the United States of America
2   3   4   5   6   7   8   9   10

This book is printed on acid-free paper.

TO M.

All the way to heaven is heaven, all of it a kiss.

—Harvey Oxenhorn
1951–1990

TURTLE MOON

Chapter One

THE last major crime in the town of Verity was in 1958, when one of the Platts shot his brother in an argument over a Chevy Nomad they had bought together on time. Usually it's so quiet you can hear the strangler figs dropping their fruit on the hoods of parked cars, leaving behind pulp and tiny black seeds. Since Verity is the most humid spot in eastern Florida, local people know enough to drink their coffee iced in the morning. The air all around the town limits is so thick that sometimes a soul cannot rise and instead attaches itself to a stranger, landing right between the shoulder blades with a thud that carries no more weight than a hummingbird.

Charles Verity, who founded the town, after killing off as many native people as he could, is said to have discovered this the hard way. He couldn't get rid of the spirits of all the men he'd murdered; they perched up and down his spine and on top of his cookstove, until he caught them in a sugar bowl, then tied the lid closed with thick brown string so they couldn't escape. Charles Verity swore he would live forever. Every night he drank a bitter tea made from the bark of the paradise tree to ensure his good health, but as it turned out he was eaten by an alligator up by the pond where the municipal golf course was later built. Each year, on Charles Verity's birthday, children parade down Main Street to the parking lot of the medical center, where a mud pit ringed with ropes is set up. For ten dollars, anyone can wrestle a papier-mâché alligator and raise funds for the burn ward. Up until the early sixties there were alligator farms all around the outskirts of Verity. At least once a year there would be a big escape, and Half Moon Road, which is now part of the Interstate, would be green and slithery for days, until a posse went out with shotguns and fishing nets. When breeding for profit became a federal offense, Verity turned its past around to suit itself, naming the high school football team the Gators, and featuring Alligator Salad in most restaurants, a mixture of spinach, green pepper, avocado, and chopped egg tinted with green food coloring.

People in Verity like to talk, but the one thing they neglect to mention to outsiders is that something is wrong with the month of May. It isn't the humidity, or even the heat, which is so fierce and sudden it can make grown men cry. Every May, when the sea turtles begin their migration across West Main Street, mistaking the glow of streetlights for the moon, people go a little bit crazy. At least one teenage boy comes close to slamming his car right into the gumbo-limbo tree that grows beside the Burger King. Girls run away from home, babies cry all night, ficus hedges explode into flame, and during one particularly awful May, half a dozen rattlesnakes set themselves up in the phone booth outside the 7-Eleven and refused to budge until June.

At this difficult time of the year people who grew up in Verity often slip two aspirins into their cans of Coke; they wear sunglasses and avoid making any major decisions. They try not to quit their jobs, or smack their children, or run off to North Carolina with the serviceman who just fixed their VCR. They make certain to stay out of the ocean, since the chemical plant on Seminole Point always leaks in the first week of May, so that the yellowfin float to the surface, bringing sharks closer to shore. In the past few years, there has been an influx of newcomers, lured by the low rents and wild hibiscus. As a result, Verity is now home to more divorced women from New York than any other town in the state of Florida. None of these women had any idea of the sort of mess the month of May in Verity could make of their lives, any more than they knew what daily exposure to chlorine could do to their hair. There were now dozens of greenheaded women all over town, all addicted to Diet Dr Pepper, and each and every one of them was shocked to discover that in Verity mosquitoes grew to the size of bumblebees and that the sea grape, which grew wild along the beach, could pull their children right into the thicket if they didn't keep to the wooden paths.

After midnight, when the heat was almost bearable and anole lizards ran fearlessly across quarry tile floors, these women never wept but did their laundry instead. While the bleach was added to the white wash and the laundry softener doled out, it became clear that although some of the children these women had transplanted were doing well, most were not. There were toddlers who called out for their fathers in the middle of the night, and boys who dreamed so deeply of the houses where they grew up they'd wake damp with sweat, smelling of cut grass. There were sullen teenage girls

13

running up astronomical phone bills, and babies so accustomed to ranch houses they got hysterical at the sight of an elevator.

At 27 Long Boat Street, just off West Main, in a pink stucco condominium facing the flat blue bay, there lived a twelve-year-old boy, a mean little Scorpio named Keith Rosen, who would have liked nothing better than to knock someone's block off. He was so mean he could cut his own finger with a serrated steak knife and not flinch. He could drop a brick on his bare foot and not cry out loud. Last week, when his only friend, Laddy Stern, dared him to pierce his ear with an embroidery needle, Keith didn't even bleed. The following afternoon he stole an earring shaped like a silver skull from a jewelry concession at the flea market over at the Sunshine Drive-In. He has never been a particularly good boy, but after eight months in Florida, he is horrid. Already, he has been suspended from school three times. He is willing to steal almost anything: lunch money, teachers' wallets, birthstone rings right off his classmates' fingers. He keeps everything in a secret stash in the laundry room down in the basement, inside a hole he punched into the plaster behind a washing machine.

Punishments are pointless. They don't work with him. He is no longer allowed to see Laddy Stern, not since they were caught cutting school and drinking Kahlúa and Coke, but who can really stop him? Laddy's mom is the hostess at the yacht club restaurant, and she works odd hours, so Keith still goes over to their condo whenever he pleases. That is where he spends most of the first day of May, and by the time he leaves, after a vicious argument that has left Laddy with a bloody nose, it is already ninety-nine in the shade, although where he bicycles, on Long Boat Street, there is no shade. He's dizzy from the Miller Lites he drank and the half pack of Marlboros he chain-smoked, and it isn't so easy to avoid the smashed turtle shells. Hard green globes the size of Scooter Pies line the asphalt and clog up the sewer traps. There is no point in Keith's trying to talk to his mother. Most days he sneaks out of the apartment while she is getting dressed for work, or he waits in bed until he's sure she's left, so he won't have to see her and pretend to be normal or cheerful or whatever it is she wants him to be.

He bikes as fast as he can, through the heat waves, past the surfers at Drowned Man Beach. He keeps at it until his lungs hurt, then he rides over the curb and into the park at the corner of West Main and Long Boat, where he pulls out the cigarettes and matches he stole from Laddy. It isn't his parents' divorce that bothers him. He could have lived with that. It was the way things just happened to him. He wanted to live with his father, but who asked him? His parents argued with each other until they came to a decision, and now his mother is stuck with him, when everyone knows they have never gotten along. He never climbed into her lap or held her hand. He knows he was a difficult child, he's been told often enough. He threw off his blanket, rattled the bars of his crib, bit baby-sitters so hard he left teeth marks in their flesh. His mother can pretend to want him all she likes, but the only thing he wants is to go back to where the heat doesn't make you break out in red bumps, and every restaurant doesn't serve grits and Alligator Salad, and some people have fathers.

Keith balances his bike against his hip, then lights a cig-arette, which he keeps cupped in his palm, the way he's seen the high school boys smoke, even though the embers burn his skin. Nothing ever happened in Verity. That was a fact. He could die of boredom, right now, his heart could give out and he'd shrivel up in the heat and turn purple before anyone thought to look for him. He'd probably fossilize before his mother reported him missing. When his heart doesn't stop, Keith props his bike up against a trash can, then flings himself on a wooden bench so he can blow smoke rings in the air. The smoke rings just hang there, dangerous white clouds going nowhere. School won't be out for another fifteen minutes, but at the far end of the park some teenagers, playing hooky, toss a Frisbee around. As far as Keith is concerned, anyone down here who is capable of enjoying himself is an idiot. The high school boys are so busy diving for the Frisbee and pounding each other on the back they don't notice the patrol car in the parking lot, idling beneath an inkwood tree. Keith sits up, interested in spite of himself when he sees "K9" on the side of the car. They don't allow dogs at the condominium where he lives. If the super discovers that you have even a guinea pig you're out forever. There's a list of rules three pages long you have to agree to before you move in. That way there's no argument when they insist you take a shower before you swim in the pool, and you can't even swim alone without an adult until you're thirteen. If Keith could have a dog, it would be just like the one in the patrol car, a big German shepherd that sits perfectly still, eyeing the boys playing Frisbee. He would love to see what the super had to say about a dog like that; just let anyone try to give him orders if he had a monster like that on a leash.

When the cop gets out of his car, Keith hunkers down on the bench. He was suspended yesterday, and technically he's not required to be in school. Still, he hasn't informed his mother of the suspension, so he figures he's guilty of something. The cop has a mean scar across his forehead and black hair that reaches over the collar of his jacket. He looks like he could pick you up and toss you, a long way. Plus he has that dog, just the turn of a car handle away. They didn't have cops like this back in Great Neck, where Keith grew up. You never saw a pickup with a gun rack attached, or dead turtles in the street. As Keith watches, the cop approaches the high school boys; before he can reach them the boys take off through a grove of cabbage palms, leaving their Frisbee behind. The cop picks up the Frisbee, then goes back to his car to let his dog out. The dog circles around the cop's legs, banging its body against him, until the cop lets the Frisbee fly. Then the dog takes off like black lightning, scaring the red-crowned parrots in the palms until they scream and take flight. Beneath a cloud of birds, Keith grabs for his bike, then hops on and races out of the park, toward West Main. He's sick to his stomach from his last cigarette, but he's also completely charged. This was almost dangerous. The cop could have turned and spied him; the dog might have attacked. You can get addicted to trouble if you're not careful. You can feel like you're flying, when all you're doing is pedaling through the Florida heat. Instead of heading straight home, Keith turns into the driveway of the Burger King, where he isn't allowed to stop before supper. As he walks inside, he reaches in his pants pocket for the money he stole out of a classmate's locker just yesterday. It's there, every cent of it, and Keith feels a wicked surge of elation. Sooner or later, he's going to get caught.

Julian Cash slouches down behind the wheel of the patrol car as he passes by the Burger King. Through the plate-glass window, he can see the little truant from the park devouring a burger and fries. Julian has seen dozens of these hotshots, boys who pretend to be fearless and dare somebody to prove them wrong. Julian himself isn't scared of much, but he avoids the Burger King. He doesn't care what anyone says, he knows the truth about the gumbo-limbo tree that grows at the edge of the parking lot. On the night of his seventeenth birthday he crashed into it, and twenty years later he still has the scar to remind him. The plain truth is, he would rather confront a psychopath hopped up on drugs than be forced to pull up to the Burger King's drive-in window.

Twenty years ago the Burger King didn't exist, and in its place was a stretch of gumbo-limbos. Julian used to park there with Janey Bass until dawn, then drive her home and watch as she climbed up the drain pipe to her bedroom window. Back then, there were still islands in the marshes around Verity, although some of them weren't any bigger than half a mile across, home to little more than cotton-mouths and foxes. The town expanded slowly, embracing the marshes with a Winn Dixie and a Mobil station, and now all the islands are connected to each other by roadways that funnel over the creeks and into the Interstate. There aren't any more coral snakes in the branches of the mangroves and you can get *USA Today* and *The New York Times* as well as the *Verity Sun Herald* over at the general store, and at Chuck and Karl's diner they now serve croissants along with their hickory-flavored coffee. The first time Julian was appre-hended, two weeks after his seventeenth birthday, he was standing outside Chuck and Karl's, waiting to be caught. He had a bowie knife hidden in his left boot and a hundred and fifty dollars in quarters, which would have seemed suspicious even if all the parking meters on West Main hadn't just been smashed open with an axe. It was May of course, and the temperature hadn't fallen below one hundred for days, and before June came around, Julian would be apprehended five more times, although he was never officially charged with anything. Those were the days when the Verity police force was made up of two men, and one of them was a Cash through marriage, not that he, or any of the Cashes, had spoken to Julian since the night of the accident.

They sent him away, to the Boys' School of Correction in Tallahassee, and that was where he first got interested in dogs. There was a hundred-and-twenty-pound bloodhound named Big Boy whose job it was to track down anyone courageous or stupid enough to scale the barbed-wire fence. Big Boy stank, and his ears were infected, but appearances didn't mean much to Julian. His own mother had fainted the first time she saw Julian and she gave him away that very night. As a little boy he was so ugly that tree frogs would go limp with fear in the palm of his hand. So Big Boy's red eyes and fleas didn't put Julian off in the least. He stole pieces of meat from the dining hall and started hanging around the kennel after lights out. It didn't take long for Julian to discover that if you looked a dog straight in the eye and thought real hard, you could get him to come to you and lie at your feet without ever having to say one word. By the end of the year, just before Julian got his high school equivalency, the director of the school got rid of Big Boy. They could hold the sweat-stained shirts of escaped boys under the dog's nose for as long as they wanted, but Big Boy would just calmly set off and track down Julian Cash every time.

In all his years of working with dogs, at the army base in Hartford Beach, and now with the Verity police, Julian has come to believe that there are two kinds of dogs that go bad. The kind that go bad slowly, whether from inbreeding or

19

being beaten it didn't much matter. And the other ones, good dogs who suddenly turned on a night when there was a full moon, hauling themselves up from the living room rug and a peaceful sleep, to jump through a window or attack a child for no apparent reason. Julian Cash attributes this to a short circuit in the brain, and that is why he no longer believes in crimes of passion. When men snapped it wasn't passion, it was only a short circuit, just like that well-behaved dog who was after a ball one minute, an arm and a leg the next. The fact that this sort of behavior is so much rarer in dogs than in people, who seem to snap like crazy, especially during the month of May, makes no difference to the nine other men and women on the Verity police force. Not one of them will approach Julian if his dogs aren't leashed, yet these officers will break up a bar fight without thinking twice. They'll stop a speeder on a deserted back road when they know damn well there could easily be a weapon in the glove compartment. They don't seem to understand that it's possible to know exactly who a dog is by looking it in the eye for fifteen seconds. This is not, and never will be, possible with a man.

Twenty years ago, when Julian drove through the hot Florida night in his Oldsmobile, he truly believed it was possible to reach up and steal the stars right out of the sky. Now he doesn't even see the stars anymore. He doesn't look up. The nature of his job as a tracker forces him to look down, and that's why he can recognize the footprint of an armadillo in the dust. He can hear a caterpillar chewing sweet bay leaves. Since he sees no reason for neighbors, he lives out in what little is left of the marshes, past Miss Giles's place, in an old cabin some people say belonged to Charles Verity. A kennel runs along the far side of the cabin, built with the strongest chain link available, and this is where Julian leaves the big dog, Arrow, since his reaction to people is much more extreme than Julian's. Julian usually has the other dog, Loretta, with him, even when he isn't on duty. When he stops for supper, he picks up something for Loretta as well, often from the Pizza Hut. Julian believes in rewarding his dogs, even if this means tomato sauce on the upholstery of his cruiser. This is not the way dogs were handled in the army. On the base in Hartford Beach, small riding crops were used on dogs that refused to perform, and the lieutenant was proud to claim there wasn't a dog born he couldn't train to attack in two weeks. It gives Julian great pleasure to know he's never once used force on a dog, and he's been asked several times to instruct the K9 corps at the base.

In all things, Julian knows, what you need is patience and time, although some talents can't be taught. Loretta is a great tracker, much better than Big Boy ever was. In seconds flat, she can search out a bundle of marijuana hidden in a packed suitcase, even if it's been locked securely inside a car trunk. Last summer, when the mosquitoes were so thick you could hardly breathe and the heat sent you reeling, she found a lost hiker over near Lake Okeechobee long after the state troopers had given up hope. With her record, Julian figures she deserves a slice of pizza now and then; hell, he would buy her a Diet Coke if that's what she wanted. It's his other dog, Arrow, who's the difficult one. He would have been put down two years ago if Julian had not seen him pacing the yard behind the animal hospital on the day he took Loretta to the vet for her rabies shot.

Arrow's owner had bought him right after her divorce, for protection and company, from a religious order that raised dogs and had greedily allowed the breeding of a bitch known to be vicious. The result was Arrow, a hundred-pound monster who was so out of control his owner could no longer walk him down the street. When Julian stood by the fence, Arrow charged him, on his hind legs, biting at the chain link, standing as tall as a man. That afternoon, Julian took him home. The vet sedated Arrow and helped lift him into the backseat of the patrol car, and when the dog awoke, trapped in Julian's kennel, he went crazy. Julian had to wear heavy leather gloves just to set his dish of food inside the kennel gate. It took six weeks before Julian could trust Arrow not to attack when his back was turned, and even now the dog can't be off his lead around people. There are times when he startles for no apparent reason other than the sound of the wind or a shift in air pressure. That may be why he took naturally to his specialized training. He sees not what is there but what isn't, and that's what makes him the best air dog in the state, with a sense of smell so fine he can gauge the slightest difference in the air around him. There isn't a park ranger or state trooper who hasn't heard about Arrow. They call him the dog from hell, and some rangers insist he be muzzled while tracking.

The officers at the Verity police station don't like Arrow, and they don't like his owner much, either. Julian knows what they say about him down at the station house: that he can't find anything right with human beings or anything wrong with dogs, that he encourages the merlins who nest in the sweet bays and bald cypresses on his property to frighten visitors away, that he's never once sat down for so much as a cup of coffee with any of his fellow officers. Well, if people want to complain, let them; let them get down on all fours and shimmy through the sea grape and poisonwood and see how they like sand up their noses and fire ants stinging their feet. Let them just try to make their way through the strangler figs and the saw grass. Chances are, not one of them would ever find a baby sleeping in the reeds.

❀

Bethany Lee, who had never heard of Verity before she drove into town, left New York last October. She didn't think about what she was doing, so she didn't begin to panic until she was in southern New Jersey. The full moon had washed the turnpike with silver light, and then, quite suddenly, a drenching rain began to fall. In the trunk of Bethany's Saab there was a suitcase, and inside the suitcase she had twenty thousand dollars in cash and three necklaces—two strands of diamonds and a string of gold and sapphires. Bethany's hands shook as she tried to keep the car steady; each time a truck passed her, a tidal wave of rain slapped against the Saab. Her baby, Rachel, who was then seven months old, was asleep in her car seat, warmly dressed in pink pajamas with feet, unaware that the rain was so hard windshield wipers could do nothing to improve visibility.

Six hours earlier, Bethany had set off to take Rachel to the park, but on this day she drove right on past. Rachel had let out a cry of delight when she saw the slide and the swings, but Bethany ignored the tightness in her own throat and stepped down harder on the gas. If she was lucky, the housekeeper wouldn't worry and phone the police when she arrived to find the doors locked and no one at home. If she was unlucky, as she had been for quite some time, her husband already knew she was gone.

She probably should have pulled over that night, but she kept going at a slow crawl, never more than thirty miles an hour, until she reached Delaware. She parked down the street from the Wilmington Greyhound station and when Rachel woke up, fussing, her diaper wet, Bethany climbed over into the backseat, told the baby what a good girl she was, and quickly changed her. Then she hoisted Rachel on her shoulder, grabbed the diaper bag, and went out to the trunk for her suitcase. She left the Saab where it was, keys in the ignition.

They washed up in the ladies' room at the bus station, got some breakfast from the snack bar, including a glass of milk to fill Rachel's bottle, then waited for the eleven-o'clock bus to Atlanta. By then, Bethany had not slept for two nights, and she barely had the nerve to ask for her bus ticket. In the past four months she had spent thirty thousand dollars on lawyers, and it had not done her a bit of good. If she had just taken off at the start, she would have had fifty thousand in her suitcase instead of twenty, but she had never made a real decision until the day she drove past the park. She'd had faith in her lawyer. She believed him when he insisted she'd easily win custody, but somehow it hadn't worked out that way, and it took months for Bethany to realize she'd been tricked. It turned out that the house in Great Neck belonged not to her and Randy but to his family's business. Even the Saab belonged to Randy's family. And now they had decided the baby was theirs, too.

Bethany had been a freshman at Oberlin when she met Randy. His sister, Lynne, was her roommate, and she'd warned Bethany that her brother was the handsomest man she would ever meet. He had dozens of old sweethearts from high school and college pestering him, but when he saw Bethany he fell in love instantly. He told her it was because she was the most beautiful girl he had ever seen, and in fact she looked more like him than his own sister, with the same dark hair and clear olive skin. But after a while Bethany came to believe that he wanted her so badly because he had never in his life met a girl quite so naive. She was perfect, if not for him, for his family. His parents picked their house and their furniture and their cars, and they thought Bethany was the sweetest thing they'd ever seen. It didn't seem to matter so much that Randy was rarely home. Bethany didn't question him when he worked late or on weekends. He managed, that way, to be both married, which his parents insisted upon, and single, which was the way he liked it. And the truth was, he seemed more relieved than upset when Bethany began to talk about a separation during her pregnancy.

He moved out five weeks after the baby was born, and he might have been happy to be a weekend father if his parents hadn't put pressure on him. Rachel was their grand-child, their first and only, and they were willing to pay any amount to a lawyer who could win her. Randy's parents, and even his sister, had testified against Bethany, and her med-ical records had been subpoenaed from the times when she was depressed, especially right after the baby was born and the marriage was already dead and she began taking Elavil. Right before God and her lawyer and everyone, she was ripped apart until she herself was almost convinced her child would be better off without her. While they waited for the court's final decree, Bethany had to let Rachel go off to visit her father every weekend. There had been strong words between them by then, and Randy said he couldn't bear to see Bethany face to face. Instead, his parents sent a driver. Every Friday night Bethany had to stand and do nothing while Rachel screamed and the driver forced her into her car seat. Often, Bethany had to turn away. She just couldn't bear to see her baby cry, and afterward she'd be sick to her stomach; she'd have the dry heaves for hours.

It might have continued that way Friday after Friday, until the final decree, and Bethany might never have driven through that horrible storm in New Jersey, if she hadn't turned at the instant when Rachel was flailing her arms and screaming and seen the exasperated driver slap the baby's face. And still, Bethany was so paralyzed she didn't run to the car and grab her daughter. She stood there, in shock, beside the automatic sprinklers that came on each day at dusk, too horrified to weep. The next morning, Bethany went to the bank to make her first withdrawal, and she went every day that week, until the one joint account Randy had not closed was all but drained. On the following Friday she refused to answer the door when the driver came for Rachel. She turned off all the lights and sat on the kitchen floor, holding Rachel and rocking back and forth while the driver rang the bell for what seemed like forever. An hour after the driver left, the phone started ringing. Bethany ignored it. She fixed Rachel a bottle and put her to sleep in her own big bed, with pillows all around her so she wouldn't roll off. Finally the phone stopped ringing and Bethany's heart no longer felt like it was going to burst. She actually thought it was over and went to get herself a bowl of cornflakes and milk, but at a little after nine Randy's car pulled into the driveway. Bethany sat on the couch, watching the door shake as he knocked, harder and harder, and when it stopped she thought, for a moment, that he had given up. She had forgotten he still had a key, although he couldn't do much more than reach his arm halfway inside, since the safety chain had been fastened.

"God damn it," he called. "Bethany?"

Bethany sat on the couch while he screamed at her through the crack in the door. She was fairly certain that she was no longer breathing. Throughout their marriage he had never once shouted at her or called her names; it didn't even sound like his voice. Then she realized, all in a rush, that they were no longer the people they had been, neither of them, and that that was what happened once you started to fight over custody.

"I'm going to break the door down," he vowed.

She really couldn't move, that was the amazing thing. She couldn't have let him in if she'd wanted to. When the door didn't give way, Randy backed off. Bethany was still on the couch when she heard the glass breaking. He had put his fist right through the living room window. Bethany's breathing was hard and sharp as she ran into the kitchen and went through the drawers. She had a rubbery feeling in her legs, as though she might collapse, but instead she grabbed the bread knife, a long one with a serrated edge, and ran back to the living room. Randy was shouting her name, as if they didn't have neighbors or a baby asleep in their bed. He had unlocked the window and was sliding it up when Bethany went to the front door and flung it open. It was an Indian summer night, and Bethany wore only shorts and a white blouse. She stood in the doorway, her long dark hair electrified, her white shirt illuminated by moonlight, waving the knife in front of her.

"Get out of here!" she screamed in a voice she had never heard before.

Randy walked right toward her. There were shards of broken glass in his hair and blood on his hand and down his arm, staining one of his favorite blue shirts. "Go on," he said. "Act crazy. That's what you do best."

"I mean it," Bethany told him.

The knife didn't feel the least bit heavy in her hands. A few months before, the most she had to worry about was picking up lamb chops for dinner and whether the gardener had planted white or purple wisteria. Now, as Randy walked closer, Bethany thought about Rachel being taken from her for no good reason, and the knife felt more and more comfortable. Randy had that serious, sweetly concerned look on his face, the one that made women go limp with desire. He had thought briefly of being an actor—he'd been the lead in all his high school plays—and although his father had finally convinced him to go into the family business, Bethany could see he would have made a good actor. He could make you believe that you needed him, that he cared.

"The decision is up to the court," he told Bethany that night. "There's no point in us fighting."

He had almost reached the door by then. Bethany jabbed the knife in the air and he stepped back. For a moment she could see she had truly frightened him.

"You can have anything you want," she told him. She'd grown up in Ohio and her voice had a sweet, flat timbre, although tonight it was little more than a whisper. "You just can't have Rachel."

"You want to tell that to my parents?" he said.

There was a dinner party going on next door at the Kleinmans', and they could hear laughter through the open windows. They used to go to those parties together. Bethany would bring her ribbon cake, and Randy a blue glass pitcher of margaritas, and when they came home they'd take a shower together and get into bed.

"If you try to take her, I'll kill you," Bethany said in her quiet voice.

"Can I quote you?" Randy said. "In court?"

Bethany lowered the knife to her side. She was a beautiful girl who had never finished college or balanced a checkbook and who needed to take antidepressants in spite of the fact that she'd married the boy everyone had been in love with.

"We should stop fighting," Randy said.

"You're right," Bethany agreed.

"We're not going to kill each other, we're just going to make each other miserable, and that's just the way it's going to be," Randy said.

That was when Bethany knew she wasn't going to win her case. She left two days later, and during the bus trip through the Carolinas she invented new names for herself and the baby. When they got to Atlanta she found a pawnshop and sold both her diamond necklaces and her wedding ring, keeping the sapphires and the two gold-plated rings she'd inherited from her mother. She also discovered that if she went out behind the used-tire shop down the street and paid two thousand in cash she could get a fake ID from the state of her choice. She chose New Jersey, so she would always be reminded of that moonlit ride when the rain came down so suddenly and she refused to stop. She, who hadn't driven any farther than the local shops during the time she'd been married, just kept on going, outdistancing the rain.

They were headed for Miami, but they got off the bus in Hartford Beach to buy diapers and milk and a decent lunch, and never got back on. The air smelled like oranges and the sky was wide and blue; the baby clapped her hands and cooed when she saw a yellow parakeet in a tall cabbage palm. Bethany bought a used Ford, cash, and drove toward the ocean. She didn't stop until she got to Verity. She bought her condo, furnished, the following day. All through that fall and winter she told herself she'd have to get a job, but she couldn't stand to be separated from her daughter, not even for an hour. She took the baby everywhere, to the hairdresser's, where she had her dark hair cut short and dyed auburn, and later, when her money began to run out, to the pawnshop in Hartford Beach, where she sold her last necklace, the sapphires Randy had given her on the night they were married.

It seemed, quite luckily, that everyone in Florida was from somewhere else. No one questioned Bethany about her past, although several women in her building gave her advice. Always, they told Bethany, ask a man if he has a criminal history before dating him. Never bad-mouth your ex in front of your child; even if you're still angry, better not to mention him at all. When her neighbors offered each other hints on how to deal with their children's problems, Bethany only pretended to listen. Her baby, who was now fourteen months old, was as sweet as ever, maybe even sweeter, as if she were being fed sugar water rather than homogenized milk and applesauce. How could a child conceived in a desperate last attempt to keep a marriage together be so good-natured? How had she been able to learn her new name so quickly, to know, instinctively, not to look at strangers, and to sit on her mother's lap down in the laundry room and not make a peep? Each time Bethany looked at her baby, she knew she had done the right thing. If there was a problem, it was only that they both suffered from insomnia, as if they were somehow more able to be their true selves after darkness fell. Bethany often did her errands in the evening, and she took the baby grocery shopping in Hartford Beach, where the Winn Dixie was open twenty-four hours a day. It was there that she first sensed that someone was following her. Bethany was in the frozen-food aisle, getting the bagels the baby liked to chew on when she was teething, when she felt someone behind her. She grabbed her cart and went straight to the checkout line. She scanned the aisles; if she had seen even a shadow, she would have picked up the baby and bolted, leaving her cart behind, but there was nothing suspicious, just a few late-night shoppers, and Bethany let Rachel play with a bag of plums while she unloaded her cart.

The parking lot was nearly empty when Bethany rolled her cart out. It was a hot, starry night. In her seat in the cart, the baby was covering her eyes and playing peek-a-boo. She had not yet begun to speak, but Bethany understood her all the same.

"I see you," Bethany had said, laughing, and then she felt it again. She looked over her shoulder. No one was there, but this time she knew she was right. She pushed the cart right up to her car, unlocked the doors, and slid the baby into her car seat. Bethany was breathing hard and her ears were burning. She opened the trunk and threw the groceries inside. She kept feeling something, like a shadow that was passing over her own. She got in behind the wheel and quickly locked all the doors.

"Ba-ba," the baby cried, wanting her frozen bagel right away.

"As soon as we get home," Bethany said.

Her hands were shaking as she backed out. It was silly; here she was, in the same parking lot she came to all the time. She drove to the exit and stopped behind a station wagon idling at the red light. An old man of seventy-five or eighty was at the wheel. Bethany looked in the rearview mirror so she could see her baby. Rachel whimpered, still hoping for her bagel.

"Peek-a-boo," Bethany sang, and then she saw the car

31

behind her with its headlights turned off. She could feel, quite suddenly, a line of ice across her back. The stoplight was still red; the old man in the station wagon was riffling through a bag of groceries. Bethany had broken into a sweat; her blouse was completely drenched.

She couldn't see his face, or even the model of the car he drove, but in that instant she decided to run. She turned the steering wheel sharply and stepped on the gas as hard as she could, so that the Ford shot over the curbstone, out into the street and oncoming traffic. In the trunk, a dozen eggs hit against each other and broke. The baby began to cry.

"Don't cry," Bethany said. "Please don't cry."

She sped toward the center of Hartford Beach. She heard the squeal of tires in the parking lot, but she knew he couldn't catch up to her. She drove for hours, down to Miami and then back up the Interstate to Verity. The baby slept curled up in her car seat, and when, at dawn, Bethany finally pulled into her parking space and lifted Rachel out of the car, she felt a wave of relief. Her baby was safe, and that was what mattered. What she didn't stop to think about, or even consider, was that she hadn't been found at the Winn Dixie in Hartford Beach. She'd been followed there. All night long, while she'd driven to Miami and back, the man who'd been sent to find her had been waiting in the parking lot of 27 Long Boat Street, and that didn't bother him in the least, since he was being paid well and had all the time in the world. Or, at the very least, he had until nightfall.

After her hair had been cropped short down at the Cut 'n' Curl, and most of the green chlorinated ends chopped away, Lucy Rosen looked about eighteen years old. From a distance, that is, in the right sort of light, late in the evening when the sky was thick with blue shadows. Lucy can still fit into one pair of jeans she bought before Keith was born, and twice she's been asked for ID at the Sea View Liquor Store, although she's far from being a teenager, as her ex-husband, Evan, recently reminded her when he forwarded an invitation to their twentieth high school reunion later this month. The invitation is shoved behind the Kleenex and the hand cream on her night table. Sometimes, as she gets into bed, Lucy sees the corner of the response card she'll never mail, and she feels shivery and somehow embarrassed, as if, after twenty years, when the facts of her life should all be settled, she hasn't even begun.

This is not the first time Lucy has had to start over. She'd been so self-reliant as a child that mothers on the block begged her to baby-sit; they offered her bags of potato chips and paid her fifty cents more an hour than any of their other sitters. Lucy's own parents, dizzy black sheep who had given up everything for music and love, rarely noticed when Lucy brought home A's or vacuumed the living room rug. Her father, Scout, played piano at bar mitzvahs and weddings, accompanied by her mother, Paula, who had once been a backup singer for Vic Damone. They were out most nights until dawn, so Lucy could easily have eaten Mallomars until midnight and read comic books and romance novels. She could have smoked cigarettes and tested all the bottles in the liquor cabinet. Instead, she did her homework and left olive-loaf sandwiches on the counter and noodle casseroles in the oven, and although her parents swore her dinners had saved them from starvation when they arrived home at four or five in the morning, the food never actually seemed to have been touched.

Scout's family, the Friedmans, whose baked goods could

be found in every supermarket in the Northeast, had sat shiva for him and cut him off without a cent when he married a Catholic girl; they left everything to his brother, Jack. Aside from the fact that no Friedmans' doughnuts or pies were ever allowed into the house, Scout believed he had gotten the best of the bargain.

"We're on a raft!" he would cry cheerfully at the end of each month when the bills came in and they were thoroughly broke. "Just the three of us on a raft, in the middle of the deep blue sea."

Actually, they were in a tract house in Levittown, and they had no idea how sick it made Lucy just to think of being on a raft with her parents, who seemed so ridiculously in love. Scout and Paula were killed at a Long Island Rail Road crossing, just before dawn, on the way home from a June wedding in Bellmore, found with their arms wrapped around each other. Lucy still wonders if they hadn't seen the oncoming train because they were too busy kissing. She was sent to live in Great Neck with her Uncle Jack, the brother Scout hadn't talked to in eighteen years. She spent all that July locked inside her bedroom, which was, she couldn't help but notice, larger than the living room of their house in Levittown. She refused the smoked salmon sandwiches and tea cakes her Aunt Naomi sent to her room; she knew and didn't care that her cousin Andrea, who was only a few months younger, despised her; and each time her Uncle Jack played the piano, she put cotton balls in her ears, rather than hear how much better he was than Scout. When Lucy finally came out of her locked room, on the night of Andrea's sweet sixteen party, her skin was as white as a calla lily and she had a careless, wild look in her eyes. It was only natural that the first boy to see her would fall in love with her and, in spite of the fact that nothing made her happy, stay in love long enough to marry her. On the night of Andrea's party, they went out behind the pool house, which was always well stocked with white wine and Tab, and there, on a stone path that led to the pool filter, Evan kissed her for the first time. In that instant, while the cicadas sang in the heat, Lucy became the mystery girl, the blonde cousin from nowhere who knew, without ever being taught, how to kiss.

In Levittown, Lucy had been the last chosen for everything. Now, after a month of starvation and mourning, all that had changed. Her gray eyes were luminous, she wore a size seven, and her pale hair fell down to her waist. When the school term began it was decided that she was the girl with talent. She was editor of the school newspaper, and president of the Honor Society, and, although she wasn't named queen of the junior prom, a title bestowed upon Heidi Kaplan, who had red hair the color of hothouse roses, she was one of the princesses. By her senior year, there were so many boys phoning Lucy that Andrea, who grew more sullen with each call, insisted Lucy be given her very own Princess phone, with a dial that glowed in the dark.

No matter how many boys were after her—and the thinner and paler she became, the more there were of them, as if she were a flickering light they couldn't stay away from— Lucy remained true to that first kiss, and to Evan. She can still recall the faces of some of the boys who followed her to her classes and hung around Uncle Jack's pool. But she always believed that eventually one of them would see through her, and Evan was so even-tempered and so thoroughly bamboozled she thought they would be together forever. Instead, it only seemed that way; they lasted nearly twenty-two years past their first kiss.

Since their breakup, Lucy has found she doesn't miss

Evan at all. She doesn't dream about him, or cry over him down in the laundry room the way some of her neighbors do on the anniversaries of their weddings or divorce decrees. Toward the end, all they had in common was Keith. They'd sit in the kitchen in the dark, drinking tea, trying to figure out what had gone wrong. Was it something they'd done or simply a nervous condition that made Keith so sensitive, ready to cry at the sound of a hornet, refusing to sleep for days on end, writing with black crayons on the walls? In spite of all this, Evan was a good father, too good, perhaps, since he'd wanted custody, and fought for it in his own mild way until it became clear Lucy wouldn't give in. Now, of course, there are times when she wishes she had. Keith has grown from a wary, difficult boy into a surly loner, a thief whose backpack has to be checked for contraband every day. When the other women at 27 Long Boat Street meet down in the laundry room or at the pool to talk about their children, Lucy keeps her mouth shut. She listens to their tales of grouchy adolescent girls who paint their fingernails purple and toddlers who eat handfuls of powdered soap, but she feels no kinship. Even physical illness cannot move her to compassion. There is, after all, strong brown soap for poison ivy, iodine for cuts and bruises, mud for bee stings, honey for sore throats, chalky white casts for broken bones. But where is the cure for meanness of spirit? What remedy is available for unhappiness and thievery? Certainly, if it were anywhere in Florida, Lucy would have already found it, since the sharp yellow afternoon sunlight hides nothing. It's the sort of light that makes it difficult to begin all over again and doesn't allow for much invention. You are what you see in the mirror above the sink—in Lucy's case, a pretty woman with slightly green hair whose son hates her.

Lucy does her best to avoid the other divorced women in her building. She confides in no one but Kitty Bass, the secretary at the *Verity Sun Herald*, who has a daughter Lucy's age and is always a great one for advice. It was Kitty who suggested Dee down at the Cut 'n' Curl, although as far as she was concerned Lucy's hair was hardly green enough to notice. When Kitty's daughter, Janey, who now owns the Hole-in-One Donut Shop over by the golf course, was a teenager, her hair turned so green from swimming in the municipal pool that a loose parakeet mistook her for a cabbage palm and flew right into her hair, leaving her with a fear of birds that persisted for years. Since whole flocks of escaped parakeets nest on the rooftops in Verity, this is not comforting news to Lucy. Sometimes when she drives home at twilight, the sky is filled with heat waves and parakeets. She can see them out of the corner of her eye, a flash of turquoise or jade feathers just above the stoplights and the telephone wires. It has gotten so that Lucy doesn't leave home without a scarf or, at the very least, one of Keith's baseball caps.

"Sugar, you're just a worrier by nature," Kitty told Lucy at lunch while they ate their Alligator Salads on the veranda of the Post Café.

Lucy had flinched each time a bird flew overhead; she shook too much pepper on her salad and then had to clean off the spinach leaves with a paper napkin.

"Don't you have anything better than birds to worry about?" Kitty had asked her, and of course she has. She has Martha Reed, formerly of Valley Stream, New York, calling her every week to report on Keith's transgressions and set up conferences in the guidance office at the junior high. She has full custody of a twelve-year-old boy who's been marking off the days on his calendar until he can finally go back to New York for summer vacation, and who now wears a skull earring. She has trouble with the cooling system of her Mustang, so that the motor cuts out whenever the air-conditioning is turned on high. And of course, she has her job at the *Sun Herald*, where she writes obituaries, and cultural pieces that are almost as deadly; earlier this week she had reviewed the high school production of *West Side Story*, making certain to mention Kitty's granddaughter, Shannon, who'd had her brown hair tinted black at the Cut 'n' Curl for her role as Anita. Lucy has not even begun to worry about the fact that she seems to be addicted to Diet Dr Pepper, or that if she keeps on devouring the jelly doughnuts Kitty brings to work every morning she won't fit into any of her jeans.

Every afternoon, at a quarter to five, Lucy begins to dread going home, because every evening she and Keith fight. They fight about his lack of privacy, as she roots through his backpack, about his failing grades and bad attitude, about the Florida heat. They have even had a particularly savage battle over the right way to replace the ice cube tray in the freezer. Their arguments seem to escalate with the humidity, and tonight the air is so damp and thick that Lucy's straight hair has begun to curl by the time she drives home. A bad sign. The sign of screams, accusations, slamming doors, sleepless nights. Every day at five-thirty the parking lot of 27 Long Boat Street is a madhouse, and the lobby isn't much better. For the past few months someone has been jimmying open the mailboxes, stealing child-support and alimony checks, so everyone wants to pick up the mail pronto, especially around the first of the month. There are thirteen divorced women in the building, and although they might reveal their baby-sitters' phone numbers or meet for dinner at the Post Café, they never, ever speak about their past histories. Occasionally, a bit of a previous life accidentally surfaces. Karen Wright from the eighth floor had also been a customer at Salvuki's, the salon in Great Neck where Lucy used to pay fifty dollars for a haircut; Jean Miller and Nina Rossi discovered they had been students at Hofstra College at the same time. But the facts of their lives mean so little; they know what they all have in common: some hard disappointment, best forgotten, which has propelled them to Florida.

That is why Lucy knows that Diane Frankel, who holds the elevator open for her tonight, goes to aerobics class during her lunch hour and eats nothing all day but two Ultra Slim-Fast shakes and a tossed salad, while she has no idea where Diane grew up or what her ex-husband's name is.

"I'm starving," Diane says as Lucy steps into the elevator.

"Yeah, right," Diane's sulky fifteen-year-old, Jenny, says from the rear of the elevator. "You look it."

"Be glad you don't have a daughter," Diane tells Lucy.

"Oh, I am," Lucy says. "Now if only I didn't have a son."

Lucy and Diane look at each other and grin, while Jenny gives them the evil eye. Jenny has long brown hair worked into dozens of braids, and, Lucy knows from conversations in the laundry room, she's already on the pill.

"That is so weak," Jenny says. "Like we asked to be born."

Lucy knows that the girl has a point, but it's a point she forgets as soon as she walks into the apartment and hears the stereo blasting. Guns N' Roses. She gets herself a Diet Dr Pepper from the refrigerator, kicks off her shoes, then counts to one hundred before she heads for Keith's room. She knocks once, knowing he can't hear her, then opens the door. As usual, all the shades are drawn and the room smells like cigarettes and popcorn. Keith sits in the center of the rug, methodically dismantling the motorized car Evan sent last November for his birthday. He's almost as tall as Lucy, and his hair is short like hers but spiked up in front, as if naturally agitated. Ever since they moved to Florida, the ridge of his nose has been sunburned. Immediately, Lucy smells french fries and oil on his skin.

"Where did you get the money for Burger King?" she asks.

"Who says I went to Burger King?" Keith says coldly.

Lucy goes to the window and pulls up the shade. "How was school?"

"Okay," Keith says, running his hand through his hair as he lies. By now he can forge her signature on a suspension notice without much trouble. "Boring."

Keith's backpack is hung over the edge of his bed. The guidance counselor has told Lucy not to feel guilty; she has a perfect right to search his possessions.

"Mind if I take a look?"

Keith salutes her as though she were a member of the SS, and he watches, grinning, as Lucy unzips the backpack. When she screams and drops the backpack, Keith scrambles to catch it. He reaches inside and pulls out the baby alligator he found behind the toilet at Burger King.

"Oh, great," Lucy says. "I can't believe you did this."

"I'm not letting it die," Keith tells her. "You can't make me."

She could fight him. She could flush the alligator or call the super and begin their last fight, the one that would end with Keith running out of the house and hitchhiking to the Interstate, where he'd stand in the dark hoping for a ride to New York, if he wasn't murdered first. Lucy knows enough to keep her mouth shut. She goes into the bathroom and runs cool water into the tub. Kitty Bass has assured her that twelve going on thirteen is the worst; if she can get through this year she can get through anything.

Keith brings the alligator into the bathroom, and they sit on the edge of the tub, watching for signs of life.

"We're not allowed to have animals," Lucy reminds him.

"We're not allowed to do anything," Keith says as he holds a piece of lettuce under the water, waving it so that ripples form.

Most probably, this alligator has been dying in the Burger King for weeks, and now it seems to be finishing the process in their bathtub.

"I think he has a fighting chance," Keith whispers.

For the first time in months he actually looks hopeful. Back home all the boys on the block have golden retriever puppies and aquariums filled with neon tetras. They have everything they've ever wanted and more. That's why Lucy doesn't think about how many times she will have to scrub the bathtub with Comet, and instead changes into jeans and a T-shirt before gathering her laundry and eating a yogurt for dinner. Keith doesn't come into the living room until the ten-o'clock news has already begun. He says he needs a break since his legs are cramping from sitting on the edge of the tub, but the truth is, he knows it's too late, and when Lucy finally forces herself to go into the bathroom, the alligator is already dead. Keith insists they bury it, and because his voice breaks, because Lucy doesn't know what else to do with the creature, she agrees. They get a shoe box from her closet and wrap the alligator in the Metro section of the *Sun Herald*. The body is very small, that's the surprising thing, that a dead alligator is so much smaller than a pair of size-eight high heels Lucy has not worn for years.

Outside, the air is thick as soup. They quickly discover it isn't easy to dig a grave in Florida. The earth is so sandy it keeps falling in on itself each time it's scooped out with one of the silver ladles, a tenth-anniversary present from Evan's mother. They are crouched behind the ficus hedge, on the far side of the pool, fearful of the super and any passing cars. The lights are on beneath the water, so the pool seems to float in space, a black hole surrounded by white moths and palmetto bugs. Finally they manage to dig a large enough hole, and Keith places the shoe box inside, then covers it with sand. They can hear a siren somewhere down Long Boat Street; they can hear the crabs that burrow beneath the sea grape during the heat of the day scuttling across the concrete walkways surrounding the pool. On someone's balcony a wind chime sways; it sounds like stars falling, or glass breaking into pieces.

Together they are shivering in the heat, beneath the black-and-gold sky. Along the shed where the chaise longues are stored, there is a vine of snowy white flowers that bloom only at night. When Keith finally rises to his feet, his breathing is shallow and much too fast.

"Are you okay?" Lucy whispers.

Keith nods, but he isn't. Anyone can see that.

"It was only an alligator," Lucy says.

"Yeah," Keith whispers. "Right."

As they walk back to the building, their rubber thongs beat a rhythm on the blacktop and the scent of the white flowers follows them. No one ever tells you how hot it can get in Florida during the month of May before you move down. No one mentions that sharks' teeth as big as a man's thumb can be found in the gutters after a storm or that the night air brings on spells of homesickness and bad dreams. When they get upstairs, Keith goes to his room and slams the door behind him. Lucy cleans out the bathtub, twice, with Comet and scalding hot water, then gathers the used towels together. When she first started writing the obituary column at the *Sun Herald*, she'd had a hard time; now it comes easy to her. She thinks in short, trim sentences of death and disease. Young alligator, dead of unknown causes, natural or unnatural, survived by no one, mourned by a single, sullen boy who would never in a million years allow anyone to know how often he cries himself to sleep.

When it is nearly midnight, Lucy knocks on Keith's door before she heads down to the laundry room. There's no answer, and, hoping he's asleep, Lucy grabs her wicker laundry basket and her detergent. Because she's so late, the laundry room is emptier than usual on a Thursday night. Karen Wright and Nina Rossi are already waiting for their clothes to dry. Karen has taken off her two gold rings, so they won't snag her baby's playsuits when she folds them, but Nina always wears her jewelry; she says it's the one thing she got out of her marriage, and she refuses to take off her gold necklaces and her charm bracelet, even when she goes into the pool. Lucy stuffs her dark wash into a machine, adds soap, then joins the other women on the plastic bench.

"You're going to be here all night," Nina Rossi tells her. "It's so humid nothing's drying."

"Lovely weather as usual," Lucy says.

"For turtles." Karen Wright grins as she fiddles with her portable intercom, which allows her to listen for her baby up on the eighth floor.

"Dead turtles," Nina adds as she unloads her dryer and begins to fold the massive amount of clothes her two girls go through every week. "I like your hair," she tells Lucy.

"Dee down at the Cut 'n' Curl," Karen guesses. "Right?"

Karen's red hair is also cut short, although nowhere as short as Lucy's.

"Is it awful?" Lucy asks Karen after Nina has taken her laundry upstairs.

"Listen, they would have charged you fifty bucks to do something like that at Salvuki's," Karen said.

"Not to mention the tip and the conditioner they would have sold me."

"They used to talk me into mousse," Karen says. "Like I need mousse."

When her baby begins to cry, Karen looks up, startled. Lucy understands exactly what a cry can do. It's a sound you never get used to, it can cut right through flesh and bone.

"Just once," Karen says as she hurries upstairs, "I wish she'd make it through an entire night."

Lucy herself didn't sleep through the night once during Keith's first five years. The disturbances came one after another: bad dreams, croup, chicken pox, fear of the dark. She can tell tonight will be a rough one for Karen. Through the intercom she can hear the baby continue her whimpering, but by the time Lucy carries her folded laundry down the basement hallway, Karen is headed back to the laundry room, her little girl in her arms.

"I give up," Karen tells Lucy as they pass each other.

Maybe it was simply impossible to sleep once you had children. You had to use that time to worry. You had to do it for the rest of your life. It's almost one-thirty when Lucy gets back to the apartment, and across the hall from her bedroom she can see a line of light beneath Keith's door. Outside, the stars are turning red with heat. Although the windows are closed and the air conditioner is turned to high, Lucy can still hear the strangler figs as they drop from the trees, and maybe that's what keeps her son awake. It's a sound that reminds you that anything is possible, right outside your front door.

Chapter Two

THE short circuit happened last night, sometime between midnight and three, when the yellowfin in the bay turn the water the color of butter. At a quarter to four this morning there was an anonymous call to the station, which could have easily been a joke, since the caller sounded like a kid, except that when Richie Platt finally got himself over there and had the super unlock 8C, there was a dead woman on the kitchen floor. In her closed fist were four quarters that had turned as cold as ice.

By ten-thirty there were four police cruisers and two unmarked black Fords parked in the circular driveway, blocking all the handicapped spaces at 27 Long Boat Street. Some of the officers, grown men who have presided at the scenes of car accidents and three-alarm fires, were so shaken they took turns going out behind the building, where they smoked cigarettes and wondered why they'd ever wanted their jobs in the first place. There is supposed to be a complete blackout, with no news leaks whatsoever, but Paul Salley, whose father owns the *Verity Sun Herald* and the radio station and just about everything else in town, has positioned himself in the lobby and won't be budged. Paul has been waiting for a murder like this ever since he got his master's degree in journalism from the University of Miami. Some people might consider him lucky; he considers himself smart. He was tuned to the police band on his radio and heard too much activity for anything less than a major crime. Greedy for facts, he hasn't even phoned in to his editor or the obit page, since he's not about to be scooped.

"One thing about Paul," the chief of police, Walt Hannen, has said. "You can spit on him and he thinks it's raining."

Nobody's giving Paul the facts or even the right time of day, although the truth is that aside from the body in the kitchen, not a thing is out of place in 8C. No one ransacked the dresser drawers or went through the closet, and there's over three thousand in cash packed inside a suitcase under the bed. As far as anyone can figure, the victim had a load of laundry going in the basement, came up with a folded load, still in a plastic laundry basket in the living room, and, while searching for change, surprised the thief, maybe even struggled with him, so that he panicked and fled before stealing anything of worth. But there's more to the crime than all this, and that's why Walt Hannen is waiting in the parking lot, smoking his third cigarette in under half an hour even though he gave up smoking last month. With Paul Salley bothering people in the lobby and so many single women in town, they can try their best to keep this murder quiet, but by tonight there's going to be a run on safety locks down at the hardware store. A lot of people will be wanting answers, and it's all going to be on Walt Hannen's head.

Julian Cash finally pulls up, late as always, just as Walt

46

takes out his fourth cigarette and lights it. The air is so heavy that the smoke doesn't even spiral upward, it just hangs there so that it's hard to see straight. When Walt hired Julian, after all the trouble he'd been in, people thought he was crazy, but Walt trusts him. Julian has a natural instinct for the way people work and an uncanny ability to connect with animals. Though nobody believes it, Walt has actually seen a red-shouldered hawk respond to Julian's whistle, stop in midair, then swoop down to a patch of grass not fifty yards away. He's heard those merlins who nest in the cypress trees along Julian's driveway raise hell, like watchdogs, whenever a car turns in, headed for Julian's house.

Julian leaves his dog in the car and comes up beside Walt, then shades his eyes and studies 27 Long Boat Street.

"Not anything you'd want to happen," Julian says.

"No," Walt Hannen agrees, figuring there's no point in griping to Julian about his being late. Behind his back, people have talked about Julian since the day he was born. They say that as a baby he had the loudest and worst cry of any child ever born in the state of Florida, and although he usually speaks softly, like a man just waking from a deep sleep, Walt Hannen would not like to see him truly angry.

"I told you last year to take early retirement," Julian says.

"You should have been more convincing," Walt says dryly.

"Well, hell," Julian says. "Let's get this over with."

He lets Loretta out, and she circles around his legs, then sits beside him. She's pure black, aside from her face markings, and Walt Hannen doesn't move an inch until Julian has clipped on her leash.

"Jesus," Julian says when they get to the lobby and he sees Paul Salley. They've known each other since grade school, and even though they haven't said two words to each other in the past five years, Julian would still like to push Paul's face in. Rich kids don't go over well in Verity, even after they're all grown up.

"The vulture has landed," Walt Hannen says.

Before they can get into the elevator, Paul Salley approaches, although he slows down when he sees Loretta.

"Hey, Julian," he says, just as if he were one of the guys, when everyone knows he could never work another day in his life and still make out fine.

Julian looks up at the ceiling like it was the most interesting thing he ever saw. Fact is, it's acoustical tile; no one on the floor beneath the murdered woman would have heard a sound.

"Just as friendly as always," Paul Salley says before turning to Walt. "You know I'm going to find out everything sooner or later. So you could just tell me, and that would be that."

"With someone of your talents that would be kind of an insult, wouldn't it?" Walt Hannen says.

"Then don't ask me for any favors," Paul says.

"Have I ever?" Walt Hannen says mildly. "Someone ought to rip that police band radio out of his car," Walt adds when he and Julian get into the elevator.

"Late at night," Julian says. "When nobody's looking."

What they know about this murder is simple; it's what they don't know that's complicated. The reason for this is that Karen Wright seems not to have existed before October. Everything—her driver's license, her car insurance, her Winn Dixie check-cashing card—was based on false information. The previous address she gave to the super, in Short Hills, New Jersey, doesn't exist. Even the color of her hair isn't her own. All they know is that she was somewhere between the ages of twenty-five and thirty and that when

she was discovered on her kitchen floor she'd been dead for
at least four hours. That, and the fact that her little girl is
missing. By the time Walt leads Julian into the apartment,
the forensic team from Hartford Beach has nearly finished.
Richie Platt, who is supposed to be in charge of the inves-
tigation, backs up against the wall like a scared rabbit when
Julian brings Loretta inside.

"Don't let Paul Salley in here," Walt Hannen tells Richie.
"Don't even talk to him."

"Nobody's talked to him in years," Richie says. "Right?"
he says to Julian.

"I know I haven't," Julian says. He's known Richie since
grade school, too. It doesn't hurt to be civil to him; for all
Julian knows, Richie may be the next in line when Walt
Hannen retires.

"I don't think we're going to like anything we find," Walt
says thickly.

From the hallway, Julian can see a line of blood on the
kitchen floor. Loretta knows it's there; she's straining, so
that Julian has to pull up on her leash and snap her metal
collar. They walk through the living room, pausing only
when Loretta stops to sniff the rug: then they head down
the hallway, toward the bedrooms. When they get to the
baby's room, Julian flips on the light, then closes the door
behind him. The walls have recently been painted pink and
there's a mobile of a moon and stars dangling above the crib.
It's not Julian's job to consider who was killed or why. He
doesn't even have to think about that. All he needs is the
baby's pillow, which, in his hands, seems ridiculously small.
The pillowcase is bordered with a row of blue bunnies, and
for some reason this makes Julian feel sick. He crouches
down, and when he clucks his tongue, Loretta approaches

and sniffs at the edges of the pillow. There is the scent of milk and baby shampoo and the thin, chalky odor of powder. But beneath that there is more, the scent of one particular human being. It's as if the essence of a person seeps into a pillow during the night, the way pollen can be caught if you open your hand just beneath a flower.

"Atta girl," Julian tells the dog as she nudges the pillow-case. He takes the pillow with him when they leave, careful to hold it by the edge so he won't get his own scent all over it.

Someone has brought Walt Hannen a black coffee, which he's gulping down, in spite of the fact that it's burning his throat. He nods to Julian and they go out into the hallway together.

"I think we've got a sighting," Walt says. "Over by the Hole-in-One."

Walt looks up at Julian and sees absolutely no clue as to what he must be thinking. Not a flicker behind his dark eyes.

"Hey, Julian, if you don't want to go, I'll send Richie."

"I thought you wanted the dog on this," Julian says. "I thought that was the point."

"Well, yeah," Walt agrees. "It is."

"Look, I don't have a personal life," Julian assures him. "If that's what you're worried about."

"Great." Walt Hannen grins.

They go downstairs and head out to the parking lot, Walt on his way back to the station, where he'll try to put a lid on any information going out, Julian forcing himself to drive over to the Hole-in-One. But Loretta doesn't cooperate. When they walk past the ficus hedges she stops. Her ears point straight up and there's a fluttery noise, low in her throat. Julian can feel the vibration move up the leash and into the palm of his hand. There it is, right in front of them, the patch of freshly turned earth.

They get two shovels from the super and call up for Richie Platt. While they dig, Loretta is so agitated she has to be tied to the bike rack. As Richie bends down and lifts the box out of the sand, Walt Hannen takes out another cigarette and lights it and doesn't think twice about what it's doing to his respiratory system.

"Want to do the honors?" Richie asks Walt as he holds out the shoe box.

"No," Walt says. "I don't even want to be here."

Julian examines the shoe box, then lifts off the top. Beneath some crumpled newspaper lies the dead alligator.

"I don't like this one goddamned bit," Walt Hannen says.

Tossed on top of the alligator are two gold rings.

"Fuck," Walt says.

Julian hands the box over to Richie. He doesn't even want to start to think about what it means.

"You just keep your mouths shut about this," Walt Hannen says.

Since Julian doesn't talk much, Richie knows this is directed at him, and he nods.

"I don't want Paul Salley to know anything," Walt tells them. "Fucking May," he adds, for in all probability he will gain twenty pounds before this business is through.

Julian Cash knows exactly what Walt means. He was born on the third day of May. The worst day of the worst month. With a birthday like that, no one needed to whisper a curse beside his cradle; he could bring about his own bad luck with no help from anyone.

As he unties Loretta from the bike rack and heads for his car, Julian is well aware that he has twenty-four hours, because after that the chances for recovery are cut in half with each hour that passes. He's not going to think about anything but the baby. He can focus that way whenever he wants. When he hit the gumbo-limbo tree going seventy miles an hour he told himself he wouldn't black out, and he didn't. If he's got something on his mind he's like a dog so intent on chasing a rabbit it doesn't notice it's sliced its foot apart in a steel trap until it's lost a pint of blood. That's why Julian can do his job in the heat, in the month of May; he can do it whether he likes it or not.

Janey Bass is still so pretty that teenage boys whistle when she walks by. She's so sweet she has to spray herself with Skin-So-Soft every morning to keep flies from lighting on her fingers and toes. It's amazing that Janey still looks this good; she'll be thirty-five in August, and her daughter, Shannon, is sixteen, and that alone can age you pretty fast. She's just got good genes. Her mother, Kitty, is fifty-eight and looks fantastic, even after going through all of Janey's traumas right along with her, or at least the ones Janey could talk about.

Janey now believes she was predestined to have that awful marriage with Kenny, even that last part when she shook her fist in his face and threatened to break his nose, because she got Shannon out of it and she learned to stand on her own two feet, which she never in a million years thought she could. She was a pretty face, period. Now she's that and something more. That's why she took back her maiden name after her divorce; she figured she deserved another chance at being Janey Bass, and she's been doing a good job at it this time around. She is actually the kind of mother who stays up past midnight sewing lace onto the hem of a flouncy skirt for her daughter's school play. She feels sorry for Kenny, who's always failing at one business venture or another, but then she can afford to pity him, since she doesn't have to depend on his child-support payments. It kind of gives her the chills to have her life turn out so completely different from anything she might have expected.

Every morning, Janey gets up at four-thirty, when the sky is still silky and black, but today she woke up before her alarm went off. She was so certain that something was haywire that she quickly untangled herself from her sheets and raced to Shannon's bedroom, satisfied only when she saw her daughter safely asleep. She went into the kitchen, where she fixed herself a pot of coffee and drank two cups, one right after the other. Janey had a funny feeling low down in her stomach, like she used to when she was Shannon's age. She was so lazy and careless back then; she could sleep till noon and sometimes her mother would have to get the plant mister and spray her right in the face in order to get her up and ready for school.

The truth was, she was boy crazy. She couldn't wake up in the mornings because she used to sneak out her window after midnight and not come home until dawn. The things she did back then she'd kill Shannon for even thinking about. She was in love with one boy but crazy about another. She'd spend all day with the boy everyone was certain she was going to marry, but at night she could hardly wait to meet the other boy; she'd be so out of breath by the time she climbed out her window and ran down West Main to his car that she wouldn't be able to speak. Each time he unbuttoned her blouse she'd nearly faint, because she knew what they were doing was so bad. They thought they had this big secret, but more people knew than they would have suspected, and no sane person would ever have guessed he'd be the one to break it off. Luckily, Verity isn't a small town anymore; you don't have to run into anyone you have a history with. You can avoid him just about forever if you try. And if you ever start to think about him, all you have to do is go into the shower and let the hot water fall down on you for ten minutes or so, and by the time you're done you're almost through remembering.

Today when Janey woke up she couldn't even decide what to wear. Usually she throws on jeans and a T-shirt; this morning she stood debating for a good fifteen minutes before she finally chose a white dress and sandals, and she took a little too long messing with her hair, as if it made a bit of difference whether or not she clipped it up with a barrette. She didn't have to worry about Shannon's waking on time; Shannon was as responsible as Janey had been flighty. She always fixed herself an English muffin and orange juice, then washed the dishes before she walked to school. Still, Shannon seemed out of sorts lately, and Janey worried about her as she headed toward the golf course in her Honda. Beneath the black sky, she kept a careful eye out for turtles in the road. Her mother has always said Janey is hypersensitive. She feels more than other people do. She can't even kill a mosquito because she knows just how bad it would feel to have your wings all smooshed together and your legs bent in half. She can't remember the last time she went to a high school football game, even though Shannon is head cheerleader, since she can't stand to see all those little Gators so excited and pumped up when she knows they're going to lose. Whenever she senses that something bad is going to happen, she feels all panicky and confused, the way she did on the night of the accident. She just knew something terrible was ahead. She was sitting alone in her room, late at night, and suddenly it felt as if she were nothing more than little bits of things—light, air, atoms, flesh—instead of a whole person.

At four-thirty this morning the streets were empty, but Janey stopped for the red lights anyway. She still got to the Hole-in-One by a quarter to five, surprising Fred and Maury, both of whom have been frying doughnuts since long before Janey's divorce, long before she came to work the counter or ever imagined buying the place.

"Hey!" they greeted her when she walked in the back door. Their hands were already white with flour.

"Early bird," Fred called.

"She may be early, but she still looks pretty good." Maury grinned. "For a boss."

"Thanks," Janey said, as she grabbed a fresh cruller. "You know it's not from following Weight Watchers."

Janey could hear the men laughing as she went out front to start the coffee urns. Her appetite for sweets was famous. Shannon always had balanced meals, Janey's made sure of that, but Janey herself eats two sugar crullers for breakfast and a jelly doughnut for lunch. Some days she fears she'll lie down and gain a hundred pounds in her sleep when all those doughnuts add up. That hadn't happened yet, so Janey took neat bites of her first cruller as she got the coffee going. Then she wiped her hands on a dishtowel and went to stand by the plate-glass window. There were still some stars in the sky. By six-thirty the parking lot would be filled; on Sunday mornings there was often a line out the door, but this morning, at a little after five, there was only a thin streak of light in the eastern part of the sky. Tiny green lizards were scattered across the parking lot, searching for drops of dew.

Nearly twenty years ago somebody broke Janey Bass's heart. Not that it matters anymore. She could have any man she wanted in Verity, married or not. There are actually some women who won't allow their husbands to come down to the Hole-in-One on Sunday mornings, as if Janey would look at them twice. She figures love and heartbreak are best suited for teenagers; she's got enough on her hands with raising Shannon, but that doesn't mean she doesn't think about the way things used to be.

She was there at the window, wondering if she should have left a note reminding Shannon to pick up a roast chicken for dinner, when she saw something moving in the shadows over by the dumpster, where the day-old doughnuts were discarded in hard, sweet piles. Janey Bass put her nose to the glass; she could have sworn she saw a baby crouched on the grass, reaching greedily for the bits of food her companion offered her. In the time it took for Janey to unlock the front door, they were gone. All through the morning rush Janey tried to figure if she had conjured up that baby or if she was just telling herself she'd imagined it, since she knew who they'd send over if she called the police. She didn't phone the station until eleven, and it was past noon when Julian Cash drove into the parking lot. He got out and slammed his door shut, but then he just stood there, leaning up against his car. He had a cup of coffee he'd picked up at the Dunkin' Donuts over by the Interstate, since he always avoids the Hole-in-One. His throat felt all closed up and tight, in spite of the hot coffee. By the time he and Loretta are through today, they will have covered so much ground Loretta's paws will be bloody. But for now she's curled up on the frayed blue army blanket in the backseat of the patrol car, the baby's pillow beside her.

Janey Bass has been waiting for him, but now she sees he's never coming into the shop, not if she waits for a hundred years. She pushes the front door open and comes outside in her white dress. Even in the harsh noon light, her skin is the color of apricots. Her neck and forehead are covered with a thin film of sweat.

"I see you're frequenting my competitor," Janey says when she sees Julian's coffee cup. She walks over but avoids looking at him. Instead, she peers into the back of the car.

"Hi, baby," she says to the dog through the window.

Janey's hands are actually shaking. She's been waiting a long time for Julian Cash to come and beg her for something, and now it seems that it just might happen. She doesn't have to stare, she knows what he looks like. She saw him outside the Value Mart one Saturday and another time at the Verity Day parade. Good-looking men can age badly. Janey has noticed it's happening to Kenny, but Julian hardly seems any different from when she knew him. Except for the scar. He didn't have that yet.

"I know you'd rather I was somebody else," Julian says, uneasy. "But they had to send me. I've got the dog."

"I never wanted you to be somebody else," Janey says before she can stop herself. "That was you who wanted that."

"They had to send me," Julian says stubbornly. "I've got the dog."

"So I see," Janey says.

A fly buzzes around Janey's hair and she waves it away with her hand. She doesn't intend to make this easy.

"Aren't you going to tell me I haven't changed a bit?" she asks.

Julian looks her over carefully, the way he used to. She

stares right back at him, defiantly. There's still a line of freckles across the ridge of her nose.

"You haven't changed a bit," Julian says.

"Oh, yes I have," Janey says, triumphant. "I've changed plenty."

"Okay," Julian says. "So I'm wrong again."

"Dunkin' Donuts," Janey says, disgusted.

"If we're finished with how wrong I am, maybe you can tell me about the baby," Julian says. "And just for next time, when you see something suspicious at five in the morning? Don't wait till eleven to report it."

"Fuck you," Janey says. "I don't have to tell you anything at all."

Julian considers this and gulps down the rest of his coffee, which has turned quite cold.

"Well, Janey," he says finally, "would you like me to go down on my knees and beg you for information?"

"Yeah," Janey says. She can't help but grin. "That would do for starters."

Julian puts his coffee cup on the roof of his car, then sinks to his knees, right there in the parking lot. Janey would throw back her head and laugh if she were able to catch her breath. He can still do that to her. She wraps her arms around herself as though she were freezing. "Get up," she tells him.

Julian rises to his feet and fishes a cigarette out of his jacket pocket. He's surprised by how painful it is just to look at her. He tries to focus on the road behind them, but it's the road that leads to the Interstate, past those marshes that were once so filled with birds that whenever you went out walking with the most beautiful girl in town all you heard was the calling of terns and the saw grass rustling like rice paper.

"I think I saw a baby, maybe a year old, or a little older, over by the dumpster at about a quarter after five. Maybe it was five-thirty."

"You think you saw her?" Julian asks.

"I saw her," Janey says coldly. "Her and the boy."

"You saw the boy, too?" Julian says, real easy, so that Janey has no idea that a second child is news to him. Bad news, probably.

"Both of them." Janey nods.

"And the boy looked . . ." He leaves room for her to fill in the blanks.

"Eleven or twelve," Janey says. "Blue jeans, I think. Blond," she adds. "Kind of skinny."

Julian nods as if she's answered correctly. "Were they headed for the Interstate?" he asks her.

"I don't know. I blinked and they disappeared. What are they? Missing children or something?" Janey asks.

"Something like that," Julian says. He opens the back door of his car and lets Loretta out.

"But not exactly," Janey says flatly.

If he looked at her now, he'd remember that whenever she climbed up the drain pipe to her bedroom window, her skirt billowed out around her. Sometimes there would be spider webs on her ankles and red dust on the soles of her feet.

"Well, that's it; isn't it?" Janey says. "Same old thing. Make certain you don't tell anyone too much, because then they might know how you feel."

Julian clips Loretta's leash on. His eyes are just as black as they ever were, revealing so little you'd think there was nothing inside.

"Did you see anything else?" Julian asks. "A car you didn't recognize? Maybe someone over there by the weeds?"

"No," Janey says. She realizes that she's tired; it's much too hot to be standing out here in the noon sun. He's come back twenty years too late, that's all there is to it. "The sky was black except for all the way east," Janey says. "Over by the ocean. You know how it is at five o'clock?"

Since he used to wait in his car with the headlights turned off until she was safely through her window, he knows exactly what it's like at that hour of the morning. There's a yellow ribbon of light and then suddenly, before you know it, the sky is wide open and blue.

"I know how it is," Julian says, because none of what happened was her fault.

Janey Bass almost smiles, then she turns and walks back to her shop. Julian appreciates the fact that she doesn't say good-bye. She's honest, that's all. There's nothing left for them to say to each other. Still, he knows that she's watching through the window as he walks across the parking lot. He also knows that eventually she'll stop; she'll move away from the plate-glass window and she won't look back and he'll never get to tell her that she's wrong. She does look the same. She's as beautiful as ever, but that never had anything to do with the reason he didn't come back to her.

Near the dumpster, the asphalt is so hot it's melting into black pools. Loretta stands still, her tail wagging slightly. When she starts that rumbling sound low in her throat, Julian reaches down and lets her off the leash, and she takes off to circle the dumpster, faster and faster, until she stops, suddenly, and puts her face down to the ground. There, along the melting asphalt, is a trail of sugar and crumbs.

They'll go as far as they have to, and if the weather permits, they'll be searching long after dark. After all this time, Julian is so methodical he can see a white moth on a white mound of sand. He can determine the direction of the wind from the sound of one leaf falling. He's made mistakes in his life, ruinous ones, but there's one thing he knows for sure. Nothing gets past him. Not anymore.

Even people who are afraid of the dark know that the worst nightmares usually happen at noon. It may be because of the gravitational pull of the sun in the center of the sky, or simply because this is the hour when everyone's defenses are down, and they expect nothing more than bread and fruit. Lucy is at the mall when she knows something is about to go wrong. She can feel a sharp edge at the back of her throat, as if she'd been forced to swallow a knife. The fifth-graders from the elementary school have built a model of Charles Verity's house entirely out of toothpicks, which has been set up on a large felt-covered table in front of the Sun Bank. This unveiling is considered a cultural event in Verity, and Lucy will actually have to write about it, but that's not what makes her feel like crying. It's those fifth-graders, with their sweet, proud faces and gluey hands. Just once, she would like to believe that her son was capable of happiness. What she wouldn't give to be able to leave for work in the morning and be certain he'll get out of bed and arrive at school on time, instead of finding his way to Laddy's place and the liquor cabinet. What she wouldn't give for just one kind word.

Instead, what she gets when she returns to the *Sun Herald* is a message on her desk asking her to phone Martha Reed at the guidance office so she can set up an appointment for Keith's reinstatement. He either doesn't know or doesn't care that a parent has to come in to school before a student can return to class after the third suspension. If he keeps up this way, Keith may break the Verity Junior High record for administrative action. Lucy tosses the note into the trash and immediately calls home. Each time the phone rings unanswered her fury multiplies, until she is ready to wring Keith's neck. Of course he told her school was okay yesterday, just not for him, he failed to mention that. He probably didn't even get out of bed today until noon, and Lucy guesses he's already hanging out at the Burger King or finding fresh trouble with Laddy Stern. Lucy wrestles with herself, then finally phones Laddy. When he answers and swears that he's alone, home with the flu, his voice actually sounds raspy and thick. Lucy can tell Laddy's not lying, but she also understands that he wouldn't tell her where Keith was if he knew. She heads for the soda machine in the hallway and gets herself a cold Diet Dr Pepper, then goes to Kitty's office and perches on the air-conditioning unit.

"You heard?" Kitty says.

Everyone knows that if Kitty had been more ambitious, or if things had been fairer, she'd be the managing editor of the *Sun Herald*. As it is, she's privy to everyone's secrets and well aware of everyone's deficiencies, and she'll cover for you only if she likes you.

"I'm at my wits' end," Lucy says.

"I'll bet," Kitty says.

"Am I supposed to hire a bodyguard to walk him to school and make certain he stays there?"

"You're talking about Keith?" Kitty says, confused.

"No," Lucy says, pausing to gulp down some Dr Pepper. "I'm talking about the preteen monster."

Kitty gets up and closes her door, something she almost never does, since her air conditioner is on the fritz.

"What is it?" Lucy asks. She feels that odd, stabbing sensation in her throat again, as if she could down a six-pack of Dr Pepper and still be dying of thirst.

"I don't know if you want to know," Kitty says. "And once you do know, you can't tell anyone, since I'm not supposed to know, and I wouldn't if I hadn't overheard Paul when he called in to talk to Ronny. That happened completely by accident. You know Paul, he wants an exclusive when a pelican drops dead on West Main Street. It's not like I intended to pick up on his line."

"Tell me," Lucy says.

Kitty sits down at her desk and leans forward. When she whispers, her voice sounds crackly, as if she were speaking through a bad phone connection.

"Someone was murdered in your building last night. And don't ask me who. I don't know."

Lucy can feel the blood drain out of her face; she looks as white as a piece of paper, all fluttery and crumpled up.

"I shouldn't have told you," Kitty says. "Shit."

"Keith's not at home and he's not at school."

Lucy is trying desperately to remember where she left her car keys. She searches her pockets frantically.

"He's probably got his music turned up high and his headphones on," Kitty suggests.

But Lucy knows she should have watched over him more carefully; if she hadn't brought him here from New York he would never have lived in a building where someone could get murdered, he'd be riding his bicycle beneath the oak trees, he'd be playing baseball with his father out in the backyard where the lilacs bloom.

"Go home, and I'll say you had a headache," Kitty tells her.

It's not only good advice, it turns out to be true. On the way home, Lucy doesn't bother to stop for red lights, and when she gets to Long Boat Street she does have a headache, a blinding one. Her heart is pounding so hard her ribs ache. Paul Salley has followed Walt Hannen down to the station on West Main, and there are now only two police cruisers in the parking lot, but an officer has been posted in the lobby, and Lucy has to sign in before she's allowed to use the elevator. She imagines Keith in his room, beautifully sullen, his headphones plugged into his ears, but as soon as she unlocks the door to her apartment she can feel the emptiness inside. There's a cricket trapped behind the refrigerator, and its song echoes above the terra-cotta tiles. It is possible, after all, to know things you shouldn't, just as Lucy knows, before she opens the door to his room, that Keith's bed hasn't been slept in. She stands in his doorway, breathing in the scent of smoke and unwashed clothes, thinking of the dozen different ways Evan can accuse her if she has to tell him their son has disappeared. When she finally can move, she runs to the kitchen and calls the police. The cricket behind the refrigerator is driving her crazy; she wraps the phone cord around her arm like a tourniquet. She wants them to tell her she has nothing to worry about. Instead, the dispatcher contacts Richie Platt, up in 8C, and sends him downstairs, so he can wait for Walt Hannen with Lucy.

Lucy sits down on a kitchen chair, her arms folded around herself, rocking back and forth. Richie Platt is afraid she's about to flip out; he won't look at her, and he certainly won't answer any of her questions. He's been told, he explains, to keep his mouth shut. By the time Walt Hannen arrives, Lucy looks so ill that Walt goes directly to the refrigerator, takes out a pitcher of orange juice and insists she drink a full glass, before she faints. He sits down beside her and when he tells her that her neighbor up in 8C has been murdered and that her little girl is missing, Lucy begins to shiver uncontrollably. Not even the blanket Walt has Richie put around her can help. Lucy tries to think of Karen, to remember her face, the angle of her haircut, but all she really cares about is the fact that two children are missing, one of them hers. She can't focus much and she can't stand to listen to Walt Hannen comforting her, but this much she understands: If the children are together, and if they are to be found today, the chances will be best before darkness falls. Someone is tracking them right this minute. Lucy needs to give them a list of her son's friends and known hangouts; then she can wait, right here in her own kitchen. She is not to panic or tie up her phone. What she can do is watch the horizon from her window, charting the exact position of the sun. She can go downstairs, and outside the glass doors she can pray for clear skies and moonlight, a condition so rare on May nights in Verity that even the most ardent stargazers usually put their telescopes away until June.

Just after dusk, Walt Hannen drives back to Long Boat Street, followed by the K9 patrol car. There are thin, low clouds in the sky and not a bit of wind. It's bad luck to have no moonlight on the first night of a search, even worse luck to see a woman waiting for you in the driveway, pacing beneath a blood-red hibiscus.

"Oh, shit," Walt says, after he and Julian have gotten out of their cars. "She's going to get hysterical."

Last May a social worker from New York jumped out her window and Walt had to drive down to her parents' retirement village in Del Ray Beach and tell them. The way he sees it, he's somehow gotten stuck with work a preacher should be doing, and he's not cut out for it.

"Get ready for a scene," he mutters to Julian as they approach.

Already, clouds of mosquitoes are gathering above the

pool. Lucy is wearing a gray sweatshirt and running shorts; her eyes are puffy from crying. All afternoon she's been falling apart. Now she's in pieces. It's possible that she's a jinx and was given the obituary column at the *Sun Herald* for good reason, since everyone she's ever cared about has disappeared. As soon as she looks at Walt Hannen she knows her son is still missing.

"You didn't find anything," Lucy says accusingly. She's so raw that Julian quickly moves back, ducking under the hibiscus, hoping she won't notice him.

"There's no reason to get all upset just yet," Walt Hannen says. He has a deep, slow voice that his wife insists is sweet enough to comfort the dead.

"Don't tell me not to get upset!" Lucy says. Her mouth is set in a tight, thin line; she looks somehow dangerous, as if she might snap in two.

"Mrs. Rosen," Walt says. "Lucy."

Lucy backs away as though he were about to strike her. When her parents were killed, all the neighbors on the block seemed to want to touch her; she'd felt that she herself would die if one more person comforted her.

"Just calm down," Walt suggests.

"Oh, yeah, right," Lucy says. "Oh, sure." She has goose bumps all up and down her arms. It's as if Keith's voice had just come out of her mouth, and the taste is unbelievably bitter.

"Julian's going back out tonight, and let me tell you, he can find a snowflake in hell," Walt says. "I kid you not."

Lucy looks over at Julian Cash for the first time. She sees the scar across his forehead and the jumble of scratches on his cheeks and hands from searching through thorn bushes. He stares right back at her. He's exhausted and filthy and he's clearly got nothing to say. Any hope Lucy might have had evaporates; she sinks down on the curb, and before she can stop herself a thin wail spirals out of her mouth. In the backseat of Julian's car, Loretta raises her head and begins to howl.

Walt and Julian exchange a look. They hate this. Walt crouches down on the curb and urges Lucy to put her head between her legs and try to breathe evenly.

"The whole situation is like a puzzle," Walt tells her. He looks up at Julian for ideas on where to take this, but Julian just stares back at him, offering nothing.

"What do we have?" Walt says, to give himself some time. He lights a cigarette. "We have a dead woman with a false identity, and two missing kids. Yours and hers. That's the reality."

After years of unhappiness, Walt now sees that the fact he and his wife could never have children may really have been a gift. The boy's mother has stopped wailing, but she's staring at him, panicked, the skin on her throat flushed with heat. For the past few years, Walt and his wife, Rose, have been breeding Labrador retrievers; each time a new litter is born, Walt sits up all night in the garage, making certain the puppies are warm enough and that each one knows how to feed. He's had only one puppy die, and that one died in his hands, before it was old enough to open its eyes. Thinking about that small death makes Walt open up more than he should.

"We don't know who took the children, or why, or if they were just frightened off. But we think they were spotted over at the Hole-in-One. And we do have one very interesting piece of evidence. We have a shoe box."

As soon as the shoe box is mentioned, Lucy sits up straight, her shoulders rigid as wire. That's when Julian Cash starts to watch her.

"We found it buried over there." Walt Hannen points his

cigarette at the ficus hedge. Julian notices that she knows exactly where to look, even though Walt is gesturing only toward the area of the pool. "It may be some kind of sign to us. Some kind of message from someone who wants to get caught. If the gold rings that were inside belonged to the victim, we may have a real lead."

"What was inside?" Lucy says. She looks truly frantic now; Julian can almost see her bones rise to the surface of her skin. "There were rings?"

"I don't want you to worry about this," Walt says.

"All right," Lucy says flatly. She's much too calm.

"Did you ever see the victim wearing two gold rings?" Walt asks.

"No," Lucy says. "I didn't."

Lucy's hair is cut short enough for Julian to see the back of her neck. Just looking at her he can feel the white edge of desire. The reason he's so attracted to her isn't simply that he can already imagine her in his bed. It's that she just lied, and she's going to do it again.

"All we want is for you to let Julian go up to the boy's room and get what he needs so the dog can do her job tracking," Walt says as he helps Lucy to her feet. She stumbles once, and Walt has to catch her beneath her elbow. "Can you do that?"

Lucy nods and starts for the entranceway. She moves like a sleepwalker, staring straight into the darkness. Before Julian can follow her, Walt takes him aside.

"Just grab something and get the hell out of there before she freaks out again," Walt says.

Lucy has stopped just outside the building, waiting for Julian. She reminds him of the merlins that nest in the cypress trees along his driveway, ready to take flight in an instant.

"Be careful with her," Walt suggests. "Don't mention the goddamned alligator."

"I won't talk to her," Julian says. "How's that?"

He stands behind her in the elevator, aware that he's making her uncomfortable. When they get to her apartment and she opens the front door, Julian remains out in the hall.

"Mud," he explains.

The wall-to-wall carpeting is a pale gray, and Julian's boots have covered acres of marshland. That's why he prefers bare wood that can just be swept once a month.

"Do you think I care about my carpet right now?" Lucy says. "Is that what you think?"

"Why don't we just get this over with," Julian says. "All right?"

Lucy opens her mouth as if she's going to argue with him, but nothing comes out. She's not going to sleep tonight and she knows it. She's not going to tell him the things she should. As Julian follows her through the apartment, he notices that it's the exact same layout as 8C. The same terra-cotta tiles in the kitchen and bathroom, the same acoustical tiles on the ceiling, the same hanging globe of light in the hall. Before Lucy opens the door to the boy's room, Julian can feel the discontent inside, a thick, blue cloud reaching from ceiling to floor. He walks past Lucy and stands in the middle of the rug, surveying the glow-in-the-dark stars on the ceiling. He can smell cigarette smoke and popcorn. He figures the window shades haven't let any light into this room for months.

"Has he ever been in any kind of trouble?" Julian asks easily as he heads for the closet. He opens the closet door, waiting for an answer, but Lucy's not talking.

"Your boy?" Julian asks. "Ever had any kind of trouble with him?"

As he takes a denim jacket from a wire hanger, Julian manages a look at Lucy.

"No," Lucy says. There's a pulse on the left side of her throat that flutters as she speaks.

"No?" Julian says. He can feel the outline of a pack of matches in the pocket of the jacket. Inside the lining there's a slit in the material, cut with a sharp knife, perfect for shoplifting. "That's rare," he said. "Most boys his age get in trouble for something. Smoking, shoplifting, that kind of thing."

"Really?"

The way Lucy says "really" makes Julian want to kiss her. His blood feels much too hot, as though it doesn't even belong to him anymore. She's going to protect her son, no matter what, Julian knows that for a fact. All his life, he has tried to understand what makes a mother love her child and what makes her cast him aside. He has seen female pelicans care for their young so tenderly they'll pluck out their own feathers to line their nests, leaving pinpricks of blood along their skin. They'll starve themselves if necessary for the sake of their brood. Certainly, there can be no uglier offspring than a baby pelican, which can't even waddle without staggering under the weight of its enormous beak. And yet Julian has witnessed this sort of devotion again and again. He's watched a twenty-pound fox stand up to Loretta, its fur a ridge of fury along its back, all because of a hidden pair of kits. He's found ants dead of exhaustion on his windowsill after carrying hundreds of egg cases to safety. Why is it, then, that a she-bear would have loved Julian more than his own mother? He was born premature, too soon for his mother to get to the hospital in Hartford Beach, a tiny baby so ugly he must have seemed like a punishment. Just two hours after Julian was born, he died. He simply stopped breathing, and he would have stayed dead if his mother hadn't run all the way to Lillian Giles's house. Miss Giles rubbed his hands and feet and breathed into his mouth; she wrapped him up in dishtowels and finally placed him on a rack in the oven, where she kept him until he was no longer blue. He has tried to remember back to that day when he was given away. He's been told he was fed sugar water, dripped into his mouth from a cloth, until he would take a bottle of milk. When he cried, the toads in the garden buried themselves in the dust, the wild limes dropped from the trees.

Although he's had no personal experience with it, Julian knows there are certain things you can't do in the presence of devotion. You can't look for marijuana seeds in the dresser drawers, for instance, or satanic messages scribbled inside a school notebook.

"How about a Coke?" Julian says. "Maybe with some ice."

"Now?" Lucy says.

"I'm dying of thirst." Julian puts a hand to his throat and realizes that it's true.

"I only have Diet," Lucy tells him.

"Diet," Julian says. "Diet's great."

Once he's gotten her out of the way, Julian goes through the desk drawers, then sorts through the clothes tossed into a jumble on the floor. He gets down on all fours and peers beneath the bed. It's not as if he knows what he is looking for, but he does know more than he'd like to about boys who search for disaster until they find it. He also knows when he's being lied to.

When Lucy comes back with his Coke, the light from the hallway forms a white circle around her. That's when Julian understands how much she knows. He reaches out suddenly,

71

and as he pulls Lucy to him, the Coke spills on the carpet. Lucy's knees buckle beneath her, and for hours afterward she will wonder why she didn't break away from him right then. He keeps one hand on her waist, while his other hand quickly moves down her leg. Lucy pushes against him, but he grabs her foot anyway and jerks off her sandal. When he lets go, Lucy stumbles backward until her spine is pressed up against the cool plaster wall.

"Size eight," Julian says as he examines the sandal. "How come I'm not surprised?"

This is the time of night when the humidity can be down-right unbearable, the ivory hour when nothing rises, not even your spirit. They stand facing each other beneath the glow-in-the-dark stars, not noticing when the stars begin to fall, one by one, pulled down by the thick, wet air. Neither of them has to be told that once someone is lost a stone forms in the place where he used to be. Rattle it once, in the smooth cup formed by your hand, and you may just draw blood.

Chapter Three

B EFORE there is any light there is the sound of birds. Their song spirals slowly upward: green heron, mockingbird, indigo bunting, kingbird. If you wake to this song, beneath the open sky, your heart may beat too fast. You may not be certain whether or not you're still dreaming until you see that the stars are already disappearing into the morning sky, flickering as they fade.

In a lair of sugar cane and strangler figs, beyond the muddy reaches of a green pond, the meanest boy in Verity scrambles to all fours, his eyes still closed, his mouth dry with sleep. His chest heaves, but amazingly enough, the raccoon at the edge of the pond methodically washing its hands isn't frightened off by the sound of the boy's heart beating. The baby who sleeps beside him remains curled up, knees to chest, her thumb in her mouth. In her sleep, the baby moves closer, until her spine rests against the boy's leg. For twenty-four hours they have lived on stale doughnuts and one Styrofoam cup filled with tepid water. At the very bottom of the boy's backpack there is still a peanut butter sandwich, found in a trashcan at the far end of the golf course. The green pond, which has begun to shimmer as the last few stars vanish, is the one where Charles Verity disappeared. Some local boys believe that an alligator still swims here. Golfers mistake its broad back for a half-submerged log. Gulls that light in the center of the pond often sink without a trace, except for a circle of ripples as the water closes over their heads. It is damp this morning and the boy's T-shirt is soaked; his jeans are coated with mud and beetles' wings. The boy gets up on his haunches, to stretch and ease the cramps in his legs, but he can't stand upright beneath the sugar cane. His lungs feel thick and wet; when he opens his mouth to cough, nasty little brown clouds come out.

There are so many things he should not have done he has lost count of them. He should never have pretended to be asleep, when all he was doing was waiting for his mother's bedroom door to close. He should have left the money he'd stolen from Donny Abrams in his night-table drawer, instead of stuffing it into his backpack and sneaking out of the apartment at three in the morning. He should never have kept his secret stash down in the laundry room, or had a stash at all, or come to Florida in the first place.

When he got down to the basement it was completely dark, except for the wavering fluorescent light above the vending machines. All he had to do was crouch down beside the second washing machine and slide his hand behind it into the hole in the plaster, then dislodge the tin box where he kept his contraband. Instead, he went to the row of dryers, drawn like a crow or a consummate thief to the two gold rings someone had left on the shelf. He scooped them up in the wink of an eye. If he brought these rings to the

pawnshop Laddy had told him about, he figured he might
have enough for a plane ticket back to New York. He should
have turned and run then, but that was when he realized
the sound of water running through the pipes overhead was
something else entirely. It was the sound of a woman screaming, and he knew, right away, just how wrong something was.

He backed up against the cool cinder-block wall and didn't
dare breathe. He doesn't know how long he stood there, but
it seemed like forever, long enough for vines to grow up
through the basement floor and wrap themselves around his
knees. And then the scream was over, and all he could hear
was the thick reverberation of somebody breathing hard and
a funny sort of static in the rhythm of a heartbeat. He saw
then that an intercom had been left on the bench, and right
beside the bench, in a metal laundry bin, slept a baby, not
much more than a year old. When she opened her eyes, he
lifted her out of the laundry bin and she put her arms around
his neck. She smelled like Ivory Snow and milk. She reached
for her stuffed bunny rabbit. He knew her by sight; her
mother always made her wear a life jacket in the pool, even
when she was just sitting on the steps. Sometimes, when
the baby's mother led her through the lobby after grocery
shopping, she'd leave a trail of Cheerios behind her. And
now, for reasons he could not begin to understand, she
seemed to be his, whether he wanted her or not.

He grabbed some diapers from the pile of laundry in the
bin, and when he carried the little girl up the stairs he found
she was heavier than she looked. But what was he supposed
to do? Leave her in the laundry room by herself, abandon
her in a stairwell, take her back to the apartment where
someone had been screaming? He went right to the ficus
hedge and set the baby down on the ground so he could dig

where the sand was already soft. He found the box and threw the rings inside. He had to. Otherwise, everyone would have known he'd stolen them. Maybe he should have turned himself in and hoped for mercy, but there was no reason for anyone to trust him. His own mother would have probably believed the worst.

He was acting purely on instinct, so when he heard the soft whir of the revolving door to the lobby he didn't think twice. He picked the little girl up and took off running, and he didn't look back until he was halfway across the parking lot. The man who had seen them was racing to his car, so the boy took the secret path he and Laddy had discovered on the far side of Long Boat Street. No car could follow them there, and after a while they'd reach the drainage ditch that ran along the Interstate. He knew he had a perfect right to be afraid. He could feel the bunny rabbit flapping against his chest as he ran; he could tell the baby's diaper was already soggy. He didn't call 911 until he dared to leave the path for a road leading to the golf course. He carried the baby into the phone booth and made certain to keep his hand over the mouthpiece when he told the officer who answered that someone might be dead up in apartment 8C. He thinks he may have lost his voice at the moment when he hung up the phone, and he still cannot speak, not even a whisper. Each time he tries, his throat closes up and he begins to choke.

The baby doesn't seem to mind that he can't talk. She's not a crybaby, and she's a good sleeper. She doesn't wake up until the dragonflies have already begun to hover over the pond and a line of pearl-colored light has cut across the sky. The baby keeps her stuffed bunny in the crook of her arm, and she scoots over, right beside the meanest boy in town. Whenever she's awake, she holds on to the leg of his jeans. At first he tried to make her let go, but she's stubborn, and he's gotten used to the tug on his leg, the constant pressure, like gravity. He has even forced himself to change a diaper, something he never in his life would have believed he'd have the stomach for. He tries not to think much about the way his stomach feels. He always laughed at Boy Scouts and nature-lovers, but now he has no idea of what's edible. Raw sugar cane, a tiny fish caught in the pond, the green figs in the branches above them. They don't have to talk for him to know that the baby is hungry. She tugs a little harder on his jeans and starts to whimper. In a little while he will have to think about what to do next. In cases like this, there is always a plan. The authorities have probably already gone through his possessions, the stolen money and cigarettes, the green birthstone ring he swiped from a classmate right before gym. How many dragonflies would it take to make a meal? How can he catch them without falling headlong into the pond? If he could speak he would tell himself not to be afraid, but since he cannot, he takes the peanut butter sandwich out of his backpack, breaks it into four neat pieces, then watches as the little girl eats every bit, including his share.

Some mothers, when handed a black-and-white photograph, taken at the instant their child committed a crime, will swear their boy spent all night right beside them on the couch. They'll hang on to their son's shirttails rather than let the police take him away. They believe not in what they see but in what they know in their hearts to be true. But when a woman hasn't slept all night, when she's left the window open so that the thick night air has given her a migraine nothing can cure, it's possible for her to believe that her child may be guilty of something. This doesn't mean she won't fight just as hard as the trumpeter swan, who will peck to death any creature that dares to approach her fledgling, and whose enormous white wings will beat against any real or imagined threat. The difference is a simple one. If a fledgling is born deformed—a broken spine, a wing cracked in half—the mother kills it herself rather than allow it to suffer. The trumpeter swan, after all, sees in black and white.

It is a little past six, on the third day of May, and after going through every possible explanation for her son's disappearance, Lucy finally telephones Evan. She knows he'll blame her, and he starts right in.

"Jesus Christ, Lucy! Don't you keep track of him? Are you saying that he gets up for school whenever he pleases and maybe he makes it there and maybe he doesn't and damned if you know!"

"You're the one who keeps encouraging him in these fantasies about going home," Lucy shoots back. "It's you."

"Yes, he's excited about coming home this summer," Evan counters. "Why shouldn't he be?"

Lucy thinks about the calendar in Keith's closet; the last day of school is circled in red with bombs going off around it. *Home,* it says in Keith's wavering script.

"Lucy?" Evan says.

He doesn't need to tell her it's her fault, and maybe that's why she can't admit how much has gone wrong. If she hasn't been able to discuss the stealing and the suspensions from school, how can she begin to explain that a murdered woman's gold rings have surfaced in a grave she and Keith dug together? She thinks about Julian Cash pulling her to him. For twenty years, Evan believed whatever she told him.

78

Lucy has always suspected that he never truly knew her because she didn't allow it; now she's not so sure. Julian Cash identified each one of her lies long before she dared to speak it.

"I'll fly down this morning," Evan says. He's an architect in a large firm, and when Lucy and he were married he never took any time off. That's changed since the divorce. Now he doesn't go into the office on Friday afternoons and he accepts less important clients, summer houses in Bellport, family room additions. "I can leave right now."

"No," Lucy tells him. "You can't. He may already be on his way to New York."

"Jesus," Evan says. "You're right. I'll stay here. God damn it," he adds. He sounds exhausted. "Look, let's not blame each other for everything that's wrong with him. We can't do that."

"We used to do that," Lucy says in a small voice.

"Well, that was okay," Evan says gently. "We were married."

She can't stand it when he's nice to her, and what's more, she can't stay home waiting for Keith to be caught. What she needs is bargaining power, just in case.

"I'll call you the minute I know anything," Lucy tells Evan, and she knows she sounds as if she really means it. After she hangs up, Lucy clicks on her answering machine, then gets dressed and washes her face with cold tap water. She puts on a pair of dark glasses to hide her puffy eyes and drives down to the *Sun Herald*. She doesn't even have to look for Paul; he comes up behind her while she's locking her car.

"Tough luck about your kid," he says.

Lucy whirls around to face him. They're both wearing

sunglasses, so neither one has the advantage. Between them heat rises off the blacktop in pale, snaky lines.

"Sooner or later a kid with his record for trouble always winds up running away," Paul says. "Statistically."

Lucy realizes that her mouth must have dropped open, because Paul grins and says, "And how do I know he's taken off?" He taps his skull gently, as though it contained a secret weapon. "Look, don't worry," he tells Lucy. "He'll wind up in Atlanta or San Francisco or back with his pop. I'd bet money on it."

Lucy smiles up at Paul; it gives her some curious, bitter pleasure to know that her son's companion is the missing baby Paul would so love to find.

"Tell me about Karen Wright," Lucy says as she trails along toward Paul's parked Volvo.

"That's not her name," Paul says. "Not her hair color, not her age, not her driver's license." He suddenly turns on Lucy. "Why? What do you know about her?"

"Nothing," Lucy says. She takes one step back and adjusts her sunglasses.

"If you ever want to get out of obituaries, you have to start paying attention to details," Paul says.

"You're right," Lucy says. She bites her lip, just a little, not enough to draw blood.

"Ever ride the elevator with her?" Paul says, as he jerks open the door to his car.

"Well, yes," Lucy admits.

"Ever sit by the pool with her? Borrow her suntan lotion?"

"I guess so," Lucy says.

"Then you probably know at least ten things about her that could lead us straight to her, if you were paying attention to details."

After Paul's car has disappeared onto West Main Street, Lucy stands on the asphalt beneath a blue cloud of exhaust. She takes off her sunglasses and pushes them up on her head. In the rich, lemon-colored light of morning, a morning that is already far too hot, Lucy has just begun to realize that, without having paid the slightest bit of attention, she knows more about her neighbor than Paul Salley ever will. She knows where Karen had her hair cut, not only here in Verity but back in her other life. Back in New York.

"Honey, you're going to fry out here," Kitty Bass says.

Lucy is so spooked by the sound of a human voice beside her that she lurches forward. Just for a moment, the voice sounded like Karen's, sweet and flat and very far away.

Kitty puts her arm around Lucy to steady her. "You shouldn't be here anyway. You should be home waiting for Keith. The question isn't whether or not he'll show up, it's how much you're going to yell at him when he does. And stop thinking about that dead woman."

"Who should I think about?" Lucy asks. "Julian Cash?"

"Are you serious?" Kitty says. "Listen, I can tell you anything you need to know about Julian." She fans herself with her hand, and the two silver bracelets on her wrist hit together and sound like bells. "Number one? Stay away from him."

"I'd like to," Lucy says. "But he's the one looking for Keith."

"Well, that's fine. He's good at that," Kitty says. "Believe it or not, he once broke my Janey's heart, about a million years ago. After that we all thought he was going straight to hell, but he went into the army instead."

Lucy promises Kitty that she'll go home, where she'll force herself to eat some solid food, then lie on the couch with a damp cloth on her forehead. But instead, she drives toward the intersection of West Main and Seventh, and she's lucky to get a space right in front of the Cut 'n' Curl.

"Lucy, I'm booked," Dee says when she sees her. "Take a number. I won't get to you until after lunch." She leaves her current client sitting in front of the mirror with a towel wrapped around her head. "I heard about your son running away," Dee says mournfully. She takes a Kent Light out of her smock pocket and reaches for a pack of matches. "I thank God my two boys are grown up and on their own. They can drive you crazy real easy, without even trying." Dee reaches up and takes a strand of Lucy's hair in her fingers so she can examine the color. "I still think you should tint this," she says. "Nothing permanent."

"You cut Karen Wright's hair, didn't you?" Lucy asks.

Dee inhales deeply and nods. "Can you believe it?" she says. "She was in here two weeks ago. From now on, I'm double-locking my front door at night."

"Did she have a boyfriend or anyone she was really close to?" Lucy asks.

"That little girl of hers. That's who she was close to. That baby would sit right in her lap and not move an inch while I shampooed Karen. I hate to think of where that little girl is right now."

"She didn't work?"

"Full-time mother," Dee says. "You say that to some people these days and it's like you're committing a crime." Dee stubs out her cigarette in an ashtray. "She wasn't a real big tipper," Dee admits. "Not that I held it against her. I think she was running low on cash. She never used a credit card or a personal check, which I appreciate. She paid cash. Whenever she was broke she used to joke about running up to Hartford Beach." When Lucy looks blank, Dee adds, "You've obviously never been broke."

"Not yet," Lucy says.

"The pawnshop's up in Hartford Beach. A lot of engagement rings wind up there when the rent is due."

It takes Lucy fifteen minutes to get to Hartford Beach, in spite of the fact that her Mustang is starting to stall at red lights, and another fifteen minutes of circling around until she finds Hallet's Pawnshop. When she turns off the ignition the cooling system just gives out and the radiator starts to boil over. Lucy jumps out and wrenches the hood open, then leaps backward to escape the hot spray of water. She knows that back in New York the azaleas and dogwoods are already blooming. Here, in Hartford Beach, the wild lime trees that grow up through the cement are wilting in the heat, and they stink, like cheap after-shave. When Lucy steps out into the street to look for a gas station, her shoes sink into the asphalt. To the right are the pawnshop, a McDonald's, and a Sun Bank. To the left is a Verity police cruiser so encrusted with dirt you'd have to look twice just to make certain it said "K9" along the side. Julian Cash gets out and leans up against the hood so he can stretch his back. He's got a warm can of Coke in one hand, which he raises in a greeting. All the cruiser's windows are rolled down, so Loretta can stick her head out and get some air.

"Kind of makes you wonder how dogs can stand it in this heat, doesn't it?" Julian says as Lucy approaches him. "Seems like they'd just go crazy and attack the first person who passed by."

"I can't believe you did this," Lucy says. "You followed me."

"You lied to me," Julian says. "You were never going to

tell me your boy buried that shoe box, so I figure I don't owe you very much."

"Oh, really?" Lucy says. "You owe it to me to be looking for my kid. That's what you're supposed to be doing."

"I just wanted to make sure you didn't know where he was."

Julian finishes his Coke, but Lucy knows that he's watching her carefully.

"I don't," she says.

"I know that now," Julian admits. "You're too busy looking for the dead girl."

"Woman," Lucy says.

"Around here we call each other boys and girls," Julian says. "Since growing up is such a tragedy."

Julian reaches for a cigarette and lights it, just so he'll shut up. He has no idea why he's talking so much; it's as if someone has pushed a button inside him and he's saying everything he never said before. Things he never even knew he thought.

"I'm sure Kitty Bass told you a whole lot about me. But you know that old joke about Kitty." He really can't stop himself; he must have some kind of talking disease. "Bigmouth Bass," he says. When Lucy eyes him coldly, he adds, "I didn't invent this joke, you understand. I'm just repeating it. Personally, I really respect Kitty."

"Are you going to continue following me?" Lucy asks. Her face is flushed and her dress is so wet it clings to her like a snake's skin.

"No," Julian says. "I'm going to call Marty Sharp's towing to come pick up your car while you go on and see what your neighbor pawned. Then I'm going back home to get my other dog."

Lucy gets a funny look on her face, as if she's holding

everything deep inside, and if she lets go, even for a second, she'll wind up in tears, right here on the sidewalk.

"I was out for four hours this morning with Loretta, and we came up empty. This other dog of mine is an air dog. That means he's supersensitive." Julian is yakking so much his mouth hurts. He's begun to suspect that if they stand here much longer a catastrophic mistake might result, a month-of-May sort of mistake, the kind that can change your life forever.

"Go on," Julian says. "I'll call the tow truck."

Julian calls in to the station and has them contact Marty's towing; then he sits in the cruiser, where the temperature must be high enough to boil human blood. He keeps his eye on the window of Hallet's Pawnshop; the green awning above the door hasn't been changed for years. When Julian was thirteen he walked here from Verity and back, twelve miles each way, just so he could buy a bowie knife. He never thought about who the hell had been so desperate he'd trade in a knife with a real bone handle for some spare change. Julian kept that knife for years, hidden behind some loose boards in Miss Giles's pantry; he used to clean the blade with rubbing alcohol and a soft flannel rag. He knows Lucy has discovered something as soon as she walks out of Hallet's door; she's got that hurried gait Loretta always has when she picks up a scent. Lucy goes to her car, circles it, then grudgingly walks over to the cruiser. When she gets into the passenger seat, Julian makes sure he's still watching Hallet's window.

"Well?" Julian says.

"If you could give me a ride home, I'd appreciate it," Lucy says. "Otherwise, I'll call a taxi."

There's less than twenty inches between them in the front

seat, so Julian leans up against the door. "I haven't mentioned to Walt Hannen that it was your boy who called nine-one-one. But you and I know it was. I haven't even told him that alligator in the shoe box wasn't some kind of voodoo offering. I think you can tell me what she pawned."

While Lucy considers this, Julian turns the key in the ignition, then pulls out and makes a U-turn.

"A sapphire necklace, less than three weeks ago," Lucy finally admits.

"She had money," Julian says.

"Had," Lucy says. "Before she got divorced." She stares out the window as they drive east, toward Verity. "It wasn't as if he killed that alligator," she says finally. "He tried to feed it lettuce but it died anyway."

"I never said he killed it," Julian says.

"It just died in our bathtub."

"All right, it died. Did it happen to have two gold rings with it when it was interred or whatever the hell you did with it?"

Lucy crosses her legs and moves so that her back is up against her door. "No," she admits. "There weren't any rings."

"There you have it," Julian says.

"What do you have?" Lucy demands.

"He stole those two rings." Julian glances over at Lucy when he should be looking at the road. "We both know he did."

"So what does that prove?" Lucy says.

"Nothing," Julian says. "Except that he's a thief." As they pass through the outskirts of Verity, where the alligator farms once stood, Julian knows that he has to get rid of her fast. He's talking like a maniac. If he's not careful, he'll be acting like one, too. "I never said he killed anyone."

"You just thought it," Lucy says icily.

"No," Julian says. "You're the one thinking it." When he steals a look at her he can see that pulse in her throat again. "Look, don't hit yourself over the head for it. You have a perfect right to be suspicious. This is a kid who's been looking for trouble. Believe me. I know. I killed a man when I was seventeen."

He can hear Lucy's breathing quicken and he knows just how far gone he is. If he doesn't stop soon, he's going to have to buy himself a muzzle.

"Is that supposed to make me feel better?" Lucy says.

The light coming through the car windows is so clear and yellow Julian almost forgets what day this is. It's his birthday, the most horrible day of a horrible month, when there shouldn't be any light around him. At least he has the satisfaction of not having blurted that out, because if she or anyone else felt pity for him he wouldn't be able to bear it. He would curl up right here, on the road that leads to Verity, and in all probability he would never be able to rise to his feet again.

The Angel lies on his back, beneath the tree, looking up through the branches at a Delta flight headed north to La Guardia Airport. He has been nineteen for a very long time, and although he can still climb to the top branches of the gumbo-limbo tree in less time than it takes to blink an eye, and still wears the same white T-shirt and blue jeans as always, his presence has never been detected. He no longer leaves footprints on the ground.

Once he had been the most beautiful boy in Verity. His hair was as yellow as butter; he had rolled over in his crib

87

and smiled at the age of two weeks. Everyone called him Bobby, except for his mother, who called him darling or sweetheart, as if his own name wasn't good enough for him. She adored him, and she had every right to, but her sister-in-law, Irene, was so jealous that she cursed the day he was born. When Bobby was two he noticed that his Aunt Irene was getting much bigger, as if she had eaten a melon seed and it had taken root inside her stomach. But she was still as sour as a lemon; she fought with Karl at the diner over the price of a cup of coffee, she wandered through the aisles of the general store, weeping as she looked for molasses and canned soup. Her face swelled up, and in the end she gained so much weight she couldn't walk without a wooden cane. When she was thin again and had no baby to show for it, nobody asked any questions. But on deep, starry nights the grownups talked about her as they sat on their front porches, fanning away the mosquitoes and drinking iced tea, and that was how Bobby learned he had a cousin somewhere.

He thought quite a lot about the baby that had been given away, and as soon as Bobby turned nine and was allowed to wander off by himself, he set off to find him. The cousin, who was seven, lived with a woman old enough to be his grandmother. Every day he sat out on her front porch, collecting small red toads, waiting to be found. After they discovered each other, the boys played every day, secretly at first, and by the time they were eleven and thirteen they were inseparable. Nothing could have kept them apart. By then, Irene had disappeared, to Virginia or North Carolina, no one was sure, and most people had forgotten that the boys were cousins. The younger boy was the shadow of the older in all things, except for one. He had a bad streak; you could see it just by looking at him. When he was angry he'd make such a horrible noise people close by had to cover their ears. As he grew older he looked for trouble. He began to drink and, what was worse, to steal, even from his own cousin, whom he loved more than anyone in the world. He couldn't seem to stop himself until he had stolen his cousin's girlfriend, although that was not what they fought about on the night of the accident.

It was the younger cousin's birthday, and he'd had too much to drink. They were driving toward town in his Oldsmobile, a beat-up old thing with a huge engine, rebuilt time and time again, arguing about a comb the younger cousin had just stolen from the general store. They had never discussed the girl, and if Bobby knew he was being betrayed he didn't let on. For some reason, that just made the younger boy more intent on being bad; he wasn't even in love with the girl, but he kept on seeing her and making love to her, and each time he did he was more bitter than he had been the day before. That night they argued over that stolen silver comb, with a sharp rat tail you could use, if need be, in a fight. A worthless thing you could buy almost anywhere; still, the younger boy would be damned if he'd take it back and pay for it. He wasn't about to take orders from anyone, not even his cousin. And just to show him, just to show off, he stepped down on the gas, as hard as he could, on a patch of road that was slick with the pulp of strangler figs, on the third day in May.

At the moment of impact, the older cousin, who had smiled so surprisingly and sweetly at the age of two weeks, grabbed for the wheel, and turned it hard, so that the passenger side of the car slammed against the trunk of the gumbo-limbo tree. The younger cousin, who refused to black out in spite of the pain, was left with nothing more than a gash in his forehead. The older one, Bobby Cash, has been waiting beneath the tree for the past twenty years, ever since the day he was killed.

The Angel knows very little of what happened next, that his cousin was sent off to the state school in Tallahassee after a summer of self-destruction, that he broke up with the girl who meant so little to him, that he cannot, to this day, look in a mirror without the glass cracking. He doesn't know that his own mother was so consumed with grief she refused anything but water for thirteen days, or that on the first anniversary of his death his parents realized they could no longer live in Florida or that when they moved to Charlottesville, Virginia, they were soon followed by nearly every other member of the family. He can't know these things because he can't go past a two-foot circle around the tree. Years ago, the sap of gumbo-limbos was boiled into glue, then spread on the branches to trap songbirds, and now it is Bobby who can't escape. Most often he appears as nothing more than a wash of low-lying mist, or a black shadow in the shape of a bird's wing. Except in May, when boys of nineteen sometimes see him as they're breaking the speed limit, and then he always makes certain to throw himself between their cars and the trunk of the tree.

For all these years, the Angel has been waiting to forgive his cousin, or so he has always believed. At the instant when he did, they would both be released, and finally Bobby would no longer have to be nineteen. But his cousin has never returned, not once, and in the meantime, just two days ago, something quite amazing happened. Bobby fell in love. He was sitting in the same spot as always, his back up against the tree, when she walked across the parking lot, headed straight for him. She was almost seventeen and her long hair was tinted black and pulled into a ponytail. When she sat down beside him, the Angel remained completely still, just as he did when hawks nested for the night.

Shannon opened a paper bag and took out a hamburger and a Diet Coke, then carefully placed her lunch on the grass. She'd heard rumors about this tree all her life; she knew people who actually believed it was haunted. No one came here, and maybe that was why the grass was so soft; it hadn't been walked on for twenty years. All Shannon wanted was a place to be alone and some time to think. At this moment in her life she truly believed she might be going crazy. No one understood her. No one noticed that something was utterly wrong. For as long as she could remember, Shannon had been planning her future. All she had ever wanted was to get out of Verity, and she always believed her salvation would be a college scholarship. Now she had actually been accepted into a summer program at Mount Holyoke for advanced high school juniors, and she wasn't so certain that she cared. Since September, she had been sabotaging herself, forgetting about papers due, leaving her books in her locker, staying up long past midnight to do nothing but stare out her window. All those extracurricular activities college recruiters so loved were going up in smoke. She hadn't yet dared to tell her mother, but she was so behind in her schoolwork that she'd been called down to the guidance office twice. She hadn't even bothered to try out for the next school play, although she was practically assured of the lead. She had boys all over her, that was part of the problem. If she wasn't careful, she'd wind up pregnant and married at eighteen the way her mother had, and then she'd be stuck in Verity forever.

She wished that her voice wasn't so breathy, as if she'd

swallowed too much air, that her eyes, which tended to wander, didn't make her look slightly confused, maybe even dumb. She could be taking calculus at school, if they offered it; instead she was wearing makeup and shorter skirts, and the future seemed more and more remote each day. It was a relief to finally be alone. Here, beneath the gumbo-limbo tree, Shannon feels at peace. Here, it seems possible that she is more than a silly, confused girl who wears strawberry-flavored lip gloss. With every minute she spends beneath the tree, she grows more sure of herself, until it seems to be the only place she wants to be. She thinks about the sunlight filtering through the leaves while she sits through her classes, and when the lunch bell rings, she runs all the way to the Burger King, edgy and confused until she sees the tree. She's drawn here even in her dreams; in her dreams she makes a bed out of twigs, she covers herself with leaves, and sometimes, in the morning, there are tears on her pillow. Already she has begun to wonder how she can ever leave Verity, how she will manage to exist among pines and sugar maples.

Each time the Angel watches her, he's filled with agony. When she goes, he vibrates like a piece of electricity; some of the leaves on the low-growing branches have already been singed. He would do anything to be able to kiss her, but since he can't, he thinks the word *kiss*. He concentrates so hard that there are times when Shannon's mouth forms a surprised O and her cheeks grow flushed. What he wouldn't give to be real with her for just one hour, to thread his fingers through hers and walk far into the field beyond the Burger King, his arm around her waist. She looks enough like her mother for the Angel to be reminded of his past, but that's not why he begins to radiate bits of light as soon as he sees her, so that the grass beneath him turns pale gold. He understands her completely, he knows what it's like to want to escape and want it desperately. When she thinks about the future, the Angel can see it right along with her, and for this he'll always be grateful.

Through all the years he's been trapped here, time has moved in instants, pure white flashes of empty space. Now, an hour without her is an eternity. And that is how it happens that, after twenty years of waiting for his cousin to show up, the Angel is reclining beneath his tree, thinking about love, when Julian finally finds it in himself to return to the scene of his crime.

"Pull in there," Lucy says as they near the Burger King.

Julian immediately feels light-headed; his hands have begun to sweat.

"I don't think so," he says.

"I need to ask if anyone's seen Keith. That's where he hangs out. That's where he found the alligator." Lucy has already pushed the strap of her purse over her shoulder. "Right in there."

Julian steps on the brakes, but he drops his hands away from the steering wheel.

"Is there a problem?" Lucy asks.

"No problem," Julian says. He feels as if he's just eaten several pounds of sand.

"Well, there's a space," Lucy says.

Julian swallows hard and then turns the wheel. He drives into the parking lot slowly and edges into a space at the far end.

"Are you coming with me?" Lucy asks as she opens her door.

"You go," Julian says.

He leans his head back and closes his eyes and listens to Lucy's footsteps on the asphalt. What he would like to do is roll up all the windows and lock the doors, but instead Julian forces himself to get out. Loretta watches him through the window, but he leaves her in the backseat. It's too hot for a dog to be out in the sun, and it's not much better for a human being. Sometimes Julian wonders if living in all this heat eventually does something to your brain. In weather like this the air turns into waves, and those waves break down into sharp white circles, so you feel that you're surrounded by stars in the middle of the day.

He begins to head toward the tree, but it's like walking through molasses. By the time he reaches the edge of the parking lot he's exhausted. He can't even hear the traffic on West Main anymore. In Julian's path is an orange salamander, frozen in fear. If the salamander stays in one place a moment longer, its feet will sink into the asphalt, so Julian kicks a small rock in its direction, forcing it to run before it's too late. As he approaches the far corner of the Burger King, Julian thinks he can recall sitting in a wooden-slatted playpen beneath the blue sky. He can remember following Bobby through the mangroves to look for those indigo snakes you never see anymore. He was Bobby's shadow moving through the red-and-black mangroves, and like a shadow he didn't exist by himself. He had to wait in a corner or on a dusty stretch of road, folded up on himself, like a piece of stocking, until his cousin's presence brought him to life. And now he's back on the last path they ever took together. Inside the Burger King, a beautiful woman is ordering him a hamburger; she thinks he's a real live person instead of a shadow. She thinks he's waiting impatiently in the car, when he's standing here terrified in a place that was once filled with gumbo-limbo trees, beneath a sky so bright it brings tears to your eyes. Julian Cash has spent his entire adult life tracking down lost people. It's second nature for him to see in the dark, to follow his dogs through the bramble bushes, to hear what other men can't. That is why he notices the dry grass rustling. And that's why he stands perfectly still.

Directly in front of him, past the gas fumes and the heat waves, his cousin stretches out, eyes closed, a smile on his face. There are leaves in his hair and his feet are bare. Julian shakes his head, but his cousin remains beneath the tree. Slowly, the Angel opens his blue eyes, and if Julian Cash hadn't fainted where he stood, he would have received his freedom, right then and there.

By the time they get to Julian's house, out beyond the palmetto and the sweet bay, about two miles past Chuck and Karl's diner, the temperature is up to a hundred and one. There's swamp cabbage growing right up to the side of the road, and the air is so thick the patrol car seems to bump against it. Julian is slumped over in the passenger seat. It took all four of the teenage boys who work behind the counter at the Burger King to lift him into the car, and he seemed so lifeless that Lucy insisted on stopping at the general store to buy him some aspirin and a cold can of Coke.

The scar across Julian's forehead has turned as purple as the skin of a plum. He's taken off his jacket, unbuttoned the two top buttons of his shirt, and tossed his gun into the glove compartment. He feels sick as hell, like he's going to explode. It does not help that Lucy has turned out to be a terrible driver. He swears she's aiming for the ruts in the road. Each time they hit one, Lucy apologizes. She keeps looking over at him, worried, as if she had a dying man on her hands. Julian told her all he suffered from was a little heatstroke but he knows she doesn't believe him. She's had a great deal of experience with liars, and actually Julian isn't too sure of the truth himself. Maybe it was heatstroke; that would make a lot more sense than a vision formed out of guilt and grief.

"Take some of those aspirins," Lucy tells him, nodding to the tin on the dashboard that rattles each time they hit a rut. No one at the Burger King had seen Keith for days, and now all Lucy wants is for Julian to get his other dog and start tracking again.

Julian takes a long drink from his Coke. At Bobby's funeral he was absolutely certain that if he waited long enough his cousin would open his eyes. The lids would flutter, then rise. His eyes would be as blue as always, so blue it could make you forget you weren't looking at the sky.

"Take two," Lucy insists. She reaches for the tin of aspirin and tosses it into Julian's lap. He won't be of any use if he's sick.

Julian slips two aspirins into his Coke, shakes the can, then downs it. He made a mistake when he followed Lucy; he knows it now and he knew it then, but he just couldn't seem to stop himself. And now look what's happened to him; he doesn't even trust himself to drive.

"Make a right," he tells Lucy when his driveway comes into view.

Lucy turns the wheel, hard, so that Julian is jostled against the door. His ribs are bruised from his fall on the asphalt; he never would have believed it possible for him to collapse like a rabbit, scared out of its wits. As they drive toward the house, the merlins in the cypress trees beat their wings and cry out as if their hearts had been broken in two.

"They always do that," Julian feels he has to explain.

Lucy watches the birds as she slowly edges down the driveway. Clouds of red dust rise up around the car. Arrow has heard the car long before it appears; when it pulls up he's already running back and forth along the kennel's chain-link fence.

"Stay here," Julian tells Lucy as he opens his door and gets out. He lets Loretta out of the back, and she trots toward the woods.

Lucy ignores him, but as soon as she opens her door Arrow leaps at the fence, baring his teeth. The flickers in the bramble bushes take flight all at once. "Jesus," Lucy says. She slams the car door shut and quickly rolls up her window halfway, in spite of the heat. "I think I'll stay here," she tells Julian.

"Good idea," Julian says.

He whistles for Loretta, and she runs to follow him up the porch steps. The house is little more than a cottage, painted gray, with a deep, shady front veranda. The yard is a jumble of overgrown bushes, but all along the porch railing is an old frangipani vine, with flowers the size of teacups. A long time ago, when Julian was a boy, he used to walk in these woods with Miss Giles. The house was deserted back then, but the vine was there. Angels drink out of those cups, that's what Miss Giles told him. They're drinking from them right now, but their thirst escapes us.

"Hurry up," Lucy calls from the safety of the car.

Julian knows that people from New York think that fast and good are one and the same. They like to call the shots and tell you how to do your job and think they're in control.

Lucy wants him to start tracking immediately, but of course she has no idea what he may find. He wouldn't want her to. Julian gives Loretta some fresh water and kibble and gets himself another can of Coke from the refrigerator, then phones Roy Schenck over at Red Cab. He's got to get rid of her now; already he's gone back to the one place on earth he fears most and had some sort of temporary nervous breakdown or hallucination. He told Lucy that Arrow is special; he's an air dog, that's true. What he left out is that another name for this is "corpse dog." Arrow isn't concerned with spirit or sound; the only differentiation he makes is between dead and living matter.

Unlike Loretta, who sleeps on Julian's bed and whines when he leaves her alone in the house, Arrow has never licked Julian's hand or allowed himself to be petted. When Julian brings him his dinner in a large metal bowl, Arrow keeps his head averted, and he won't touch his food, no matter how ravenous he is, until Julian has left him alone. Sometimes when Julian sits in his kitchen, eating a TV dinner or some reheated pizza, his own aloneness comes down on him so hard he can't stay in one place. On those evenings, he throws his uneaten supper in the trash and goes out to the kennel. Arrow never acknowledges his presence. All the dog wants is to be left alone in the moonlight. Given half a chance, Arrow would leap the kennel walls and run as far as he could. Julian understands that desire, he's had it himself: to disappear into the woods and never once look back, to get as far away from whatever's been caging you in as fast as you possibly can.

Julian has that desire to run as soon as he goes back out to the porch. It's worse than he anticipated; Lucy is crying in the car. Her tears are so hot they leave little red spots, like match burns, all down her cheeks. Julian goes to stand by Lucy's half-open window.

"Don't do this," he says.

The Red Cab pulls into the driveway and honks. In the kennel, Arrow gets up on his hind legs and claws at the fence.

Now that Lucy has begun to cry, she can't seem to stop. She thinks about lost children, guided by the position of the stars in the sky. She thinks about boys who vanish forever, tangled up in weeds, trapped in drainage ditches, small bodies washed out to sea, where the fish pick their bones clean.

Julian opens the car door, but Lucy doesn't move. In desperation, Julian looks over at the kennel, where Arrow is pacing, still growling and showing his teeth.

"Look at that dog," Julian tells Lucy, and he waits until she does. "He's a maniac, but let me tell you something about maniacs. They see and hear things no one else can. That's why this dog's going to find your boy."

As soon as he's said this, Julian knows it's too late for him to turn and run. He never makes promises, and although he never said whether it would be dead or alive, he should have kept his mouth shut. This is what happens when you're born on the third day of the worst month of the year. Everything you ever did or loved or wanted comes back to haunt you. And if a woman happens to cry in your driveway, beneath the cypress trees, you may actually believe, however briefly, that it is still possible to fall in love.

"Just don't cry," Julian says. "Don't even think."

Lucy looks up and nods, then wipes her face with her hands. Together, they walk toward the idling taxi while the merlins above them swoop through the still air. The wing span of each bird's shadow is so wide a full-grown man could lie down on the road and not see a bit of sunlight. Lucy tries

99

her best to take Julian's advice as the taxi starts down the driveway. The dust comes up in small cyclones and there is the sharp scent of bay trees. In the backseat of the cab, Lucy lists inconsequential things, apricots, peaches, and plums, fruit so sweet you can taste it before you take a bite. And then, before she can stop herself, she thinks about desire, how it lives within you and yet is separate, surfacing when it chooses, without permission, in the harsh afternoon light, at the moment when you least expect to find it.

Chapter Four

N the heat of the day, when the dragonflies rest on the
surface of the water so their wings won't catch on fire, the
meanest boy in Verity follows the drainage ditch along
the service road between the Interstate and the golf course.
The ditch hasn't held a drop of water since winter; it's filled
with dust and small black toads. Whenever the boy walks
beneath an overpass, into a dark concrete tunnel, his heart
echoes louder than the traffic above him. Inside his throat,
there is now a lump the size of a golf ball; he can't grunt or
hiccup or sigh. A line of hot red skin runs across the bridge
of his nose, and his bare shoulders and back are already
blistering. The baby has fallen asleep in his arms; he's covered her head with his T-shirt to protect against sunstroke,
and as he walks the little girl's feet swing back and forth and
hit him in the stomach. Each time a car passes, the boy
freezes, but no one seems to notice him. All those cars have
their windows rolled up and their air conditioners turned on
high. They pass by like the wind, flushing birds from the

saw grass, traveling so fast they leave no trace on the melting asphalt.

The boy has already realized that the problem with a baby is that you have to take care of it. It holds on to your fingers and makes whimpering sounds and expects you to find food and water. It puts its arms around your neck and presses its hot cheek against you as it falls asleep, convinced all will be well when it wakes. The meanest boy in Verity would sit down in the dust and cry if he weren't so dehydrated. He's made of straw and bones and teeth, furious and ignitable. If someone came up behind him and tapped him on the shoulder, he would turn and bite, then run. Everything that has ever happened to him before has dissolved. There is no before and no after. All he can see and remember is this blinding sunlight, the slow, steady breathing of the baby, the lurch of his own pulse.

Like a wolf, he is headed back to the place where he knows there is food. When the baby sees what he's found for her, she'll smile and coo; she'll unwind her fingers from his neck, letting go of him only long enough to eat. They'll sit in the long green shadows and drink orange juice and cold coffee from discarded cups, and they'll fill themselves until their bellies are fat and their fingers are sticky with sugar. The idea of the dumpster, and all that it contains, is so compelling that the boy starts to jog, though it strains his back to run while carrying the baby. She's a big baby, and her arms and legs are red where she's scratched at her mosquito bites. She smells clean, though, in spite of how dirty she is. When she's asleep her breath comes out in warm little puffs; her eyelids flutter, as if she is able to see with her eyes shut tight.

At the end of the drainage ditch, when the Hole-in-One

Donut Shop is finally in sight, the boy sits down in the tall grass, exhausted. The baby wakes up, and the boy unwinds her arms from his neck and plops her on the ground. But as soon as he goes to stand, she grabs on to his leg and won't let go. The boy waits, and when the baby turns her head, he quickly tries to edge backward, but she scrambles right next to him just as quickly. She's not about to let him out of her sight. He has no choice but to pick her up and carry her across the road, in full view of a line of passing cars. He runs to the dumpster, sits the baby down on the curb, then raises himself up so he can root through the garbage. The boy brushes the fire ants off the first piece of jelly doughnut he finds, then crouches down and hands it to the baby. She holds the lump of dough in two hands and devours it, making a humming sound as she eats. While she's occupied, the boy searches the dumpster again, pulling off the tops of Styrofoam cups, his hands shaking. He finds half a cup of coffee and gulps it down; it is the most delicious thing he's ever drunk in his entire life, in spite of the lipstick marks around the rim of the cup.

It is so hot now that the air crackles. Aside from that, and the occasional car passing by, the parking lot is silent. There are no birds foolish enough to fly in this heat, and all the insects have crawled into the burrows they've dug in the sand. Behind the screen door of the Hole-in-One's kitchen, Shannon is watching. She wears shorts and a T-shirt and a pink apron; her long hair is gathered into a ponytail. She works at the Hole-in-One on weekends and afternoons after school, and ever since she came to work the register today, Shannon has been chewing ice and thinking about the future. She's beginning to wonder if it's some kind of obsession, the kind that makes it impossible to live your life day to day. How can it be that she wants to get out of town so badly, and yet each time she leaves the gumbo-limbo tree she's torn apart? Today she missed lunch because her math teacher had her stay in to make up her missing homework, and now she feels all empty inside, as if she's lost the most important part of her day. It's not as if the tree is waiting for her, and yet she feels she's betrayed it. She could almost believe that sorrow will wind its way along the tree's branches, chasing away the birds that nest there.

How can she go on living her life when no one on earth really knows her? Her mother keeps cooking her nutritious dinners and touching her head for fever. Her grandmother has suggested vitamin B and iron, as if what is wrong with her was a dietary ailment. She's gotten so used to masking her true feelings that when she sees the children at the dumpster she doesn't appear to have any reaction. She continues chewing on a piece of ice; she keeps one hand on the meshing of the screen door and her back remains straight. But deep inside, she feels as if she's just discovered something important. She knows how to be quiet, since it's the only way to have any privacy when you live in a tiny house with a mother who thinks every sniffle is pneumonia. With no noise whatsoever, she turns and goes to the refrigerator, gets out the milk, and pours a tall glassful.

"Oh, no!" Maury kids her as he cleans out the fryers. "Don't tell me you're eating healthy. You can't be your mother's daughter."

That's exactly what Shannon herself keeps wishing and then she feels horrible for wishing it. She loves her mother, she's crazy about her, she just doesn't want to be anything like her.

"Calcium," Shannon tells Maury. She grabs two chocolate

sugar-frosteds and grins at him, then heads back to the screen door. As far as she can tell, the boy is about thirteen or fourteen, tall and thin and absolutely filthy. His little sister is nothing more than a baby, with some kind of rag over her head and streaks of mud on her arms. She's like a little doll eating garbage. It's pitiful; she's so quiet and serious and she keeps one hand gripped on the boy's jeans. Shannon opens the screen door with her toe and edges onto the back stoop. She used to do this at their house when her parents were still together and deer came into the yard; she could get less than a foot from them before they noticed her presence and fled. Now she bends down and places the milk and doughnuts on the step. She's concentrating hard; her tongue darts out between her lips the way it always does when she's thinking, and she backs up into the kitchen slowly, on raised toes.

It's the screen door closing behind her that the boy hears. He turns his head, the way the deer used to in the tall grass in Shannon's backyard, then stands there frozen. The little girl holds tight to his leg and makes a high-pitched humming sound. The boy sees Shannon through the screen, sees her pink apron and the arc of her profile as she reaches out to steady the screen so it will stop creaking. They stare at each other across the parking lot, where the asphalt is melting and the heat waves rise like butterflies. In the kitchen, the frying vats sizzle as they're tossed into a sink of green soapy water. The smell of oil is heavy and rich; mixed with the heat, it can make you feel faint. Shannon runs her tongue over her lips. Someday, she'll live where there's frost in the early morning and the sky turns orange in October. But right now it's in the high nineties, and in this kind of weather milk can sour in a matter of minutes. So Shannon leaves the

105

screen door and goes out front to the counter, where she works the register. An hour later, after convincing her mother that she doesn't have the flu and the pink on her cheeks isn't fever but blush-on, Shannon goes back to the kitchen. When she looks out the door, she sees that the glass of milk has been drained and the doughnuts eaten, and the footprints on the steps are white and powdery, pure sugar that will disappear as soon as the raccoons venture out after dark.

Just before suppertime the next day, the only customers at the Hole-in-One are the high school boys who lounge at the counter, drinking Pepsi and eyeing Shannon as she counts the singles in the cash register drawer. Lucy sits in her Mustang, with the air conditioner turned off, since Marty from the towing service has warned her to get a new radiator before she uses it. She watches through the plate-glass window as the boys blow their straw wrappers over the counter, begging for Shannon's attention.

Lucy is here even though she knows that Keith is too smart to retrace his steps; if he saw her parked car, he would probably run in the other direction. She feels no comfort being in the last place he was seen; the air is mild and orange, but the deserted parking lot is spooky, the asphalt looks like a wide, black sea.

Lucy gets out of her car and goes into the doughnut shop, then sits at the far end of the counter.

"I'll be right with you," Shannon calls from the register.

Since Keith disappeared, Lucy's nerve endings seem too raw; she's susceptible to forces she's never even noticed before. Fluorescent lights are much too bright; change tossed on a Formica counter echoes. She wonders what it would be like to put her arms around Julian Cash, what it would be like for him to hold her. Would she be frightened by the sound of his heartbeat? Would she lose her nerve and run? Lucy is so busy trying not to think about Julian that she doesn't notice when Janey Bass comes out of the kitchen to clear the shelves behind the counter.

"Are you guys buying?" Janey asks the high school boys. "Or just breathing my air-conditioning?" She's been working since five in the morning, and she still looks beautiful, even though she's dying to close up and go home.

"They just ordered more Pepsis," Shannon tells her mother.

"Sure," Janey says. "Like they're here for the drinks."

As soon as she spies Lucy, whom Kitty's pointed out to her twice at the Winn Dixie, Janey nudges Shannon. "I'll take care of her. You go on and ring us out."

Janey gets two cups of coffee and brings them to the far end of the counter.

"You're the one with the fear of parakeets," Janey says, as she puts a cup of coffee down in front of Lucy.

"I thought that was you," Lucy says.

"No," Janey says. "That used to be me. Now it's you."

Janey goes to the covered racks of doughnuts, gets a jelly-filled cruller, and brings it back to Lucy on a white china plate. "Your favorite, right?"

Surprised, Lucy nods.

"You know the joke about my mother," Janey says. "Big-mouth Bass."

Over at the register, the boys gather around, paying Shannon for their Pepsis. She's probably the prettiest girl in her class, but she doesn't look twice at the boys; she just hands

107

them their change, and when they head mournfully for the door she calls, "Mom, we're all set to close."

"Go ahead and wait for me in the car," Janey says, then she turns back to Lucy. "Who would have thought somebody like me would have an honor student for a kid? Go figure."

When Janey laughs she arches her neck. She has three beauty marks, two on the left side of her face and another at the base of her neck. Lucy tries to imagine Janey Bass and Julian together, but she just can't do it; they're the least likely couple in the world. Just looking at Janey makes Lucy doubt herself. She must have been crazy to cut her hair so short. She was thinking about comfort in the heat without once considering how she would look.

"I hear you've had a lot of problems with your boy," Janey says.

"Let me guess," Lucy says. "You and Kitty have been talking about me."

"You're right," Janey says.

"How nice for you." Lucy's not sure why, but she feels as though she's just entered combat.

"I was the one who saw your boy, you know," Janey says. "And I guess I don't blame him for running away after all the trouble he's been in, although he kind of screwed himself even worse by taking that baby with him, didn't he? And don't worry, I didn't tell my mom he had the baby with him, not the way she talks. I only told Julian."

Lucy pushes her cup of coffee away. She can feel herself get all flushed.

"Uh huh," Janey says. She's got a smile on her face, but it's like a cat's smile—you don't know whether or not to trust it.

"What's that supposed to mean?" Lucy asks.

"Like I said." Janey nods. "It used to be me. Now it's you."

Lucy takes her hands off the counter. She can feel a pulse vibrating in both her wrists. "Whatever you think you know, you're wrong."

"Oh, come on," Janey says. "You know exactly what I'm talking about. I thought you were going to faint when I said his name. I'm one of the few people in the world who understands completely." When Lucy looks blank, Janey tosses her head, impatient. "How bad you want him. It's all over you."

Janey's not one hundred percent certain she's right until she sees Lucy's reaction: she looks so guilty you'd think she'd just committed a crime. For a moment Janey feels ashamed for making Lucy so uncomfortable. Janey's never been the jealous type, she's never had to be. It's not even that she wants Julian anymore. She just remembers how much she used to. She remembers so well her throat aches.

"You know what I think?" Lucy gets up, reaches into her jeans pocket for a dollar, then tosses it on the counter. "I think you and Kitty ought to find someone else to dissect."

"Hey, I didn't mean to offend you," Janey says.

"Oh, yes you did."

Lucy is shaking as she heads for the door. When she gets outside she has to stop and fish through her purse for her car keys. What's bothering her isn't so much what Janey's said but her own reaction to it; there's something fierce inside her, and she doesn't even know what it is.

"Wait a minute," Janey calls. She's come out of the shop and has begun to follow, but Lucy clutches her purse and heads for her car.

"All right," Janey says. "Run away."

Lucy turns then to face her. "You think I'm afraid of you? You think I care about anything you have to say?"

"There's one thing men will never understand," Janey says. She walks over to Lucy. "We really don't give a damn about the way they look. They think we care, because they care, but that's not what drives somebody crazy. I know how it feels when Julian wants you."

Lucy has finally found her car keys; she keeps her fingers tightly wrapped around them, till they cut into her flesh.

"Maybe I'm jealous," Janey says. "Maybe I should have gone after him when he broke up with me. But I started to listen to all the people around me, and they all told me I was nuts, so I never did."

Across the parking lot, Shannon presses down on the Honda's horn.

"I kind of forgot about her." Janey grins. "I guess I should have kept my mouth shut about Julian, but there you have it. Bigmouth Bass."

Tonight, when the sun goes down, the sky will clear to reveal constellations Lucy has never even seen before. Standing here, with Janey, she feels as exposed as those orange flowers on a trumpet vine.

"You want some advice?" Janey asks.

"No," Lucy says.

They look at each other and laugh.

"Not about Julian," Janey says. "Considering I did everything wrong."

Shannon leans her head out the car window. "Mom," she calls.

"Hold your horses," Janey calls back. "Use lemon juice on your hair," she tells Lucy. "Some people don't believe it gets rid of the green ends, but it always used to work for me."

As Lucy drives home beneath the coral-colored sky, she misses two turns. Instead of driving around to doughnut shops, considering the effects of passion, she should be doing what Paul Salley and the Verity police probably never will. She needs to find out who Karen Wright was and who really killed her. It's the only way to deflect attention from Keith. If there are any doubts, and they catch him, he'll be destroyed. It's not a question of innocence or guilt, it's what he'll believe about himself. If he manages to prove himself despicable, he may never be able to turn back: the small lies will grow larger, like well-fed fish in a pond; the thefts riskier and more expensive, a string of beads formed into a noose around his neck.

And so instead of going straight to her apartment, Lucy goes to 1A, where the super lives. She doesn't have to pretend to be flustered when she tells him she needs to get into 8C. It's silly, of course, but there's a blouse she lent Karen that she'd like to reclaim. The super, a man in his sixties relocated from the Bronx, grumbles and tells her the apartment has been sealed off by the police. Lucy has to plead. She tells him that the blouse was bought on sale at Macy's, that she'll never find another like it, and in the end, he leads her upstairs, tells her she's got two minutes, and waits for her out in the hall.

It doesn't make any sense to be terrified by an empty apartment. The air conditioner's been turned off and the rooms are stifling. Someone has washed the kitchen floor, and the scent of industrial cleanser lingers. Lucy avoids the kitchen completely and goes directly to the master bedroom. But when she turns on the lights, she's momentarily paralyzed. The bedspread is one Lucy's seen over at Bed and Bath on West Main: huge, wild roses on a mint-green background. Those roses could break your heart if you looked at them too long. She throws open the closet door and grabs the first blouse she sees. She never in her life lent Karen Wright anything, and now she regrets it. The blouse is white linen, with pearl buttons, but Lucy doesn't stop to examine it. Instead, she goes to the night table; she knows where you keep what's most important. She opens the top drawer and rummages through the earrings and cough drops until she finds what she's looking for. It's a photograph of Karen and her daughter, taken at the beach on a day when the humidity was bearable and the sky stretched out forever. It's even worse than those wild roses, so Lucy slips it into her pocket, then goes to shut the closet door.

Later, she'll take the photograph out and prop it up on her bathroom counter. After she phones to reserve a plane ticket back to a place where she never thought she'd return of her own free will, she'll memorize each one of her neighbor's features until they've become as familiar as her own. And when she's done, she'll take some lemons and halve them and rinse her hair twice, but not because Janey Bass told her to.

❀

Arrow moves through the thickets and the thorns, his huge head down, his tail raised. For the past three days he has unearthed dead moles, the remains of sea gulls, lifeless crickets, curled up and blackened from the heat. Whenever he and Julian work together there is silence, except for the sound of their breathing and occasionally the crack of a branch beneath their feet. Nothing distracts Arrow, not the planes overhead or the heat or the golfers on the fairway.

Julian keeps the dog on a forty-foot leash, so it's almost

112

as if he is free. A regular tracking dog might overlook a body that has been in the grass so long Spanish moss has begun to cover it, replacing the human scent with the rich odor of earth and growing things, but an air dog can gauge the extra molecules in the air when something dead is near. So when Arrow stops at the edge of the pond where Charles Verity died, Julian also stops. He's been thinking about his cousin too much. If he didn't know it was the thorn bushes that tore at his skin, he would almost believe the streaks of blood on his hands were the physical proof of his guilt. If he doesn't focus soon and stop thinking about Bobby, he'll walk right past the trail he's looking for, he'll mess up in a big way, all because he was scared by a ghost.

Julian takes out a cigarette, and waits for Arrow's next move. The sun has already begun to set, faster than would seem possible. Soon the night birds will begin to wake. As Julian follows Arrow in a circle around the pond, evening falls. Mosquitoes rise up from the shallow water, and the air grows heavier. Julian can feel something, right between his shoulder blades, and he stands absolutely still. It's just like what they say about damp evenings such as this: the air's too thick for spirits to rise. It comes as no surprise to Julian that he would attract a loose soul, since he is alive purely by accident. Twice he was supposed to die, and yet here he is. He can tell by the way Arrow looks at him: the dog knows the truth. He's a dead man whose heart beats. For no reason at all, he's alive when others are not, whether or not he deserves to be.

The weight on his back, the spirit or dead air or whatever it is, pushes Julian forward. He lurches toward an overgrown thicket of sugar cane and Arrow looks up at him, startled. The dog growls, low down in his throat, then charges into the thicket. Julian is strong, he can beat a man fifty pounds heavier than himself in a fight, fair or not, but he can't hold Arrow back. He's dragged into the sugar cane, over wild rose thorns, till he's flat on his belly. When he's no longer pulled, Julian crawls farther into the thicket, following Arrow's slack lead. In the center of the clearing the dog is stretched out, his ears pricked up. In the darkness his eyes are like black stars in a black night. Between his paws is a stuffed white bunny, held tight.

"Good boy," Julian says.

Julian sits up and lights a match so he can see the hollows where the children have slept. Arrow looks up at him and blinks in the sudden light; in his own good time the dog approaches and lays the bunny at Julian's feet.

"Atta boy," Julian says, as he picks up the bunny and strokes its ears.

They go back the way they've come, this time in the dark. Arrow traces the children's path along the drainage ditch, trotting fast, so that Julian has to take care not to stumble over the weeds. When they near the first concrete tunnel, Arrow stops. He raises his head to the sky and makes a sharp yelping noise, like an SOS no one can decipher. A long time ago, Julian Cash used to come here when he had nowhere else to go. Often he'd bring along a six-pack he'd talked one of the Platts into buying him up at the general store. He came here for weeks after the accident. He'd sit with his back against the cool concrete, thinking black thoughts that no boy is old enough to have. He's still having those same damn thoughts, and it may be that he'll never understand why human beings have such a horrible need not to be alone. It doesn't make any sense, since that's what you are, from your very first breath.

Julian reels in Arrow's lead so the dog won't get it into his head to attack. They walk side by side into the tunnel, where field mice are burrowing in the dry earth and blue crabs scuttle along the concrete. The children are huddled together, their arms looped around each other. For some reason, Julian can't bear the thought of waking them. He watches them sleep, while beside him the vicious dog who would think nothing of tearing a man apart tilts his head back and whines.

The boy shifts in his sleep. He can never get comfortable. He has lost his voice and all his courage, yet when Julian finally bends down and shakes his shoulder, he's ready to run. He scrambles to his knees, out of breath and shivering from his dreams. He reaches blindly for the baby beside him, and when he finds that instead he's clutching a huge dog, he's no less amazed than Julian to discover that the dog who has tracked these children into this tunnel now lies down beside the meanest boy in Verity, and refuses to budge.

Last week, Lillian Giles had three willow trees cut down and carted off her property. She had considered having these trees chopped down for a long time, nearly thirty years, since she was tired of warning visitors not to trip over their twisted roots. Sooner or later someone would break a leg, so she finally had them hauled away, and she can tell, already, it was a good decision. There, where the willows once stood, a circle of apple mint has already begun to spring up.

Lillian has always kept hutches full of brown rabbits, all of whom she calls Buster, although some are certainly female, since every spring there are new baby rabbits who sit in the palm of her hand, begging for leaf lettuce and sunflower seeds. Lillian has cared for more foster children than anyone in the county; all the social workers call her by her first name. Not too long ago, one of the children she raised, who's grown up to be a tax accountant in Orlando, bought Lillian a satellite dish, so now, when her feet begin to ache, she can rest them on a hassock and turn on *Oprah*, and that's a relief.

Lillian has always had a knack with babies and could put even the most difficult ones down for a nap within minutes. She still keeps a long-handled axe over by the shed for big, angry boys who need to chop wood. She never called any of the big boys in for supper, no matter how much wood they chopped, until they were good and ready, and then she'd fix them franks and beans, with brownies for dessert. She has two cribs stored in her back room, and two roll-away cots, and several large wicker laundry baskets filled with toys. Although she can't recall the name of the host of the *Today* show whom she watches every day, she remembers every child she's ever taken in, even the ones who stayed just for a day. In all these years she's never had a favorite, except for one, and that was Julian Cash, who was probably the ugliest, fussiest baby ever born. Time has gotten mixed up on Miss Giles. It seems like yesterday that she changed Julian's diapers and years ago that he drove up to make certain the men she'd hired were taking the willows out by their roots, since it was the roots that were causing the problem. She knows, in fact, this isn't possible, since some of the lemonade she served Julian and the yard men is still in a pitcher in her refrigerator. That's one thing some of the children complain about, that she never adds sugar to her lemonade, but after a while they all get used to it, and when they grow up they can't bring themselves to drink the store-bought stuff; it's way too sweet for their tastes.

A long time ago, Lillian was in love with Charles Verity's great-grandson, but he went to New York and married a rich girl, and Lillian stayed put. It was simply her good fortune that somebody's burden was another person's delight, because that's the way she got Julian, and she's been taking in children ever since. She may be a little deaf, but that's no crime, and she can still tell Julian's car as soon as it pulls in her driveway. His car parks in front of the house tonight when it's very late and the frogs in the hedges are singing the same song they sing every May. Lillian has always been a light sleeper. She gets out of bed and pulls on her robe and hopes that she has enough food to fix Julian something, since she knows he never cooks for himself. When she goes to the front door to watch him get out of his car, her heart just about flips over. She opens the screen wide enough for him to bend down and kiss her.

"I brought you a little something," Julian says.

"How little?" Lillian knows he's not talking about a satellite dish or a microwave oven.

"A year or so," Julian says. "You know I can't judge."

Lillian peers out the door and sees Keith's sleeping form, slumped against the car window. "Looks a little older."

"And a twelve-year-old," Julian admits.

"Pick them up by the side of the road?" Lillian asks.

Julian grins at her. That's what she used to tell him whenever they had a new child in the house. She just happened to be out walking when she picked this one or that one up by the side of the road. Once there was a baby so small and dehydrated that Miss Giles had to feed it with an eyedropper, the way she sometimes feeds the baby rabbits. Julian stood

117

next to her, beside the rocking chair, dressed in his pajamas, listening to her talk that baby into opening its little pink mouth. He used to believe Miss Giles had night vision, like an owl, since she was the only one who managed to find all these children by the side of the road. When he got older, he would hear the social workers' cars pull up, at odd hours. Sometimes he would put his ear up to the bedroom wall and discover there was a woman wailing in the kitchen. He opened his door a crack one night and saw a woman pulling on her hair, rocking back and forth in Miss Giles's chair as she held a baby in her arms. Maybe it was only the moonlight, or maybe there really was a silver pool of tears on the linoleum floor, or maybe it didn't even matter, since in the morning both the silver tears and the woman were gone and there was a new baby sleeping in the spare room.

Tonight, as they stand at the screen door, Julian realizes that Miss Giles has grown smaller. She's been shrinking and he hasn't even noticed. He guesses she is somewhere in her seventies, but he doesn't know for sure. All he knows is that when he was sent away, Miss Giles packed his suitcase and gave him a dozen brownies wrapped in tinfoil for the bus ride, then went into the bathroom and locked the door so he wouldn't hear her cry. Each week she wrote to him on thin blue paper. *Baby*, she'd write, *somebody here is missing you so she's losing a quarter of an inch of herself every day, and it's all coming out of her heart.*

"You'd better bring in those little packages," Lillian Giles tells him.

While Lillian goes to make up a crib and a cot with clean sheets, Julian walks out to the car. In the backseat, Arrow paces behind the metal grating. Julian had to pull him away from the boy down in the tunnel, then tie him to a telephone pole in order to get close to the children. Now, as Julian opens the driver's door, Arrow begins to growl.

"Jesus," Julian says under his breath.

He doesn't expect Arrow's obedience, but he'll be damned if he lets his own dog keep him out of his car. The little girl is curled up on Keith's lap, but she doesn't wake as Julian lifts her up. He carries her to the porch and she startles, just a bit, when he hands her over to Lillian.

"Ssh," Lillian says. The baby's eyelids don't even flutter when Lillian smooths her knotted hair and takes her into the house.

Walking back to his car, Julian knows he's making another mistake. Actually, it's a done deed. The mistake was made as soon as he started driving to Miss Giles's instead of heading directly to the station. That woman from New York has got him so messed up he's thinking about her even when he doesn't want to. It's that time of year when you have to be careful even when you can't. It doesn't help that the boy seems to be some kind of mute; every time he tried to speak to Julian all that came out was a croak. He fell asleep in spite of himself; dreaming, shirtless, he looks younger than twelve.

Julian gets into the car. "Wake up," he tells the boy.

The meanest boy in Verity nearly jumps out of his skin. When he sees Julian, then realizes that the baby is gone, he gets that wild look that Arrow has when he's cornered.

"Relax," Julian says. He raps on the wire meshing behind them to try to quiet Arrow, who's still growling.

The boy stays absolutely still, but all his muscles are tensed, just in case he has to make a run for it.

"Something wrong with your throat?" When the boy doesn't answer, Julian shrugs and adds, "It's probably a good thing you can't talk. This way you can't bullshit me."

Julian takes the pack of cigarettes from the dashboard and shakes one out, then takes out another and holds it toward the boy.

"Go on," he says when the boy doesn't move. "I just told you. You can't bullshit me."

When Julian lights the cigarette the boy inhales deeply, then coughs his dry, brown cough. There's panic all over him, so Julian speaks softly, as if talking through the chain link of the kennel.

"You got yourself into a mess, all right. But I'll tell you what I'm going to do. I'm not going to turn you in."

The boy cups his cigarette in his palm and narrows his eyes. Julian notices that his right hand is on the door handle. He'd be fast if he decided to run.

"Anybody ever tell you how stupid you are?" Julian asks. "Anybody ever tell you that everything you've done so far has made you look guilty of just about anything, including murder?"

He can see the boy's fingers tighten on the door handle. "You can run now," Julian tells the boy. "But whoever did kill that neighbor of yours might just catch you and slit your throat. One thing you can be sure of—I'm not about to kill you."

The boy lets go of the door handle and wraps his arms around himself so he's all hunched up.

"Okay." Julian nods. "You made a good decision right there. Now just put out that cigarette before you burn a hole in my upholstery, and follow me into the house."

The boy is shivering, but his mouth is set in a fierce line. Julian can't help but remember exactly how much he had to prove at that age. He used to climb out his bedroom window and meet his cousin where the willow trees stood until last week. They could easily find their way along the road without a flashlight, even on nights when there was no moon.

The boy has reached through the wire meshing, into the back, so that Arrow can sniff his fingers.

"Want to leave that dog of mine alone?" Julian says as he swings his door open. "He's vicious."

After going around to the passenger side, Julian opens the door and waits. The boy looks up at him, then gets out. His hair sticks up on one side, from sleeping all folded up against the door.

"Just watch out for coral snakes," Julian says, in case the boy gets it into his head to take off.

The boy is shivering so badly that his teeth hit against each other, and Julian wonders if he should have offered him his own shirt. As they near the house, Julian realizes just how run-down the place has become; the porch is sagging and the roof is covered with leaves. Miss Giles stands at the screen door, holding her robe closed. In the dark, with the wind coming up, Julian figures this could easily look like a place where they popped you in the oven, then ate off your fingers and toes.

"Don't tell me you're scared?" Julian says softly when the boy hesitates.

The boy gives him a look of pure hatred, then continues up the steps. Julian knows that when he was twelve he didn't want anyone too close to him, so he makes certain to walk a pace behind. At the top of the steps, he reaches past the boy and pushes open the screen door, and when he sees that Miss Giles is holding her long-handled axe, Julian has to bite his lip to stop from laughing out loud. It's a test. If they can't trust the boy, they might as well find out right now.

The boy looks terrified of Miss Giles, who greets him in her robe and the fuzzy slippers she always refers to as mules.

"If I'm going to make you hot chocolate, then I need some wood," Lillian Giles says. She holds out the axe and the boy stares at her; Julian can see the lump in his throat. "Right out by the back door," Lillian says.

The boy takes the axe, but then he sees the stuffed bunny, so badly stained with chocolate and dirt, and it becomes clear to him that he's not going anywhere without the baby. He opens his mouth but nothing comes out.

"He doesn't talk?" Lillian asks Julian.

"He's having a problem with his throat," Julian says. "I don't know, maybe he's got strep."

The boy keeps on staring at the bunny, running his fingertips along the smooth handle of the axe. He looks as if he's been swimming in mud; when he turns his head, little clouds of gnats fly out.

"I'll let your mother know you're all right," Julian tells him. "All you have to do is chop some wood and keep your mouth shut, which shouldn't be too hard for you to do."

But the boy still refuses to move, and that's why Miss Giles leads him to the spare bedroom. She waits in the hall till the boy gets up enough nerve to follow her; then she opens the door so he can see the baby in her crib, filthy and safe, sucking on her thumb.

"Now you go out by the back door," she tells the boy. Bossing around runaways who carry sharp axes has never bothered her in the least. The boy has no choice; since he's not about to run and leave the baby behind, he does exactly as he's told. The dog in the car is watching him as he walks to the woodpile. Arrow makes a soft whining sound that makes the boy shiver even more. Shirtless and cold in the moonlight, he's afraid of coral snakes and death and his own loneliness, but he starts to chop wood anyway.

They can hear him in the kitchen, where Miss Giles heats up a pan of milk. She hasn't had a wood-burning cookstove for years, not since one of her foster children grew up to manage an appliance store in Hartford Beach, but sometimes chopping wood is what's needed anyhow.

"You're exhausted," she tells Julian as he lights a cigarette off the back burner of the stove. "You're getting that froggy look around your eyes."

Julian grins and heads for the living room, but he stops and turns back in the doorway. "You're sure I can leave you with that?" he asks, nodding toward the back door.

"Baby, you can leave me with ten more just like him," Lillian Giles says.

If Julian weren't who he is, he would put his arms around her. He always loved to watch Miss Giles make hot chocolate; she used a big wooden spoon and round motions that made it appear she was using all her strength.

"You've got diapers and all that?" he says, hesitating.

"I've got everything," Miss Giles assures him. "Scat."

Julian walks out to his car just as the quarter moon appears in the sky. He gets in behind the wheel and works the wipers once, just to get some of the mosquitoes off the windshield. In the back, Arrow stretches out and groans, then licks at the torn pads of his paws. As Julian hears the boy chopping wood, he remembers that all you needed was three strokes to split a log. But to get a pile big enough to suit Miss Giles took a lot of energy. By the time that boy was done, his shoulders and arms would ache, his palms would be bloody and raw, and he'd be just about tired enough to crawl into bed and sleep the whole night through.

Chapter Five

Lucy is asleep on the couch when he phones her. It's only
natural that she thinks at first that it's Evan, who's
been calling her constantly. As soon as she does recognize Julian's voice, she sits up straight, completely awake.
He tells her that her son is safe, but that isn't enough. Even
after he explains how isolated Miss Giles's place is, after he
gives in and tells Lucy exactly where the house is, she isn't
satisfied. She needs to know how long she has before Julian
turns Keith over to the police for questioning. It's late, but
Lucy quickly gets dressed. She chooses her clothes carefully:
a short black skirt, a silk blouse, high heels. When you are
going to beg you must never look like a beggar. That's
common sense. You need to look like you deserve what
you're asking for, and in Lucy's case all she wants is time.

She drives toward the marshes, but in the dark everything
looks different; she's not certain she'll recognize his driveway
until it's right in front of her. She parks out on the road,
near the sweet bay, which leaves its scent on her clothes,

then walks down Julian's driveway. As she finds her way in the dark, she rehearses what she will say to him. She'll say *Please* and *Thank you* and *If you had a son, you would know.* But mercy is more difficult to ask for than to grant, and when she nears the house, she hesitates. She doesn't notice the toad that scrambles across her path. When she stumbles, the dust rises around her in a cloud and the dog in the kennel begins to bark. It's an awful, bellowing sound, as if the dog had been wounded.

Is it possible that Julian Cash waits for prowlers? He's wearing jeans and has already stepped into his boots when he comes out to the porch. He's holding tight to the female shepherd's collar, so she can't break away. When he sees Lucy, there in the dark, almost at his front door, she looks like something he dreamed, as though she belonged to him. Julian quiets Loretta and has her sit. There are white moths trying to get inside his open front door, and his porch is lined with rotten boards. Julian can't look away from Lucy; he's hypnotized by the way she opens and closes her hands when she speaks, as if she were using sign language. Behind her, the black sky shimmers with living things, mosquitoes and night beetles and moths.

"I want to make a deal with you," Lucy is saying.

Julian signals for Lucy to follow him. Maybe he didn't hear her, maybe that's why he's leading her into his house and maybe that's why she's going. Loretta goes directly to her place beside the door. It's a small house, basically one room, with a couch and an unmade bed and a braided rug, which is dusty no matter how many times it's hung over the porch railing and beaten with a broom. In the kitchen there are the shadows of everyday things: a toaster, a plastic dish rack, a blue tin pot used for boiling water. Right in the center of the ceiling there's a circular fluorescent light, but when Lucy reaches up to pull the string, Julian stops her. He doesn't want her to see him. He doesn't want her to know how hot he is in this tiny kitchen where the windows don't budge unless you hit the frames with a can opener. The white moths smack their wings against the small panes of glass as Julian sits down on a wooden chair. He takes out a cigarette, and when he strikes a match there's a sudden flare of yellow light. Quickly Julian shakes out the match without bothering to light his cigarette.

"I could make coffee," he offers.

If you drank hot coffee in this kitchen you might faint from the heat. You might lose all your willpower.

"No," Lucy says. "Thanks."

"Good, because I make terrible coffee. All I have is Cremora," Julian says. He knows he sounds like a complete idiot.

"I don't want you to tell anyone where the children are," Lucy says. "Just for a few days," she adds after he looks at her. "Until I can find out who Karen Wright was and why someone would want to kill her."

He doesn't argue with her the way she expected he would; he doesn't ask why she thinks she has a better chance at the truth than the Verity police or Paul Salley. He just keeps looking at her. He's not going to stop.

"I don't want Keith to look like he's guilty," Lucy admits.

"He does," Julian says. "Look it." He places his unlit cigarette on the table and studies it. "And what do I get out of this?"

"You get the identity of the dead woman and maybe the person who murdered her."

Julian should reach for the phone and call Walt Hannen

127

right now. When he looks up, he sees that one white moth has managed to find a crack in the glass; it sweeps in from the night air, wings beating.

"I don't think that's what I want," Julian says.

In the doorway to the kitchen, Lucy can feel him wanting her. If it weren't so dark, she'd be able to see that the mark across his forehead has turned scarlet.

"You should tell me to go home," Lucy says from the doorway.

"Go home," Julian says, and he means it.

But in this place, in the middle of the night, they are light-years away from reason. Julian would never make the first move. He knows if it were day she would run, and who could blame her? He doesn't have to look in a mirror to know who he is. As a boy, he was frightened not of ghosts and spiders but of his own reflection. Drawn by his desire, Lucy steps through the kitchen doorway, and once she's done that it's impossible to go backward. Julian reaches for her hand, and when he pulls her onto his lap, he knows he'll never be able to stop himself.

Lucy can feel his hands under her blouse. She can feel his heart beating. It's so hot in the kitchen it's unbearable, hotter still when he kisses her throat. It is possible, in heat like this, to find yourself dissolving. When he takes her face in his hands and kisses her on the mouth he wills her to close her eyes, and she does. This is what they call May madness, when you do things you never expected or even imagined yourself capable of. It comes upon you suddenly, and it doesn't let go. Lucy feels his shoulders, his back, the ladder of ribs that hides his heart. Her skirt rides up, past her thighs, as she moves to wrap her legs around him. That's when he stops kissing her, abruptly, leaving her gasping. He

128

wills her to open her eyes; he gives her one more chance to really look at him, and to flee.

Right then, Lucy decides to forgo daylight and perfection, simple thoughts and reason. She lifts her mouth to his ear and whispers that she wants him, and he takes her to his bed, where the sheets are blue and unironed. He pulls off her skirt and her underpants, he can't do it fast enough; he lifts her on top of him, cross-stitching himself onto her skin. The noises he makes sound as if he were in pain, and when he moves inside of her he has his fingers laced through hers.

Lucy kisses him on the mouth, certain she's under a spell. For this one night she's crazy, crazy to be in his bed, where he keeps her until it's no longer possible to tell what part of the heat is outside and what part is made up of their own flesh and bones. By the time the stars have begun to fade, the sheets are soaked and the heat has risen into an arc just below the ceiling. Never in his life would Julian have believed he could have fallen asleep with someone in his bed. Still, it comes as no surprise to him that when he wakes up, he's alone. It makes perfect sense that he would be awakened by the barking of dogs and the sound of a woman running down his driveway in the pale first light of morning.

No child has driven Lillian Giles crazy, not yet. She pities parents, it's such a thankless job and so many of them mess up so badly. She probably would have done the same with her own, would have scolded too often or not often enough; she might have whacked her truant boy with a hickory stick or sent her fresh-mouthed girl to bed without supper. As it is, she's more patient than the spider who's been living in her rafters for years. She's convinced she's so good with children because of Julian. Once you bring a child back from the dead, nothing he does can distress you. After that, everyone else seems easy.

She lifts her curtain and watches through the window. That baby is still trailing after the boy, playing in the tall, dry grass. She's just about the best-natured child Lillian has ever seen; this morning, when she was fed her oatmeal with cinnamon sugar she opened her mouth like a bird whenever she wanted more. Lillian does not plan to get overly attached, since sooner or later someone will come along to claim the child. She's getting a little too old to have so many emotional ups and downs, but it's hard to stop herself from loving this baby. Just once, she would like to raise a child all the way through. She almost did it with Julian, but then he was sent off to that boys' school, and anyway, he was never anyone's baby, not really. From the start, Miss Giles knew enough not to hug him; even as an infant, he never liked to be held and preferred to be in his playpen, set up outside in the fresh air.

This baby girl would be different. This one you could take in your arms and rock, you could tell her stories and she'd look at you, with those wide brown eyes, and listen to every word. The Social Services Department has decided that Miss Giles is too old for their list, but they're wrong. This baby's going to need her, since her heart's going to be broken real soon. The way she looks at that mixed-up boy sends shivers down Miss Giles's spine, even though she's drinking a hot cup of lemon tea. When they finally have to separate these two, and they'll have to, that baby's going to cry hard enough to wake the dead. She's going to have sleepless nights and beg for her bottle, even though she's just about outgrown it, and Miss Giles would like to be able to comfort her.

She's tried her best with the boy, with no success at all. She's given him licorice cough drops and honey and he still can't say a word; she's had him sit on the rim of the bathtub with the hot water turned on full blast, so the room is steamy and gray, and his throat is as closed up as ever. She's had him chop more wood than any boy in her memory, aside from Julian, and he doesn't complain. Last night, Miss Giles dropped her big iron pot, the one she uses for boiling corn, on his foot, purposely, just to get him to cry out loud, but he didn't do anything more than blink, then turn white with pain.

Early this morning, when the sky was still gray, and the boy was at the kitchen table, adding raisins to the baby's cereal, Miss Giles went to fill her teakettle, and that was when her heart nearly stopped. She let the water go on running as she looked through the window above the sink. Behind her, the baby was banging her spoon on the table; the milk Miss Giles had put up for hot chocolate had begun to boil. Out in their cages, the rabbits were growing restless, because over where the willow trees used to stand was a woman looking through the kitchen window; only it wasn't Miss Giles she was staring at, it was the boy.

It took a few seconds for Miss Giles to understand that this woman was real; as soon as she understood that, she knew this was the boy's mother. It gave her the chills, it really did, it made her feel that the first baby she ever loved had been given to her yesterday. She turned to see exactly what this woman saw: the boy at the table, sleepily eating his breakfast; and when she looked back out the window, the woman was gone. Miss Giles took the pan of milk off the stove then, and set her teakettle down; as long as she lives she will never figure out why it is that some boys refuse to see that somebody loves them.

And now there he is, out in the tall grass. To Miss Giles it looks as if he's studying weeds, but the boy is simply considering his options. He can't help but wonder if there's a man somewhere in town who would like to kill him. He's sure that the man who watched them run across the parking lot that night got into his car all set to follow them. He remembers the white moon of the man's face reflected in a windshield, he may have seen a line of blood on the man's shirt. Although he's not certain about the blood, he gets all shaky just thinking about it. Would he be able to recognize this man in a lineup? He doesn't know, but he's fairly certain that the man would be able to pick him out in a crowd. The boy has no idea of how he could disguise himself; all he can think to do is to take the skull earring out of his earlobe and throw it, as far as he can, till it disappears into the tall grass.

The baby is wearing a red sundress Miss Giles has kept stored in a dresser drawer. Her hair has been washed and brushed and she's got on white sandals that Miss Giles found high up on a shelf in the front closet. She keeps one hand on the boy's ankle while she pulls up blades of grass and pats them into a pile. The boy is as sure as he can be that her face was hidden that night. She was leaning against him, and it was so dark no one could have identified her features. No one could know her mouth was a little crooked when she smiled, or that she had a small scar on one knee, or that when she insisted on holding your hand in hot weather your palm got all sweaty.

The baby can't know what's happened to them; all she knows is that they're in this together. The boy can feel her watching him for a signal: Should they run or stay? Should they eat the cereal they're offered or spit it out? By now, Laddy Stern has probably got himself a new best friend, since they never meant that much to each other anyway. He figures that a thousand miles from here on the street where he grew up, the boys have all forgotten his name. He thinks of his mother, and for some reason he's reminded of a night soon after they moved to Florida when he lay in bed, in despair, wanting desperately to call out for her and not allowing himself to. Now he couldn't call out if he wanted to. It's a punishment, that's what he thinks; he's said so many awful words that his wicked tongue is paralyzed. He's actually grateful that the baby can't really speak; not one horrible word has come out of her mouth. She doesn't have to wish she could take it all back.

The meanest boy in Verity watches dust, dragonflies, low white clouds above him in the sky. When the sun is in the center of the sky, he leads the baby back to the house. She does whatever he wants her to, and because of that he has to do what he's told. He has to go inside to the kitchen when Miss Giles calls them for lunch, otherwise the baby would never eat her chicken soup with carrots and rice. He has to mind Miss Giles so the baby will, and after lunch he has to lie down on the cot, otherwise the baby would refuse to stay in her crib for her nap.

He stretches out and stares up at the cracks in the ceiling, listening to the mockingbirds that pull at the last remaining roots of the willow trees. In her crib, the baby is falling asleep; she turns on her side and slips her thumb into her mouth and hums to herself the way she always does when she's tired. There are clean white pillowcases and sheets, washed so many times they're as soft as snow. The boy can hear Miss Giles's slippers, and the sound of the old brass hinges as she opens the bedroom door to check on them. He has never in his life taken a nap, but for some reason he closes his eyes and when he dreams he dreams about the dog who found him, he dreams about another place, far from here, where you don't have to speak in order to be free.

❀

Walt Hannen is having coffee in the last booth at Chuck and Karl's diner. The coffee tastes like rocket fuel, but that's not what's working on his ulcer. He knows what can happen with these goddamned May cases. There's a good chance that somebody who happens to up and disappear during the month of May might never be found. It's the yellow light at dusk and the damned humidity. Before you know it, clues start to evaporate in the palm of your hand.

Someone with experience can tell when these cases are slipping away, and Walt Hannen's got a feeling it's happening again. He's even more certain of it when Julian's car pulls into the parking lot. The hair on the back of Walt's neck rises up when Julian comes into the diner. For the first time since Walt's known him, Julian is grinning.

"Hey," Julian says as he slides into the booth.

"What the hell is wrong with you?" Walt asks.

"What?" Julian says, confused. He's forgotten to comb his hair and now he runs a hand through it.

"You're smiling," Walt says.

"No. I'm not," Julian says, stricken.

"All right," Walt Hannen says to soothe him. He calls for two more coffees and takes out a pack of Camel Lights. "I'm quitting tomorrow," he tells Julian as he offers him a cigarette.

134

"I won't hold my breath," Julian says. He's looking straight at Walt, but it's Lucy he's thinking about, and he knows he has to stop. He can shut down a whole section of his mind if he wants to. He'd have to be out of his head to jeopardize everything just for a woman he's taken to bed. "You know these missing kids?" he asks Walt.

"Unfortunately," Walt says.

"I want you to ease up on the case over the next couple of days," Julian says after the waitress brings over their coffees.

Walt Hannen holds one hand to his ear. "Excuse me?" he says. "Pardon me?"

"You can keep looking for the killer and all that," Julian says, since he's gone way beyond his better judgment and straight on into stupidity.

"Well, thanks," Walt Hannen drawls. "I'll do that."

"Just hold off looking for the kids." Julian turns and looks for the waitress; this coffee needs milk and sugar and a detonator.

"Are you telling me you found them?" Walt says.

"I didn't say that." Julian takes a sip of his coffee, then shoves the cup away. "Can you drink this stuff?"

"Jesus Christ, Julian," Walt says. "What exactly are you telling me?"

"I just need a couple of days."

"Yeah?" Walt says. He puts his elbows on the Formica tabletop and leans forward. "And what are you going to give me in return for this favor?"

"What do you want?" Julian asks.

This is the most consecutive talk Walt Hannen has heard out of Julian's mouth in the ten years they've worked together, and it's disconcerting.

"I want you to tell me who you fucked last night." Walt

grins and reaches for another cigarette, but when he looks up he sees Julian has leaned back and he has a closed-down look, like an electrical wire that's been crossed. "That was a joke," Walt says. "Or at least I thought it was."

Walt can't help but wonder if his wife, Rose, is right. Maybe he is a little bit psychic. He knew her brother would lose all his money up in Atlantic City, and he guessed Disney was going to buy a piece of Florida long before he ever took over Orlando, and now it looks like he's right about Julian, too. He's not a gossip and he'll keep his mouth shut, but boy, he'd like to talk this one over with Rose and see who on earth she could figure as a match for Julian. In the past two days, Walt has had to speak at two town meetings; he's had to bite his tongue each time someone mentions the series on local crime Paul Salley is writing in the *Sun Herald*. If they could produce the children and have their photos on the front page of the *Herald*, some of the heat on Walt would die down in spite of the murder. If anyone else in town gets hurt, never mind murdered, it will mean Walt's job, not to mention his pension. That's why he won't dare discuss any of this with Rose. She would hit the ceiling if he did, and she'd have a perfect right, since Walt has already decided he's going to trust Julian's instincts.

Twenty years ago this May, Walt Hannen was just starting out; he'd been injured and decorated in the service and had recently married Rose. He'd been on the Verity police force for three weeks when the call came through from the dispatcher. He was the only officer on duty, and he felt like the only individual on the planet as he got into his new patrol car and drove through the thick, wet night, his tires sliding over turtle shells. He followed the white line in the road, too inexperienced to have remembered to switch on his siren, his adrenaline racing. All the windows in the car were open and the air moved through in dense waves and he didn't take his foot off the gas until he found the skid marks leading to the gumbo-limbo tree.

Walt jumped out of his car, and while he ran to the scene his ears were ringing. He groped around in the black air, blinded by the Oldsmobile's headlights. The car was all crumpled up on itself, and Walt circled it until he found Julian, down on the ground, cradling his cousin's head.

"It's okay," Walt said.

He knew he sounded panicky, but he couldn't help it.

"I'm calling for an ambulance right now. Do you hear me?" he asked, because it was much too silent. He got down on one knee and reached out to pat Julian's shoulder. Julian turned on him then, as if he'd kill him if Walt even attempted to touch his cousin.

"Let me try for a pulse," Walt Hannen said.

Julian threw back his head and howled, and his cry cut right through Walt Hannen, it cut through the night and brought tears to Walt's eyes before he had time to blink. Walt knew the sound of a soul torn in two, just as he knew there was no pulse before he grasped the dead boy's wrist. He sat there on the damp ground, helpless, beneath the tree that was as red as a man's blood, listening to Julian weep. Seeing a man like that makes you owe him something; you know him the way no one else does, whether you want to or not.

So they shake on their agreement, in the last booth at Chuck and Karl's. They don't discuss it any further now, nor will they ever. They don't mention what the board of selectmen might say if they knew about the bargain that had just been made between two public officials. They argue over the check, just enough to be polite, and nod their good-byes easily, as if they hadn't both done something that could get them fired.

Julian immediately goes to the pay phone in the parking lot to call Lucy. So he wants her, that's not a crime. It doesn't necessarily mean he's crazy. What's crazy is the way he feels when she doesn't answer her phone. It's a churned-up feeling and it won't go away; it just gets worse each time he calls her and finds no one at home. All that afternoon he searches out telephone booths, and by evening he has her phone number memorized. If she were anyone else, he'd go knock on her front door, but he can't quite face her. He tries not to think about her when he gets home, although it's because of her that he can't sleep in his own bed and instead spends the night in an easy chair. In the morning he tries to call before he's had his coffee; he can't eat and he can't keep his mind on anything, and if that's not crazy he doesn't know what is.

He wastes the whole day, driving through town, stopping at phone booths, cursing himself for being a fool. He parks at Drowned Man Beach for over an hour, trying to make sense out of the things he's done in the past few days. But the fact is, he can't; there's no sense to it. Finally, at around suppertime, he drives over to Long Boat Street. He's relieved when he sees her parked car, but when he goes up to the seventh floor, no one answers the door. He stands there, considering, then takes his MasterCard from his wallet and jimmies open the door. She needs a better lock, that much is certain.

He moves quickly through the apartment. Nothing seems out of place, but in her bedroom a dresser drawer is open, and it's only half full. Julian reaches into the drawer and takes out a white silk slip, and that's when he knows she's already gone. When the telephone rings he goes to the night table, picks up the receiver, and holds it to his ear.

"Lucy, honey?" a woman's voice says.

It's Kitty Bass, so Julian has no choice but to hang up on her. She'd recognize his voice instantly; she disliked him enough to still remember. Julian takes the phone off the hook and rests it on the night table, and that's when he sees the white envelope. He studies it, then pulls out the invitation to Lucy's high school reunion. He searches the night-table drawer until he finds Lucy's most recent child-support check, not yet cashed, then jots down her ex-husband's address on a piece of notepaper. On the way out, he notices Lucy's car keys on the coffee table, and he slips them into his pocket. He's never been on a plane, and he doesn't intend to start flying now; he certainly can't be inconspicuous if he's driving a Florida police cruiser up north. When he goes down to the parking lot, Diane Frankel spots him just as he's unlocking Lucy's Mustang. She watches him, suspicious, one arm thrown protectively around her sulky teenage daughter.

"Radiator," Julian tells her. "Mrs. Rosen's having us check out the cooling system."

He can see this neighbor of Lucy's loosen her grip on her daughter, but she keeps an eye on him as he starts the car and pulls out onto Long Boat Street. There have been so many police cars here recently, no one will make much of his cruiser parked at the far end of the lot. All the way out to the marshes, he's thinking shoulder bone, collarbone, all those pieces that can be so easily broken if you're not careful. Driving down a road he has taken a thousand times before, he is convinced that Lucy is headed for nothing but trouble. He plans to give the boy one more chance to talk.

It's almost seven when he gets out to Miss Giles's. He

honks the horn twice and reaches for a cigarette. When Keith comes out and sees his mother's car, he stops right outside the back door.

"Your mom's got a nice car," Julian calls through his open window. "If only the air conditioner worked."

Julian remembers how he was tormented by his dreams during the summer when he was twelve. He'd wake suddenly, frightened, uncertain as to what was real and what wasn't. On some nights, a stone would be thrown at his window, and he'd scramble from his bed and peer outside, in a fog of sleep and terror, to see Bobby Cash, there behind the willows, grinning, motioning for him to sneak outside. That was the summer when Julian stuck his head into Miss Giles's old cookstove. It was the same oven in which she had warmed him when he was just a few hours old in order to bring him back to life. The old stove burned wood, which meant they ate mostly salads and boiled frankfurters, but Julian must have believed that all ovens used gas. After twenty minutes with his head inside the oven, his cheeks were sooty and his hair smelled like toast, but he had accomplished nothing. He pulled his head out, then had a piece of peach pie and went off to collect toads.

The boy is looking at the Mustang expectantly, and it takes Julian a second before he realizes that he isn't looking for his mother; he's checking out the backseat for Arrow.

Julian gets out and walks to the porch. "I don't have the big guy with me, if that's who you're looking for."

The boy has hooded eyes; quickly he looks away, as if he didn't give a damn. He's wearing clean blue jeans and a black T-shirt washed so many times it appears gray. If Julian Cash isn't mistaken, he wore these clothes when he lived here.

"I don't want you to get the wrong idea about the dog,"
Julian says. He studies the boy's face, looking for any re-
semblance to Lucy and finding none. "He's not a pet. He'll
bite you as soon as look at you."

The boy shakes his head. How much more of this does
he have to listen to?

Julian takes out a cigarette and points right at the boy.
"I've got your number," he says.

The boy blows air through his lips. Yeah. Right.

Julian holds the cigarette out, and when the boy doesn't
take it, he places it on the porch steps, along with a pack of
matches.

"I used to spend hours out here." Julian sits down on the
last step. He can see that one of those goddamned May
turtles is crawling under his left rear tire. "I used to think
about maiming people and spitting right in their faces and
whatever the hell else it is you think about when you're
twelve."

The boy's muscles tense, all at once. If he wanted to, if
he didn't have to worry about the baby, he could take off
right now. He's younger, he's faster, he might just pull it
off.

"Take the goddamned cigarette, will you?" Julian says.

The boy looks him over, then reaches for the cigarette.
He's so high-strung he's like a piece of wire.

"Your mother and I made a deal last night," Julian says.
The boy has lit his cigarette and inhaled, but as soon as
Julian mentions his mother, he coughs. "I'm giving her a
couple of days before I turn you over. Mostly because I'm
an idiot."

Julian moves sideways on the step so he can get a good
look, but there's still no reaction. The boy's eyes are all

141

cloudy; you'd barely guess he was alive. "Just jump in here anytime," Julian says. "Feel free to put your two cents in." He smokes his own cigarette and grins. "Oh, right," he says. "I forgot. Cat's got your tongue. So I'll ask you some questions. You don't have to use actual words or anything. You can just nod."

The boy stares at him through a curtain of smoke.

"Did you find the baby in the apartment?"

Nothing.

"In the laundry room?"

The boy's eyelids flicker, so Julian knows he's scored.

"You found her in the laundry room after you'd stolen the rings, and then you took off like a guilty bastard. You should have just left her there. You know that, don't you?"

The boy's breathing shifts slightly; he knows that was his biggest mistake.

"Burying those rings in the shoe box was pretty stupid, too." Julian shakes his head. "You should have just thrown them in the bushes. They never would have turned up."

The boy's growing more and more fidgety. He reminds Julian of the ferret he and Bobby once found in a hunter's trap. The damn thing wouldn't let Bobby get near enough to save him. He bit Bobby on the forearm and he would have fought to the death if Julian hadn't hit him with his boot to stun him. Even then, he bit Bobby one more time, on the thumb, deep enough to draw blood, before they could get him out of the trap.

Inside the kitchen, Miss Giles taps on the window and motions to Julian.

"You stay right here," Julian says to the boy. "Don't fucking move."

As Julian walks inside he passes the pantry, where Miss

Giles keeps a shotgun, behind the Hoover and the mops. Her father used to shoot at raccoons that came to steal pickles and butter from their larder. He taught Miss Giles how to shoot. She's always kept the bullets hidden, but for years Julian has known they're inside a tin on top of the flour canister.

Julian goes to the refrigerator and gets himself some lemonade. He used to do this every day; back then it was the only thing that could quench his thirst.

"The baby's asleep," Lillian Giles says. "You know, that boy is the first one I've ever had who won't say a word. Not even 'Pass the ketchup.' "

"I don't want anyone to find these kids for the next couple of days," Julian says. "Just in case somebody comes looking for them."

"I can take care of these children," Miss Giles says. "Don't worry about that."

Julian puts his empty glass in the sink, as he's been taught. "I'm not worried," he insists, although he's never really thought about how far she is from her nearest neighbor or a hospital.

Julian can see the porch from the window above the sink; the boy hasn't moved, not an inch. He still doesn't move when Julian comes outside, not even when the screen door slams shut. His shoulders are so rigid it's painful to see; the sneakers Miss Giles has given him to replace his own are a full size too big. Somehow, Julian has become more of a sucker than he ever would have thought possible.

"Come on," he tells the boy.

The boy looks at him, but doesn't budge.

"I know I told you not to move, but I changed my mind. Move."

The boy rises and grudgingly follows Julian to the car.

"I don't want to hear that you're giving Miss Giles any trouble," Julian tells him as they get inside. "Put your seat belt on."

The boy curls his lip, but he buckles up.

"You know, I've never been out of Florida," Julian says as he heads down the driveway. "You watch what I'm doing now," he adds as he turns onto the road. "Make a right out of the driveway and go half a mile."

The boy is ignoring him, so Julian elbows him, and he sits up in his seat with a little growl.

"I've never seen snow," Julian says. They pass Chuck and Karl's and the Mobil station. "Here at this telephone pole? Take a left."

As if the meanest boy in Verity could give a shit about directions. He puts his head back and closes his eyes, but Julian steps on the brakes, hard, so that the boy shoots forward in his seat, then is snapped back by the harness of the seat belt.

"Now do I have your attention?" Julian asks. "You make a sharp right into the driveway."

The boy slowly nods, and Julian continues toward the house, past the merlins in the cypress trees. Both dogs are barking, Loretta from inside the house, Arrow from his kennel. When they get out of the car, Arrow charges the kennel fence, but when he recognizes Julian and the boy, he stops. Julian walks on ahead, then signals for the boy to follow him. Outside the fence there's a silver trashcan filled with kibble; the cover is weighed down with a brick to discourage raccoons. Julian opens a small gate, about the size of a cat door, and lifts out a metal bowl.

"Fill this with eight cups," he tells the boy.

As Julian roots around for the plastic measuring cup, the boy places his hand against the wire meshing of the fence. Arrow comes to put his nose against the palm of his hand.

"Are you listening?" Julian says.

The boy obediently begins to fill the bowl, so Julian goes inside. He takes his suitcase from the closet, and throws in some socks and underwear along with a clean pair of jeans and some .38 rounds. He stops in the kitchen for a bag of Doritos and a six-pack of Coke. Most people, when they take off, wind up heading for home. Julian turns off his kitchen light, then calls to Loretta and snaps on her lead. Out on the front porch, he puts down his suitcase and has Loretta sit. The whole time he's driving he'll be thinking of Lucy; he'll be covering up her fingerprints on the steering wheel with his own.

It's already dark, and Julian should get on the road, but he's held by the sight of the boy stroking Arrow's neck while the dog gobbles his dinner. Julian knows if he stuck his hand in the feed door and tried to touch the dog while he ate, he'd be bitten. What makes Arrow so quiet tonight, almost docile? When he's finished his food, the dog lies with his head on his paws while the boy pets him.

Julian leads Loretta down to the car, opens the back door for her, and tosses his suitcase inside.

"You'd better keep your hands out of there," he calls.

The meanest boy in Verity is embarrassed; quickly, he stops petting the dog and latches the feed door. He's still crouched on the ground when Julian comes up beside him.

"I have to go out of town," Julian says. "I need you to feed him."

The boy looks up at him, puzzled.

"Forget about him and he starves, so don't forget about

him. He looks like he likes you, but don't start thinking you can let him out of his kennel, because you can't. He'd tear most people apart."

When the boy rises to his feet, Julian has the urge to tell him not to talk to strangers, but he keeps his mouth shut. This isn't any of Julian's business; he can't keep tabs on the boy, he won't even be in town. By morning he should be in Virginia, where he'll let himself sleep for an hour by the side of the road. Still, he knows what it's like when no one trusts you; it turns you so inside out that your shadow is the one that leads the way and all you can do is follow wherever it takes you. He knows for a fact that bad boys don't necessarily run away, even when they're given the chance. That's how they get into trouble in the first place. They don't know when to back down.

"You want a ride to Miss Giles's, or you want to walk it?" Julian says.

The boy turns his face to him and Julian can tell he doesn't believe he's heard correctly. It takes a good while for the boy to understand that he has. After Julian gets into his car, and the key is turned in the ignition and a cloud of blue smoke spills into the black air, the boy finally allows himself to believe. It's easy to tell when the car reaches the end of the driveway; the merlins begin to call in the tops of their trees. The meanest boy in Verity listens to the sound of birds in the night. It's all right if he's out here by himself. It's all right just to look at the sky. Soon, he'll be on the road, all on his own, and as he walks beneath the stars, finding his way will be easy as pie.

Chapter Six

I N Great Neck, in the month of May, you can smell lilacs and freshly cut grass and the sharp, stinging scent of chlorine as pools are cleaned and readied for the summer. On Easterbrook Lane, where the shade trees are more than a hundred years old, it's nearly impossible to see some of the houses from behind their hedges of rhododendrons, although Lucy manages to spy her front door as soon as the taxi turns the corner. It's a white colonial with green shutters, actually quite pretty, and although it was several steps down from her Uncle Jack's house in Kings Point, Lucy is astounded to see how large it is, how well kept since her departure, almost as if her presence had made the shutters fall off their hinges and crabgrass sprout up along the brick path to the door.

It's cool here in the mornings; Lucy had forgotten that. The air is blue and fresh, and you can hear dogs barking in the fenced backyards. Lucy pays the driver and collects her suitcase and purse, but after the taxi has made a U-turn and disappeared she is still standing on the brick path. Someone has planted a new rose bed, and by June there will be huge pink roses lining the walkway. From the moment she left, Lucy erased bits and pieces of this house, until it had become no bigger than a toy she could hold in the palm of her hand. But here it still stands, rooted and sturdy with its red brick chimney. At the front door, Lucy puts her suitcase down on the white wooden bench she once mail-ordered from Smith & Hawken, then runs a hand through her hair. She had to spend the night in Atlanta, where she curled up in a plastic chair and slept fitfully, and now the front of her hair stands straight up, as though she's had a bad scare. She has brought almost nothing with her; her suitcase is filled with tank tops and jeans. It is possible that she may not even have brought a comb.

She knocks twice, and it's a while before the lock slides open and Evan appears at the door. She's woken him, and standing there in his blue robe, he's sleepy and confused. He's a good-looking man, tall, with the same thick, fair hair as Keith and a face so open it hides nothing, not even the fact that for a moment he doesn't recognize his ex-wife.

"Lucy," he says finally. All the color has drained from his face and he doesn't open the screen door. "What happened? Where's Keith?"

"He's fine," Lucy says. It's so much easier if you take a deep breath before you begin to lie. "He went to a friend's and didn't bother to tell me. You know how he is," she adds when Evan looks doubtful.

"You came here to tell me that instead of phoning?" Evan says.

"Actually, I came for the reunion," Lucy says. If she didn't have this cover story, she would have to invent one; the truth would only reignite Evan's desire for custody.

Along the street, some of the automatic sprinklers have switched on; there's the sound of water spraying and the scent of rich earth.

"You're here for the reunion?" Evan says, more confused than ever. "You didn't call me to let me know Keith was all right. I thought he'd been kidnapped. I haven't been using the phone in case a ransom call came through. I haven't left the house in case Keith appeared at the door."

"I'm sorry," Lucy says, for more than he'll ever know.

"I have a right to know these things," Evan says. "I mean, Christ, I'm not some outsider."

Lucy swallows hard. "I agree."

"Where exactly was he all this time?"

Lucy tilts her face upward; the pulse in her throat is throbbing. If Julian Cash were here, he'd know she was lying.

"At his friend Laddy's."

"Jesus," Evan says. "All that worry. Something's seriously wrong here, Lucy. It really is."

"Why does this sound like you think it's my fault?" Lucy asks.

"Because he's unhappy."

"Well, that's nothing new, is it?" Lucy shoots back. "He's been unhappy since the day he was born, and that was before I had a chance to screw him up."

"I didn't mean that," Evan says.

"Look, do you think I could come inside?" Lucy asks.

"Maybe it's good that you're here," Evan says, still speaking to her through the screen door. "We need to talk seriously about Keith. I didn't want to hurt your feelings, but ever since winter vacation I've been getting letters from him. He's been calling me collect. He wants to come home."

Lucy stares at the man she married when she was twenty-one, when her hair was still so long it reached her waist, when she thought she had all the time in the world.

"For good," he says.

She had forgotten you could actually get a chill here early in the mornings. It's so unlike Florida, where the heat doesn't bother to wait until a decent hour to strike.

"I'd really like some coffee," Lucy says.

"Coffee?" Evan says. "Here?"

It was never that difficult to win an argument with Evan; he was far too kindhearted to go for blood.

"I sat in Atlanta all night." But still he doesn't open the door. "You don't want me inside," Lucy says flatly.

A woman's voice calls tentatively from the hallway. "Evan?"

Lucy is embarrassed to discover that she's never once thought of or imagined Evan with another woman; she didn't feel proprietary about him even back when they were married, so she's not at all certain why she suddenly feels so uncomfortable. Evan looks completely distressed, as though he'd like one or both or all of them to disappear into a puff of smoke.

"It's okay," Lucy tells Evan through the screen door. "You're allowed."

"Look, Lucy, I think you should call before you do something like this."

The woman appears behind Evan; she's dressed but still sleepy. Her hair hasn't been brushed yet.

"Evan?" she says when she sees Lucy out on the front porch.

The woman has long dark hair, and Lucy can tell, right

away, that she's younger, possibly by as much as ten years.

"You remember my wife," Evan says to the woman. He turns back to Lucy, flustered. "Melissa Garber," he reminds her. "Kindergarten."

Lucy sees that the dark-haired woman was indeed Keith's kindergarten teacher. They'd had endless conferences about Keith's misbehavior, even back then. Melissa came up with the idea of making him the permanent hamster monitor, to build his self-esteem and sense of responsibility, but it hadn't worked. He'd continued destroying the library corner and stealing pocketfuls of Legos, and Lucy had had the damned hamsters to care for over every school vacation.

"Right," Lucy says. "Melissa. Miss Garber, right?" she says to Evan.

What Lucy can't help wondering, as Evan finally opens the door and leads her into the kitchen and Melissa excuses herself, is how long this has been going on, whether it was already starting all those years back, during their parent-teacher conferences. It hits her, all in a rush, that she may not have been the only one who was unhappy in their marriage—a possibility she has never once considered before.

"It's very strange to be here," Lucy says. She is sitting at the kitchen table watching Evan fumble with the coffee grinder.

"It's very strange to have you here," Evan admits, and they both have to laugh.

"So you don't mind if I stay for a few days?" Lucy says once Evan's got the coffee going.

"A few days?"

"You keep repeating everything I say, only when you say it it sounds like I've committed some sort of criminal offense."

"What about going to Jack and Naomi's?" Evan suggests.

"You're not serious?"

"Actually, I saw him a few weeks ago. He said they hadn't heard from you once since you moved."

"Look, I'll stay in the guest room," Lucy says. "I promise I won't bother your girlfriend."

Evan frowns as he hands Lucy her coffee. She remembers these mugs; she bought them in Bennington, Vermont.

"I wish you wouldn't call her that," Evan says.

"What do you want me to call her?" Lucy asks. "Miss Garber?"

Evan is so uncomfortable that he turns his back to her, exactly as he used to whenever he didn't want to fight.

"All right," Lucy says. "If you let me stay I'll talk to you about Keith." She doesn't mention that she won't tell him a single bit of truth, but she feels justified in that, since in only a few hours she'll know the identity of her murdered neighbor, information she feels is powerful enough to clear Keith of any charges against him. "I'll discuss it calmly," Lucy promises.

"You'll consider letting him come back?" Evan says.

She can't stand to be with Keith, she does nothing but argue with him, she's not even certain she likes him very much, yet her hands instantly begin to sweat.

"I said I'll talk," Lucy hedges. "I'm willing to do that."

Evan has come to sit across from her at the table. He has something of a grin on his face. "What happened to your hair?"

Lucy fluffs up her bangs. "Is it awful?" she asks.

"It's very unusual." Evan smiles.

"Oh, great. Thanks. You never liked anything I did with my hair."

"That's not true," Evan says. "Exactly."

Melissa has been standing in the doorway. She has a quilted tote bag over her shoulder, filled with the clothes she's hurriedly collected from the bedroom.

"You don't have to leave because of me," Lucy tells her, although she's not sure if she means it.

Melissa looks uncertainly at Evan. He was never much good at awkward moments; Lucy sees now it's because he's too honest to attempt false cheer.

"No. I'll go." Melissa waits a moment to see if anyone is about to stop her. "How's Keith?" she asks Lucy when nobody does.

"Great," Lucy says. "All he needed was to be switched into a decent school system."

It's a cruel and untrue thing to say, and they all know it.

"I'm sorry," Lucy says. "I'm just exhausted. I have to go lie down," she tells Evan.

"Here?" Melissa says.

Lucy plans to rest for only a few minutes, but once she stretches out on the living room couch, which she bought on sale at Bloomingdale's one Labor Day weekend, she falls into a deep sleep. When she wakes, the living room is dark, and she bolts from the couch, frightened, unsure of where she is. Even when she turns on the light, she's confused. She had not remembered owning so many things: good china and silverware, lithographs and thick wool rugs, woven to last a hundred years. She goes outside, even though it's already dusk, too late to go to Salvuki's. Instead, Lucy walks down Easterbrook Lane, past lawns so deep and green it almost seems like midnight. When Lucy first came to Great Neck, after her parents' deaths, she was mesmerized by all the greenery; she felt as if she could go to sleep for a very long time, lulled by the mockingbirds and the mourning doves. It's happening to her all over again; it's an effort just to walk half a block. She used to take this route with Keith in his stroller, and now she sees a boy about his age, maybe one of his old friends, she can't tell at this distance, dribbling a basketball as he heads for a neighbor's house, a springer spaniel behind him, lunging for the ball each time it hits the concrete. Lucy can see the boy is wearing the hundred-twenty-dollar Nikes that Keith has begged for, sneakers Lucy wouldn't buy him even if she could afford to. The Nikes are clean and white, and they'll probably stay that way till the boy has outgrown them and been given another pair.

Evan is waiting for her when she gets back to the house. He's brought a pizza, which they wolf down together in silence. They're used to doing this; they spent most of the last year of their marriage avoiding conversation.

"Are you sure you're all right?" Evan asks when Lucy insists she has to go up to bed at a quarter after eight.

"Jet lag," Lucy says, though it's nowhere near the truth.

She keeps thinking about the way Keith looked as she peered through the window of Miss Giles's house. In the early-morning light, his hair seemed blonder, he was leaner than before, all sharp angles. He looked like a stranger, a boy found in the woods, covered with bramble scratches, but dressed in clean clothes, and safe in that kitchen where there was cinnamon sugar to sprinkle over the cereal.

When she's not thinking of Keith, when she's not careful, she imagines Julian Cash, and each time she does she feels edgy, and nothing can cure that but sleep. Up in the guest bedroom there is a yellow bedspread Lucy doesn't remember, no doubt chosen by Melissa, since Lucy has always disliked bright colors in bedrooms. Lucy sleeps in her clothes, her arms wrapped around herself. By the time she wakes in the morning, Melissa's car is already idling at the curb.

"She doesn't trust me," Lucy tells Evan down in the kitchen.

Evan lifts the window shade and waves to Melissa. "She has nothing to worry about," he says. "You know what I mean," he adds when he sees the look on Lucy's face.

"I know exactly what you mean," Lucy says. "Since she's picking you up, can you lend me your car?"

Evan grudgingly hands over his keys, and when Lucy gets dressed and goes out to the garage, she understands why he hesitated. He has a brand-new red Celica convertible. He's always wanted a convertible, and Lucy appreciates that he would trust her with it, especially in the shape she's in. She heads straight to Middle Neck Road, the main shopping district of town, and she's lucky enough to find a parking space just two blocks up from Salvuki's. When Lucy moved here all the girls wanted Capezio ballet slippers, whether they were dancers or not, and the boys wore loafers and high-topped sneakers or, occasionally, well-polished Frye boots. Her Aunt Naomi bought Lucy her first pair of Capezios, thin pink slippers that didn't make a sound when she walked and made her size-eight feet seem as delicate as one of the roses that will soon open beside Evan's front door. As she locks up the Celica, Lucy realizes that she still has a key to that door in her purse. She just never would have thought of using it. Even when she lived there, especially toward the end, she felt as though she were breaking and entering each time she brought the groceries home.

She has that same feeling walking into Salvuki's, even though there is still a pot of coffee at the front desk, and a tray of flaky croissants. The air here always smells like coconut shampoo, which costs twelve dollars a bottle and never seemed to get your hair truly clean. This is where Lucy had her hair cut off to shoulder length just before her wedding, and then she wept all night long, even though her Aunt Naomi assured her that a married woman shouldn't have all that hair. Clearly, Salvuki can't help her now; she actually cringes when she sees her reflection in the mirror behind the receptionist's desk.

"I'm looking for Salvuki," Lucy says. Actually, she has to say it three times before the receptionist turns her gaze on her.

"Mr. Salvuki is out today. He's doing an entire wedding party," the receptionist informs her. "And he's not taking any new clients, since he's booked with his regulars."

"I am a regular," Lucy informs her right back.

The receptionist studies Lucy's green-tinged hair and doesn't believe her for a second.

"Well, I used to be," Lucy admits. "I moved to Florida."

"God. What did they do to you there?" the receptionist asks.

"My aunt, Naomi Friedman, is one of his regular customers," Lucy says. "She's one of his best customers."

"Mrs. Friedman." The receptionist nods. "She was in yesterday."

Lucy reaches into her purse and brings out her neighbor's photograph. "You haven't ever seen her, have you?"

"Never," the receptionist says, eyeing the photo, then quickly handing it back. "But believe me, she didn't have her hair colored here."

Lucy wanders over to the sinks and shows the photograph to the shampoo girls, but neither of them recognizes the

murdered woman; they haven't even been working for Salvuki for more than a few months. Lucy herself doesn't remember the other stylists, but she recalls that no one worked
for Salvuki for long; he was, and probably still is, too much
of a screamer. There's nothing Lucy can do until tomorrow;
the entire day is wasted, and maybe that's why she's so
susceptible to the white strapless dress in the window of a
shop on Middle Neck Road. The dress is gathered into
hundreds of tiny pleats; it's a dry cleaner's nightmare and
much too expensive. But it's gorgeous, like a slice of moonlight, and there are silver-colored sandals, which the sales-
woman also convinces Lucy to take. She will have to go to
the reunion after all, and by the time she's done shopping,
Lucy has spent three hundred dollars she can't afford, all
because she's back in Great Neck, where the saleswomen
don't bother you with anything as trivial as the price until you're
already rung up and the credit card is out of your hand.

When she gets back to Easterbrook Lane, Lucy pulls into
the garage, then goes into the house through the garage door,
which leads to the kitchen. She hangs Evan's car keys on
the hook by the telephone, just the way she used to. She
has a cup of coffee, thinking, in spite of herself, about Julian
Cash, how impressed he'll be when she hands over the real
name of her neighbor, how willing to keep Keith out of
this mess completely. She thinks about the way he looked
at her when he told her she should go home. Maybe she
should have, because now something's happened. It was so
late at night, and the shadows were so blue, she may not
have been seeing straight. Here in Great Neck, so far from
that Verity madness that happens every May, she cannot
believe the things she did in his bed. She won't even think
about that.

Lucy washes out her coffee cup in the sink before carrying her shopping bag upstairs. In the guest room, she shakes out her new dress and hangs it in the closet, and then she finally dares to walk down the hall to Keith's room. She's been avoiding it, and now she knows why. It's like opening the door into another lifetime. Lucy had worked so hard to make his room perfect; she'd special ordered mini-blinds in the hues of the rainbow, she'd had shelves built in that were deep enough for fish tanks and globes of the world. Keith hasn't been here since school vacation in February, but there is still a pile of comic books he left beside the bed. His yellow rain slicker is hooked over the closet door. From the window it's possible to see the whole backyard: the swimming pool and the climbing structure Evan ordered on Keith's sixth birthday, a green grid of slides and swings and monkey bars. There is the herb garden Lucy so carefully put in, although she left before it could be of use. There is the birdhouse, still in the magnolia tree. A child would have to be crazy not to want to come back here. He'd have to favor man-o'-wars and dust, heat waves and an old single bed bought at the Sunshine flea market.

Lucy closes Keith's door and goes to the guest bathroom. She takes a long shower, and when she's done she lies down on the yellow bedspread, just for a few minutes, but she winds up falling asleep, with her hair still wet, so that all her dreams are cold and blue. Since she's come back, she's amazingly tired, as if she were recovering from a fever, and she sleeps longer than she has in months. She's out for hours and doesn't wake until she hears Evan come home. As soon as she gets off the bed, Lucy knows her hair will be a disaster for the reunion. She finds some mousse in the bathroom cabinet, slicks a little over her hair, then slips on the new

160

white dress. She can't wear a bra with it, which makes her self-conscious, and the silver sandals are half a size too small. But when she turns and sees herself in the full-length mirror, she understands why some people are willing to pay so much for clothes. It's a wonderful dress. She doesn't even look like herself. With her hair cut so short, and no jewelry, her neck is as long as a swan's. All those tiny gathered pleats look like feathers, or layers of abalone shell.

Lucy knows the full effect of the dress when she goes downstairs and Evan stares at her the way he did a long time ago, when they'd meet in her Uncle Jack's garden. If Julian could see her now, he'd be lost. He'd be hers, if that's what she wanted.

"You're really going to the reunion?" Evan says.

"I told you I was," Lucy says.

"I thought you hated the past," Evan says. He's carrying a dry-cleaning bag and inside is a gray suit Lucy doesn't recognize.

"What?" Lucy is annoyed that he presumes to know how she feels about anything.

"That's how it always seemed," Evan says. "You never talked about your parents. I don't think I know one fact about your first sixteen years. I just assumed you'd never want to see anyone you went to high school with. Melissa's in the middle of compiling her family history. It's really pretty interesting. There's a whole branch of her family that settled in New Orleans."

"Oh, great," Lucy says. "What do you do? Compare her to me, and if she does the opposite she gets an A-plus?"

Evan doesn't answer, but he tightens up, just as he always did when he was hurt. Still, Lucy can't stop herself.

"What do you plan to do?" she asks. "Marry her, then

161

sue for custody because you live better than I do? So what?
Most divorced men have three times the income of their ex-
wives."

"I'm not like that," Evan says, wounded. "I offered you
this house, you didn't want it. You never wanted anything
from me."

He turns from her, defeated, but actually, he's right. She
never got anything from her marriage, because she didn't
want it; sometimes when he brought her presents, earrings
he spent too much for, a silver chain he'd ordered weeks in
advance, she'd put them in a dresser drawer and never touch
them again.

"I want something now," Lucy says. "Take me to the
reunion."

"I have two tickets, and I'm taking Melissa," Evan tells
her.

Lucy has not come back to New York for her high school
reunion, and now she's desperate to go. She has never looked
back, Evan's right about that; she has locked up the past,
much the way Keith keeps the Indian-head pennies Evan
collected for him in a glass jar. There are times when she
could swear she's heard something rustling in her own
kitchen, her mother's skirt as she backs up against the linoleum counter so that Scout can wrap his arms around her
and kiss her.

"It's not *her* past," Lucy says. "Is it?"

She goes to wait in the driveway, so Evan can make his
decision, and when he comes out, nearly twenty minutes
later, showered and wearing the gray suit, she knows that
he's called Melissa. He was always generous, and he still is;
in spite of everything, they do have a past together. They
don't speak on the way to the country club, although they

are both thinking of all the other times they drove up this winding gravel road. Evan waves to the guard at the iron gate; he still comes here on Sundays to play golf with some of the boys they went to school with, and Melissa has suggested they have their wedding reception here. Twenty years ago, at their prom, Lucy wore a pink chiffon dress and refused to dance with anyone but Evan. She didn't know it then, but he'd already decided to ask her to marry him.

Tonight the golf course is so green it shimmers in the twilight; the hedge of mock orange is still just as lush, emerald leaves sprinkled with stars. Lucy and Evan look good together as they walk across the parking lot. They always did. Lucy wanted the exact opposite of her parents' marriage and that's what she got, and she knows, even now, that she has nobody but herself to blame.

"It's great that you found Melissa," Lucy tells Evan. "Keith will be happy when you tell him about her." Probably he'll adore her; she has everything Lucy does not: youth, patience, no blood tie.

"You think so?" Evan says hopefully.

"As happy as Keith can be," Lucy amends.

She says this as they're entering the club, and Evan touches her elbow lightly. It's the touch of commiseration, and it reminds them both of all the hours they have spent trying to understand Keith's unhappiness. There is a crush of people filling in name tags, grownups in linen and silk, all unrecognizable to Lucy after twenty years. Several people greet Evan, old buddies and acquaintances, but it's not until they walk into the ballroom that a woman approaches Lucy.

"You look incredible," the woman tells Lucy. Whatever that means. The woman glances over at Evan. "I thought you two were divorced."

Lucy realizes that this stranger is Alison Reed, whom she used to sit next to in algebra.

"We are," Lucy says. She cannot for the life of her remember ever talking to Alison, not even in class. "It's a friendly divorce."

Lucy waves to Evan as he turns to look back at her before making his way to the bar.

"No alimony," Alison says knowingly.

Lucy forces a smile, then excuses herself and heads for an hors d'oeuvres table. There is some sort of vague Hawaiian theme, echoing their prom, with lots of sliced pineapple and a band whose members wear leis over their white dinner jackets. The room is a little too cool and Lucy has the sense that everyone here knows one another, except for her. She felt that way in high school, although now, when she stops at a table piled with tea sandwiches, she instantly recognizes Heidi Kaplan. Heidi's red hair is just as thick and luxuriant as ever, especially when set against her silky black dress. For years, Lucy has been guessing that Heidi would have grown coarse and fat, when in fact she's more beautiful than ever.

"Lucy Rosen," Heidi says, coming up to Lucy as she piles a plate with crabmeat sandwiches and pineapple. "Everyone thought you disappeared off the face of the earth."

"No," Lucy says. "Just Florida."

"Year round?" Heidi says, shocked. "We go to Boca in February, but the rest of the time we're in the city, except for the summer, when we're out at the beach."

People here seem to be starving; they circle around the hors d'oeuvres, so that Lucy is pushed uncomfortably close to Heidi.

"So what do you do with yourself in Florida?" Heidi asks. "You were always so smart."

Lucy smiles and takes a bite of pineapple. "Not really," she says. She looks over her shoulder; the lights are dim and she doesn't recognize anyone out on the dance floor.

"Oh, yes you were," Heidi tells her. "I was actually jealous of you."

They both laugh at that, a ridiculous schoolgirl folly. All Lucy has to do is listen politely while Heidi talks about her husband, an oncologist whose practice is on Madison and Seventy-third, and then she manages to get away. When she reaches the bar she can see Evan talking to a group of old friends. The women seem to have aged better than the men, many of whom are balding and paunchy. These men look about the same as their own fathers did, back when the boys were seniors in high school. Lucy's Uncle Jack wasn't much older when she came to live with him. Her parents were just about the age she is now on the night they died. Though she doesn't drink, Lucy orders a margarita. It's a cash bar, and Lucy has to rifle through her purse for some singles. She accidentally pulls out the photograph of her neighbor and while she looks at her neighbor's face she can feel the air-conditioning blowing on her shoulders. She slips the photograph back into her wallet and pays for her drink, and when she turns from the bar she realizes that she's being watched. Over by the French doors that lead to a stone patio bordered by azaleas is Andrea Friedman, Lucy's cousin. Beneath Andrea's gaze, Lucy feels as if her white dress were shrinking, exposing too much skin. She takes a long sip of her margarita and then, because she has no choice, crosses over to the French doors and stands beside Andrea.

"No one looks the same," Lucy says. "That's for sure."

They have not seen each other for three years, and actually they never saw each other more than once or twice a year after their disastrous tenure in the same household. As it's turned out, Andrea was ambitious. She's a corporate lawyer married to one of her partners, a large, intelligent man who wouldn't be caught dead at a twentieth high school reunion. And the truth is, Andrea does look the same, only she wears contact lenses and her mass of dark, curly hair is considered exotic rather than a curse.

"I take it my parents don't know you're in town," Andrea says. She's still staring at the bar; she has a glass of white wine and seltzer.

"Well, no," Lucy admits. "I didn't plan this trip. It just happened."

Andrea turns and appraises Lucy, staring at her hair. "That took guts," she says.

"Guess what?" Lucy says. "We still have nothing to say to each other."

They sip their drinks and watch the dance floor, where Heidi Kaplan is dancing with one of her old boyfriends.

"What a bitch," Andrea says bitterly.

"Heidi?" Lucy says.

"She told everyone you were on the pill," Andrea says. "That's why she was the prom queen and you were only one of the princesses."

Lucy looks closely at her cousin. "Where did she get that piece of information?"

Andrea sips her white wine.

"Thanks so much," Lucy says to her cousin.

"I only come back here to see my parents," Andrea says. "I avoid this town like the plague. You have no idea what it was like not to be pretty here. You were so wrapped up in yourself, you can't imagine the things I had to do." Andrea finishes her wine and places the glass on a windowsill. "There they all are." She nods to their left.

Lucy sees a group of men; somewhere inside those men nearing forty are the boys who used to follow Lucy down the hallways.

"None of them ever looked at me twice," Andrea says. "I would have agreed to a lobotomy if they only had. Well, most of them look like shit now," she adds, signaling to a waiter for another glass of wine. "Is that poetic justice?"

"Only if you care," Lucy says.

"Did you come back because of Evan?" Andrea asks. "Because he's involved with some kindergarten teacher. My parents have seen them together."

Lucy lets that pass, the way she always let things pass when they were forced to live together. She used to double-lock her door, she used to ignore Andrea completely when they walked by each other in the hall.

"Sorry," Andrea says. "It's an old habit. Gossip served me very well. I knew the name of everyone we went to school with, and every ugly little secret, and believe me, there were plenty of them."

Andrea is watching the dancers on the floor; she holds her glass of wine against her cheek. Lucy reaches into her purse and takes out the photograph.

"Do you know her?"

"She didn't go to school with us," Andrea says. "She looks too young."

"Then maybe you've seen her in town. Last year or the year before? She was a friend of mine in Florida and she just took off."

"Kind of like you did." Andrea shrugs and hands the photograph back to Lucy. "I've never seen her before. Although it's interesting that you actually have a friend."

"Meaning?" Lucy says coldly.

"Let's not fight," Andrea says.

"You always said that after you started a fight," Lucy says. "And you know it."

From behind them, in the doorway leading to the patio, a man's voice says, "Lucy."

Lucy recognizes Randy immediately. He was one of those boys Andrea would have been lobotomized for, and he's just as handsome as he was back then. Lucy slips the photograph back into her purse so she can take Randy's outstretched hand.

"No wedding ring." He grins. "Isn't that a nice surprise."

"You remember my cousin," Lucy says, since Andrea is watching them grimly, "Andrea Friedman."

Randy turns and looks blankly at Andrea.

"I gave you a blow job after Teddy Schiff's bar mitzvah," Andrea says.

Randy turns pale, but Lucy laughs, completely shocked. It is the most human thing she has ever heard Andrea say.

"Call my parents," Andrea says as she walks toward the bar.

"Who was that?" Randy says, still flustered.

"Well?" Lucy says. "Is it true?"

Randy has a slow, sweet smile and dark green eyes. "I'll take the fifth," he says. "Seriously, I thought you were married. I keep track of what happened to all the beautiful girls."

"Evan and I got divorced," Lucy says.

"Same here," Randy says. "Last October. That's why I think this is fate."

"Just a statistical probability," Lucy says. But she's flattered in spite of herself. She remembers now that she'd actually considered dating Randy, but he seemed too handsome, too full of himself, to ever be true.

"I always thought we'd be good together," Randy says.

He moves closer to Lucy, and although she should back away, she doesn't. She remembers the odd rush of triumph she used to have each time the phone rang; she used to enjoy looking in the mirror and seeing the girl they all thought she was.

"Back then, I could never be with one girl. I wasn't ready for that," Randy tells her. "But I've changed."

"Really?" she says. "You're still flirting with me. That hasn't changed."

People have begun to look at them, and Lucy realizes that if she doesn't move away from him soon they will be a piece of gossip. By tomorrow, their names will be linked no matter what happens.

"I never got to dance with you at the prom because Evan was always around."

He has already circled her waist with his arm. Lucy remembers that he had a way of looking at you that made you feel there were no other people in the room. She remembers that Andrea used to write his name on her loose-leaf notebook. There is a slow song playing, and Lucy lets him lead her out to the dance floor, past Heidi Kaplan, past the classmates whose names she no longer recalls. That one dance turns into half a dozen. He's had a lot of practice at this, he knows what to whisper in your ear and how to move his fingers up your spine. Sometime after midnight, when Evan approaches them, Lucy finds that she isn't ready to leave. She doesn't have to think about anything when she dances with Randy, she doesn't even have to make a decision, since he offers to take her home.

"Are you sure you want to do this?" Evan says, after Randy's gone off to get Lucy another margarita.

"Why? Will I be in danger? Is he a terrible driver?"

"You know what I mean," Evan says. "He was the kind of guy who got whatever he wanted."

"You're worried," Lucy says brightly.

"I used to worry about him," Evan admits. "I thought he'd try to steal you away from me."

"I'll be fine," Lucy says.

And she is, until it's time to leave and they go out into the parking lot and she realizes she's had too much to drink. The stars in the sky seem to be moving too quickly; the ground is a little too shaky.

"Where do you want me to take you?" Randy says. He's got his hand on her bare back and he ignores several people who say good night as they walk to their parked cars. Randy has a Porsche, the same color as the one he had in high school, but a more expensive model.

"I'm staying with Evan," Lucy says. When Randy raises an eyebrow she adds, "Not in that way. We're really divorced."

"You could stay at my place," Randy says.

He's taken her purse out of her hands and placed it on the hood of his car. She was attracted to him in high school; everyone was. What might have happened if Randy had been invited to Andrea's sweet sixteen party, if he had been the one she'd wandered out to the pool house with that night? What would happen now if they spent just one night together?

"This isn't high school," Lucy tells him.

"Thank God," Randy says. "Come on," he urges her. "Let's go to my house."

If she had married him instead of Evan, they might still be together, their child might be home in bed right now, sleeping peacefully, under a hand-sewn quilt. He was the kind of man she was supposed to have married, so why is it that she finds herself wishing that the asphalt in the parking lot would turn to red dust beneath her feet? Why is it she thinks about the white moths and blue shadows and the merlins that guard their trees so well they refuse to migrate in April?

"Not tonight," Lucy says.

"When?" Randy says. "Tomorrow?"

"This is silly," Lucy says. "I don't even live here anymore."

"Sunday night?" Randy insists.

"I might be gone by Sunday. I'm going back to Florida."

"Palm Beach?" Randy asks.

"Someplace you've never heard of," Lucy tells him.

"Try me," Randy says. He's got that smile the girls could never resist.

"Verity," Lucy says.

"You're right." Randy laughs. "That's a new one."

He leans toward her and kisses her. Lucy quickly takes a step back.

"Really," she says. "No."

"Then let me take you out to dinner. No strings," Randy says. "Sunday night."

"All right," Lucy finds herself saying.

Randy grins and opens the passenger door for her. "I believe in fate," he says. "I believe we both came to this reunion for a reason."

But Lucy is no longer listening to him. She can feel the knot in her stomach, and her throat is dry as dust. If she isn't completely mistaken, that is her car parked at the edge of the lot. It's right there, beside a magnolia thick with cream-colored flowers.

"I don't know what I was thinking," Lucy says. "I've got my car."

The night suddenly seems much darker; the green sloping hills behind the country club are really nothing more than man-made mounds of earth, built to amuse golfers. Someone once told Lucy that years ago the country club mail-ordered fireflies and let them out of their big cardboard boxes in June, so when you looked out through the French doors you'd see them in the bushes and above the greens, just as if they belonged there.

"You won't forget?" Randy says, because she's already turned from him.

"Sunday night," Lucy says. "Maybe. We'll see."

As she walks across the empty parking lot in her white dress, she's aware of how much her feet ache from dancing in tight shoes. She's aware of the crickets singing in the grass and the sound of her own heartbeat. Her car is parked at an angle, with all the windows rolled down. The radio is playing, and although Lucy doesn't recognize the song, she finds herself running the rest of the way, faster than it would seem possible in her new shoes.

Chapter Seven

THE meanest boy in Verity knows the price you pay when you hesitate. He's known it for a long time. An opportunity presents itself to you, you take it, whether it's a wallet left unguarded, a record store clerk looking in the opposite direction, or a dark, empty road, which leads in two directions. Stop to think and the momentum fades away, imagine a baby waking in the morning after you're gone and searching the house for you, imagine a dog slowly starving to death in the heat, and you'll wind up trotting back the way you've come instead of heading for the Interstate, the way you'd planned. All that night the boy stayed awake wondering why he didn't run when he had the chance, after Julian had disappeared down the driveway, and in the morning, while he ate his oatmeal with raisins, he was still kicking himself for the chance not taken.

He doesn't plan to miss his chance again, he's not about to stick around until someone figures he's guilty of murder or kidnapping or even petty theft. Yes, he brings the breakfast dishes to the sink for Miss Giles and he fills up the little wading pool for the baby and holds her hand so she won't slip while she's hopping around in the tepid water, but that doesn't mean he's staying. The baby loves to play in the water, he remembers that from Long Boat Street, how she'd sit on the steps of the pool beside her mother with a plastic watering can and a pink plastic sieve while he and Laddy splashed each other and held each other's heads underwater for as long as they dared. This little girl is never going to hold someone's head underwater in a swimming pool; the boy can tell that already. She's thoughtful and cautious; when the boy lets go of her hand, to sneak a cigarette behind the woodpile, the baby sounds like she's about to cry, and he has to come right back and watch her as she sits down carefully in the water and wiggles her toes.

He doesn't have to be responsible for her and he's not going to be. He doesn't have to notice that she looks up at him, quickly, each time he moves, just to make certain he's still there. So what if she steps out of the pool as soon as he nods to her and picks up her towel when Miss Giles calls them in to lunch; that doesn't mean he owes her anything. No one could guess what the boy was really thinking or planning. He eats his franks and beans, even though they turn his stomach. He lies down beside the baby till she falls asleep at nap time. He even hangs the laundry on the line for Miss Giles without being asked. He doesn't care about anyone and nobody can make him. He doesn't care as he sits at the kitchen table and watches Miss Giles stir her batter for icebox cookies, he doesn't give a damn about anything any of Oprah's guests have to say, he couldn't care less that his mother hasn't even bothered to try to find him.

"You've got a funny look to you today," Miss Giles says

to him after the baby has woken from her nap and reattached herself to the boy's leg.

The boy makes his face go all innocent and confused, but he can tell Miss Giles isn't so easily fooled. Little by little, she's been getting the baby to like her, and now the baby will leave the boy's side long enough to go out to the yard with Miss Giles and feed bits of lettuce to the rabbits. She even let Miss Giles wash her old, muddy stuffed bunny, though she sat right out on the porch with it until it dried. Miss Giles may be smart, but if she thinks the boy's got a funny look to him she doesn't have to worry. It's the last one she'll ever see on his face. If people are stupid enough to trust him they deserve whatever they get. Actually, he'd bet good money that Julian Cash would have done the same exact thing when he was his age. He would have gotten the hell out of there as soon as he could; he probably would have traveled a hundred miles on the Interstate by now.

It's not easy to sit through the rest of the afternoon, and then through supper and a plate of the icebox cookies Miss Giles baked. The baby lets Miss Giles put her to bed tonight, a first, since she's always made a big fuss if the boy isn't the one who tucks her in and gives her the stuffed bunny rabbit to sleep with. It's just as well, it's better this way, it doesn't really matter one damned bit. He'd have to be nuts to be jealous, since he's not about to have this baby hanging on to him for the rest of his life. He watches the big clock in the kitchen, waiting for the sky to fill with orange light, then begin to darken. At a little before nine, when the baby's asleep, Miss Giles looks up from her day-old issue of the *Sun Herald* and says, "Don't you have a chore to do?"

Like he'd ever forget, like he hasn't been waiting all day just for this. The boy nods politely and swings open the back door, and then he's free. By now the sky has turned dark purple, the color of the quilt his mother and father used to keep on their bed. It is not so difficult to make a left rather than a right when he reaches the end of the driveway, and so instead of heading to Julian's place, the boy takes off running in the opposite direction. He runs along the edge of the road, through the damp, purple night, his heart beating fast. He figures it won't take him long to hitch a ride north once he gets to the Interstate, so he lets himself slow down. He fishes a wrinkled cigarette he stole from Julian's kitchen out of his jeans pocket and lights it with a wooden match, then inhales greedily. The sky above him settles into blackness and the white moths appear, as if out of thin air. All he has to do is clear his mind and keep walking, and before he knows it, he'll be home.

Up ahead of him, on the back steps of the Hole-in-One, Shannon is waiting for a sign that will tell her what to do with the rest of her life. Today at noon, as she sat beneath the gumbo-limbo tree, she began to wonder what it would be like to be rooted in one place forever. She thought of all the things the tree had to endure, gas fumes and woodpeckers, termites and hurricanes, and as she rested her head against the peeling bark, she began to weep. She has to choose, otherwise the future will just happen to her; she'll sit beneath this tree for what will seem like only hours, but when she finally rises from the ground, she'll discover she's an old woman, with long gray hair that twines down into the grass. If she goes north this summer, it will change her whole life. She'll come back for her senior year, and after that for Easter and Christmas vacations, but she won't be the same person anymore, and she's not sure how anyone is ever ready for that.

Tonight, as she stands outside her mother's shop, it is just as possible that she'll spend the rest of her life in Verity as it is that she'll be on a plane headed north for the summer session at Mount Holyoke. She looks up, but there aren't any stars. She can hear her mother joking with Maury and Fred as they get ready to close up, late, the way they always do on Fridays. Her mother's been working here since the summer she turned eighteen, not very much older than Shannon is now. Nobody offered her any fellowships or plane rides. Shannon can't even remember her mother taking a vacation, except for the time she took Shannon up to Disney World a few years back. They went on every single ride— Pirates of the Caribbean, Big Thunder Mountain Railroad, Mr. Toad's Wild Ride—and they kept a log so they wouldn't miss anything, since they both knew they probably would never come back. People thought they were sisters, but instead of being flattered Janey was downright annoyed. "I paid my dues," she told Shannon.

Just thinking about her mother makes Shannon feel like crying, and she doesn't know why. She breathes in quickly, short little breaths that make her feel slightly dizzy, so that she's not quite certain what she's seeing when a figure appears on the road. She stays real quiet, and when he draws a little closer she recognizes him as the boy she saw at the dumpster. She feels a little fluttery, as if maybe he's the sign she's been waiting for, and without stopping to think, she walks out to meet him.

The boy is startled when he sees her; he takes several steps backward, just the way the deer in her yard used to.

"Are you running away?" Shannon asks.

The boy stares at her, then nods his head.

"I'm thinking about it, too," Shannon says, because right now that's exactly the way it feels to her.

The boy takes one last step back. He should have dodged

her before she opened her mouth to speak. Just because she's stupid enough to hesitate doesn't mean he has to do that too.

"I can't make up my mind," Shannon admits. "I think I have and then it turns out I haven't. I feel like I'm driving myself crazy."

The boy can feel the momentum begin to drain out of his fingers and toes.

"Where's your little sister?" Shannon asks. "The baby I saw you with?"

If the boy could speak, he would tell her that the baby is asleep in a crib, beneath an old cotton blanket, almost five miles down the road. He would say that she's too young to know she's been abandoned. She won't understand, even after she wakes to find that he's gone. But nothing comes out of his mouth. All he can do is scowl and wish this girl would disappear. She's a complete stranger; he doesn't have to feel the doubts she has, he doesn't even have to consider them. He can be on his own in two minutes flat, he can do it and not look back. What does he owe anyone? Absolutely nothing. What does he feel on this road, so far from home? Nothing at all.

A car appears out of the darkness and passes nearby, and as its headlights sweep across the road, Shannon and the boy step closer to each other. It's the moment the boy's been dreading, the instant when he hesitates. As soon as the car has gone by, the boy looks at Shannon as though he were frightened by everything—the dark, the car's headlights, the sweet smell of lemons in the air—then he takes off running, back the way he's come.

"Wait," Shannon calls after him, since it's too soon to tell whether or not he's the sign she's been waiting for.

178

The boy is amazingly fast, running down the road until the night closes in behind him. You would think he'd never been there at all, unless you had been close enough to feel his warm breath, because he's gone now, without ever having said a word. Shannon fans herself with one hand and holds her long hair up off her neck with the other. She's used to hot weather and mosquitoes; she's seen those white moths appear each May all her life, then disappear again in June. She hears Fred and Maury head out to their cars. She hears her mother calling from the back steps, the way she used to when Shannon was a little girl and woke early, so she could go outside and wait for the deer. It never occurred to Shannon to leave the back porch and walk over to the woods where her father kept a block of salt, just as it hasn't yet occurred to her that she's already made her decision. Standing in the road, listening to her mother call to her, she's already left home.

Julian Cash sleeps in the car, just as he has for the past two nights, hunched up in the front, so that Loretta can sprawl across the backseat. The only difference is that now Lucy is sleeping less than two hundred yards away, in the guest room of her ex-husband's house, and that just a few hours ago, while the sky was still inky and everyone else on the block was asleep, what Julian wanted to happen did, and it's driving him crazy.

Since she's gone inside the house, he hasn't been able to sleep more than an hour at a time. Every time he wakes he's startled by the moon above him, as if it were a piece of Lucy's dress, which tore when he touched it, so that his

179

hands seemed filled with light. He thought she would be angry with him when she first got into the car, but she wasn't. She leaned against the door and pulled her legs up beneath her. She had a way of looking at him that made him think she might bolt and run at any second.

"Are you here because you think I can't do this by myself?" she had asked him.

"No," Julian had said, and it was the truth. He had been parked outside the country club for hours, with Loretta curled up in the backseat, listening to people enjoying themselves, because he couldn't not be there. When the guy with the Porsche leaned down and kissed Lucy, Julian went to the glove compartment for his gun. It was just a reflex, he didn't act on it. But he wanted to, and he knew what that meant. He had lost the ability to focus; if somebody didn't stop him soon, he wasn't going to be able to stop himself.

"I can get the name of this woman on my own," Lucy had told him. The white dress was so short it moved halfway up her thighs and she had to tug at it. "Whether you think I can or not."

"I think it's a good thing you didn't go home with him," Julian had said, as he steered the Mustang down the country club driveway. He actually said that; he heard the words come out of his mouth.

"We'll never know, will we?" Lucy had said. "Since I didn't."

"Oh, we know," Julian had said.

He was certain then that the madness had followed them. It had seeped into their bones, and even a thousand miles between them and Verity didn't make a difference. He wanted her all the way back to her ex-husband's house, but he never would have done anything about it if she hadn't leaned toward him, suddenly, and looped her arms around him. It had happened with so little warning, as soon as he'd parked in front of the house, that neither of them could think straight. But before Lucy could change her mind, or even take another breath, he slid his hand between her legs, and when he felt how hot she was, he knew it wasn't over yet. He couldn't stop kissing her. He held her to him, so that her spine was pressed up against the steering wheel, and the most amazing thing was that she didn't stop him. She wanted him to pull her dress down. She must have, because when he did she arched her back and let him go on kissing her. She didn't run away when he jammed his seat back, or when he pulled down the zipper of his jeans, or even when he moved on top of and then inside her. She didn't even close her eyes.

He could have sworn she told him not to stop. Somebody told him that. Parked beneath the streetlight, he could hear her whispering to him. Even if this never happened again, he didn't care, and he wouldn't let her go, not until the sky turned milky and gray and they heard *The New York Times* delivery truck turn the corner. And now his mouth is sore, and his head throbs, and he feels her all over him, as if she were still with him. He wants more than he promised himself he would, and because he doesn't dare hope for anything, he finds himself hating New York and everything about it. He can barely breathe here.

It shouldn't matter one bit that her ex-husband's house is so big, or that there were thirty-one Jaguars parked at the country club last night. It shouldn't matter that he had to show ID to get past the guard at the gate, when he noticed that no one else was being stopped. Lucy told him, as she got out of the car, clutching her dress around her, not to follow her anymore. You'll make people nervous, she told him. He's thought about what she said and he knows it's true. He's been making people nervous all his life. He does it to her; he could tell from the way she backed away from the car. Sooner or later someone on Easterbrook Lane will pad out across a green lawn to pick up *The New York Times*, spot him, and call the police, and then he'll have to report to the New York State police for permission to carry a gun.

He's never given a damn about cars or houses before, and he sure as hell isn't going to start caring now, but he thinks he may have a virus, or maybe it's just that something's wrong with the air up here. Loretta, snoring in the backseat of the Mustang, doesn't seem to notice the difference between New York and Florida, but she must because you can smell it, you can feel it on your skin, like pollen.

When Lucy finally comes out of the house, at a little after eight, Julian slouches down behind the wheel. She and her ex-husband are in the middle of an argument, probably about the boy. Julian had felt he'd done the right thing in giving the boy his freedom; now he's not so sure. A boy who grew up here on Easterbrook Lane couldn't possibly know the difference between a daddy longlegs and a scorpion; he wouldn't know enough to look out for ferrets and horned owls; he'd never manage to find his way in the dark. A boy from here wouldn't think to avoid drainage ditches after a rainfall, or make certain to wear shoes, even on the hottest days, because of the fire ants. If Lucy knew her son was walking the roads by himself at night, putting his hands into Arrow's feed gate, she'd probably be arguing with Julian instead of her ex-husband. If she knew how much he wanted her, still, she might actually slap him. He wouldn't blame her if she did. Lucy and her ex-husband argue until a white Volvo pulls up to the curb and honks. The ex-husband grins at the driver and waves, then walks over, although before he opens the door he turns to watch as Lucy backs the Celica out of the driveway.

Julian lets her get a good distance ahead of him before he pulls away from the curb. He follows her through the town of Great Neck, into the village of Kings Point, where the houses are bigger than most of the motels Julian has stayed in. They probably have better service and clean white sheets, ironed so well there's not one wrinkle. He's never going to mention what happened between them if she doesn't. He's already decided that. He'll keep his mouth shut and stop wanting things, and when he gets back home he'll just go on with his life, the same way he always has. He'll be out of New York before he knows it, and he never has to come back.

Still, when Lucy drives through the iron gates leading to a house hidden behind weeping beeches, Julian finds himself wishing he had come here at a different time of year. Maybe then he would have seen snow. He has pulled over onto the shoulder of the road, and from where he's parked he can see the blue outline of the Throgs Neck Bridge. He gets out and lets Loretta run for a while, making sure to whistle when she strays too far onto someone's lawn. He imagines that snow must be a lot like the mock orange petals that fell to the ground when he turned his wheel a little too hard and sideswiped the bushes on the shoulder of the road. A shower of pure, cool white; walking in it would be like walking through a cloud. He would have preferred winter; maybe then he wouldn't still be hearing bees, like the ones that hover in the perennial garden behind those iron gates. When he wasn't more than five years old, Julian stumbled into a bees' nest hidden within the roots of one of Miss Giles's old willow trees. The bees swarmed around him, so many that the air was pure yellow, and that's the way Miss Giles found him. She washed him in a bath of oatmeal soap, but she didn't find one sting, and that made perfect sense to Julian, even then. Miss Giles thought it was some sort of miracle, but that wasn't it at all. If he'd reached out and plucked a single bee from midair, its wings would have stopped beating beneath his gaze.

Past the beeches, and the gate, not much has changed since Lucy first came here. On that day, she was wearing a pleated skirt and a blue blouse with a round collar. She had two suitcases with her, and her long hair was pulled into a ponytail. As soon as she walked through the door and stood in the marble foyer, she felt sick. She barely made it to the powder room, where she threw up in the pink-veined sink with its gold-plated handles. And although that was more than twenty years ago, Lucy feels queasy again when she rings the doorbell. She decided to come here sometime near dawn; it is the sort of decision that seems shakier when considered in the bright light of morning. When she'd left Julian, she went up to the guest bathroom and ran the shower as hot as she could, and still she couldn't stop shivering. After she folded her white dress into the wicker trash basket, she ran her hand over her throat, where he'd left a line of raised love bites. Since then, Lucy has thought, again and again, of her parents' final embrace in their car. She can almost taste their last kiss. A kiss so sweet and deep it could turn you inside out. They seemed so ridiculous to her, the way they couldn't keep their hands off each other, the way they'd reach for each other in the morning, at the kitchen table, still sleepy from being out so late. At sixteen, when she came to this house, and locked herself in her bedroom for nearly a whole summer, she'd had no idea why her mother had always seemed so flustered when Scout grabbed for her hand instead of the coffee she set before him on the table. A silly woman, so careless she hadn't heard the train headed straight for them. And now, standing here, at her aunt and uncle's door, Lucy finally understands how this might have been possible; she herself had not heard the news vendor's truck this morning until Julian quickly threw the torn dress around them so they wouldn't be seen.

When she rings the doorbell a second time, Lucy expects a housekeeper to answer, but instead it's her Aunt Naomi. For just the slightest instant, Naomi doesn't seem to know who Lucy is; she has that put-upon look she always had when Lucy didn't come down to dinner on time.

"You should have phoned," Naomi says. She quickly embraces Lucy, then draws her into the foyer. "I could have canceled some of the appointments I have today."

Naomi has always been able to make Lucy feel guilty; during dinner she would stare at Lucy across the table just at the moment when Lucy happened to knock over a goblet of water or drop her butter knife on the floor.

"I saw Andrea last night," Lucy says. "Didn't she tell you?"

"Actually, she did," Naomi says.

Naomi is nearing sixty, but she looks very much the way she did when Lucy first moved in. Her hair is a little blonder, her jewelry smaller and more expensive. "But I know you never come to visit us," she says. "God forbid."

They go into the airy dining room, with its arched windows that overlook the gardens and the pool, and Naomi pours them both hot coffee. Lucy reaches for her cup and immediately spills some coffee on the white linen tablecoth.

"That's all right," Naomi says smoothly, but her forehead puckers as she frowns.

Lucy looks out to the garden. There is the pool house she remembers so well, and the stone path bordered by rhododendrons and lilies. Someone is already swimming laps in the pool. Her Uncle Jack.

"His heart," Naomi says. "There's nothing wrong with it," she adds quickly. "We just want to keep it that way." She takes a sip of her coffee, then adds some low-fat milk. "What did you think of Andrea?" she asks casually.

"A big success," Lucy says.

"Well, she deserves every bit of it," Naomi says. "Her reaction to you was our fault." She has clearly been wanting to say this for a long time. "Actually Jack's."

Out by the pool, Lucy's uncle rises from the water and grabs a thick towel.

"He had so much damn guilt about your father that you instantly became his favorite, and that wasn't easy on Andrea."

"I wasn't his favorite," Lucy protests.

"You were, for all the good it did him. Did you know he turned sixty last month? Did you consider sending a card?"

Lucy puts down her coffee cup. She remembers that her mother often wore a bathrobe until noon and sang along with every song that came on the radio. Lucy could hear her mother's deep, sweet voice, even when she tried not to, when she fled into her room and slammed the door shut. She could hear her father slide back his kitchen chair and applaud at the end of each song.

"Pardon me for being honest," Naomi says. "He idolized your father. Did you know that? But he did what his parents told him and cut Scout off, and he's had to live with that."

Lucy looks down at the linen tablecloth. There is a vase

of pink roses in the center of the table. Naomi has always preferred pink to red, which she thinks of as vulgar.

"You never knew Grandma and Grandpa, but everyone did what they said, or else. Except for Scout, of course, who never listened to anyone."

"So what's your point, Naomi? My father's dead. Is there some further punishment you'd like to dole out to him?"

They stare at each other over the roses. Unless Lucy's mistaken, Scout once bought her mother a chiffon scarf that was exactly the same shade of pink; she wound it around her hair on windy evenings and let Lucy borrow it to wear with a burgundy jumper.

"No," Naomi says thoughtfully. "I just wish he'd never existed in the first place."

The glass doors slide open and Jack comes in, wearing a long terry-cloth robe.

"I don't believe my eyes," he says. "Lucy?"

Lucy rises and goes to kiss his cheek. He tastes like chlorine and suntan lotion.

"I saw Andrea last night," she tells him.

"Ah," Jack says proudly. "My attorney."

That's when Lucy knows her Aunt Naomi is wrong. She was never his favorite, though he might have tried to make himself believe it.

"Did she tell you she was pregnant?" Jack asks. "It took them forever trying."

"Jack!" Naomi says.

"It's good news," Jack says. "Good news should be told. Of course, she's still too skinny."

Jack sits down and accepts the coffee Naomi pours him out of a separate pot.

"Decaf," she tells Lucy.

If Scout were alive today, Lucy doubts that he'd be drinking decaffeinated coffee, but you never know. He wasn't yet forty when he died. He didn't have to think about decaffeinated coffee and life insurance and what staying out all night could do to you, let alone what it meant to be out on a raft when you entered middle age.

"Where's the boy?" Jack asks as he breaks apart an onion roll. "Where's Keith?"

"No fats," Naomi tells him when he reaches for the butter.

"He's back in Florida," Lucy says. It's true; she doesn't have to feel guilty about saying that.

"Still as smart as he always was?" Jack asks. "Will you stop?" he says to Naomi, who has pushed a tub of butter substitute toward him. "This woman is my health consultant all of a sudden," he tells Lucy. "Did you get your M.D. while I wasn't looking?' he asks Naomi.

Lucy's aunt and uncle smile at each other, but that doesn't stop Naomi from handing him the butter substitute.

"I should have called you when I moved to Florida," Lucy says. "But things got so complicated with the divorce."

"Divorce is never pretty," Jack agrees.

Lucy runs her fingers over the coffee she's spilled. She sees now how easy it is to be cruel without even trying; children do it every day.

"I'm sorry," Lucy tells her uncle.

"Don't worry," Jack says. "The tablecloth can be dry-cleaned."

But it will never be the same, Lucy knows that. There will always be a slight yellow stain, and, if it's not thrown out, the tablecloth will never again be used with the good china. They drink their coffee and have their onion rolls and discuss the traffic on the Long Island Expressway until enough time has passed for Lucy to leave politely.

"Scout," Jack says suddenly, after he's walked her to the door. The name escapes out of his mouth. He has never said his brother's name in Lucy's presence, and when she came here she was almost grateful for that. She took nothing from her parents' house, except her own clothes, and now she regrets not searching for her mother's pink scarf, for Scout's battered briefcase filled with sheet music. When Lucy looks at her uncle he explains, "It's just with your hair so short, I can see him in you. The profile. The nose."

They can hear Naomi in the dining room, as she clears the table. They can hear the hum of the pool filter out back.

"I was the baby," Jack says. "Believe it or not."

After Lucy leaves their house she finds she's having trouble breathing. She remembers she's always been slightly allergic to lilacs. Keith was the same way. His nose was sniffly from May until July, then again during ragweed season at the end of August. When he was a baby, Lucy used to keep him indoors as much as she could during these months, but even before he could walk, he'd bang on the screen door until it opened and he could escape into the yard. She takes a hard left out of Jack and Naomi's driveway, so that fine bits of gravel hit against the paint of Evan's Celica, but when she reaches Middle Neck Road, she slows down, since it must be much more difficult to tail someone here in New York than it is in Florida. More traffic, for one thing, and faster, ruder drivers. She should probably be angry, since she told Julian not to follow her, but at least he's staying far behind. Still, it's disconcerting to be trailed, even when you know it, as if your shadow were lagging three blocks behind, instead of following right at your side.

If she tried to figure out why she wanted him so much last night, she would never be able to. This is not rational, it's way beyond that. She's not going to think about Julian, that's all there is to it, although not thinking about him takes so much energy that Lucy is exhausted by the time she finds a parking space in the crowded municipal lot. When she gets to Salvuki's she has to introduce herself to the receptionist all over again before she's allowed access to Salvuki himself. She approaches him as he combs out a white-haired woman who already has a terrific tan, even this early in the season. Salvuki pauses for a moment after Lucy tells him who she is; he studies her reflection in the mirror.

"You haven't been here in almost a year," he says accusingly. Salvuki looks more like an accountant or an assassin than a hairdresser. "What did you let them do to you?"

"I had a problem with chlorine," Lucy admits. "It's almost all out."

"I don't know if there's anything I can do with that," Salvuki tells her.

"Actually, I'm just trying to find someone who was a client of yours," Lucy says.

She roots through her purse and brings out the photograph of her neighbor. Once he identifies this woman, Lucy will be free. She can swoop down on Verity with the victim's name, dazzling both the Verity police and Paul Salley; she may be able to rescue her son and get herself a front-page byline all at the same time. If she's lucky, she won't even remember Julian Cash, she won't think about him every time she closes her eyes.

"This woman wasn't my client," Salvuki says, handing Lucy the photograph and reaching for his comb.

"She was," Lucy presses. "She told me. Just look at her one more time."

"I'd remember that hair color," Salvuki says. "I'd remember that face."

"The hair color is new," Lucy says, panicked. She has never imagined the possibility of his faulty memory. It is quite conceivable that if someone had brought Salvuki a photograph of Lucy, with all her hair chopped off, standing beneath the Florida sky at noon, he would have never known her. She sees now that as Salvuki combs out his client, he's studying only her hair; the rest of her is nothing more than baggage.

"Please," Lucy says. "Think back."

"Look, if you need help, I'll try," Salvuki says. "But I can't make any promises. Your hair is too damaged for that."

Outside, standing on the sidewalk, Lucy can't catch her breath; it's as if she were caught in a net of lilacs. She has nothing to show for this trip, nothing to show for all her certainty. She had one simple fact and it isn't enough. Without a name, Keith will be the only lead; when they take him into the police station for questioning, he'll freeze, or he'll spit and utter a hundred curses, and if they finally have to restrain him, they won't believe a word he says. Lucy stands facing a children's shop whose window is decorated with a castle made of Legos. Soft pink dresses hang above the castle like clouds. She remembers this place; she used to come here for birthday presents for Keith. On impulse, Lucy goes inside. She picks up a puppet in the shape of a dragon, with soft green wings made out of satin, and silk fire shooting from its mouth.

"Great, isn't it?" the owner of the shop calls.

Lucy carries the puppet up to the counter and takes out her wallet.

"Is it a boy or a girl?" the shop owner asks. When Lucy looks at her blankly, she adds, "The new owner of the dragon?"

"A boy," Lucy says. One much too old for such nonsense as puppets.

"Boys love any sort of monster, don't they?" the shop owner says.

As Lucy reaches for her MasterCard she sees the dead woman's face right in front of her driver's license.

"Is that Bethany?" the shop owner asks.

Lucy looks up; she can feel her heart race.

"It is. I remember that adorable baby."

"That's right. Bethany," Lucy says evenly.

"She used to come in twice a week," the shop owner says as she rings up the dragon. "And then she just stopped. She special-ordered one of those." There is a pink rocking horse decorated with rhinestones and garlands of hand-painted flowers at the rear of the store. "She gave me a deposit, then never came back to get it."

"She did that?" Lucy says.

"If Bethany's a friend of yours, you might want to remind her about the rocking horse. I can't hold it forever."

"No," Lucy says. Her lips are dry, and she runs her tongue over them. "Of course not."

Most probably, Lucy is standing in the exact same place where her neighbor stood when she put down the deposit for the rocking horse. An impulse buy, Lucy thinks, a toy so exceptional she wouldn't have cared about the expense, or maybe, back then, she didn't have to care.

"I haven't seen her in ages," Lucy says. Her heart skips one beat as she lies; she imagines the same thing happens to Keith all the time. "If I had her address, I'd go right over. That rocking horse is so cute it's a shame not to have it."

"Well, no one responded to the cards I sent," the shop owner says. "And when I phoned I got a recording, because

192

the number had been changed to an unlisted one. But maybe you'll have better luck."

She looks up the address in her card file and writes it down for Lucy, then has Lucy sign her MasterCard receipt.

"Your little boy will love this," she tells Lucy.

Lucy runs all the way to the parking lot. She throws the dragon into the backseat of Evan's car. She's in such a rush that she doesn't look at the address until she is stopped at a red light and can finally pull a local map out of Evan's glove compartment. As it turns out, she has to head back toward Kings Point. The street where Bethany used to live is lined with lilac hedges, and Lucy's eyes start to water even though all the car windows are rolled up. When she sees the house number, her stomach lurches. It's a lovely house, bigger than hers and Evan's; there are baskets of potted fuchsias hung along the porch ceiling and the driveway is paved with heavy bluestone. Lucy parks halfway down the block and walks up to the house, but when she gets to the door, all she can think of is her neighbor down in the laundry room and the look on her face when she heard her baby cry. Lucy realizes that she may have to give someone horrible news. She has always wondered how it was decided that her next-door neighbor should be the one to tell her that her parents had died; she'd wondered, back then, why it was her neighbor who broke into tears when Lucy was the one who had suffered the loss.

Standing beneath the fuchsias and a blue-painted ceiling, she finally rings the bell. She's rummaging through her purse in search of a comb when the door opens.

"I thought I was picking you up tomorrow night."

This is the voice of her neighbor's husband, and it turns Lucy to ice. She has to shield her eyes against the sunlight so she can see him. He's just showered and he's wearing slacks and a clean white shirt.

"Don't tell me." Randy grins. "You couldn't wait."

"Right," Lucy says.

She goes in through the open front door, into the cool foyer, her cheeks and throat burning hot.

"What did you do?" he asks. "Follow me?"

"My cousin Andrea knows where everyone lives." It's amazing how easy it is to continue lying once you've started. You don't even know why you're doing it; it just feels necessary. "It's a beautiful house," Lucy says.

"Let me show you around," Randy says, leading her into the living room. "I just had it redone. I think it might be too much."

"I'm sure it's great," Lucy says. She really doesn't want to go any farther than the front hall. "Look, I have to talk to you about your wife," she tells him. This is going to be horrible and she knows it. He may not believe her, he may break down and cry.

"Ex," Randy corrects her. "I'm no longer married. Remember?"

"Right," Lucy says.

"She was Dutch," Randy says. "I met her when I was traveling through Europe, and after the divorce she went back. She took the kid, naturally. That's the roughest part, the damned custody."

He has such beautiful eyes; they keep changing color as he lies. If she hadn't lived with a liar for so long, Lucy might not have noticed the way he ran his hand through his hair, she would never have recognized the flicker of yellow light behind his eyes.

"Now it's my turn," Randy says. "I get to ask about your past."

There are bands of panic expanding around Lucy's neck and shoulders. She had considered going home with Randy last night, she'd wanted to.

"Were you sleeping with Evan in high school?"

Each time Randy was in a drama club production, the first three rows in the auditorium would be filled with girls, and every one had made certain to apply extra mascara and lipstick. Andrea wouldn't go into the lunchroom until she knew what table he was sitting at and could position herself near him. Lucy wonders if he was a liar, even back then.

"During senior year," she says.

She will admit to anything, but she won't tell him about the rocking horse, she won't say a word about Bethany.

"I thought so!" Randy says. "I could always tell. Now there's only one more thing I need to know." He has moved much closer to Lucy. "Are you sleeping with me?"

"Never on a first date," Lucy says.

Randy studies her carefully. "Then why are you here, Lucy?"

She has Evan's car keys in her hand, and without thinking she moves them between her fingers, as though they were a weapon.

"If I came here today, tomorrow wouldn't be our first date," Lucy says.

"Ah." Randy smiles.

It's the smile he has used so well a million times before.

"Let's forget about the restaurant," he says. "Why don't you just come back here tomorrow."

It is so hard to breathe in this house, Lucy can't imagine how Bethany managed it. Randy moves toward Lucy; his hair smells like coconut shampoo. He kisses her once, a brief, practiced kiss that has always left women asking for more.

"Seven-thirty," he whispers, and Lucy nods before she

goes out the door. She walks down the driveway and along the street, but when she reaches Evan's Celica, she doesn't stop. It's not morning anymore, yet the street is quiet, except for the droning of hedge clippers in the backyards as landscapers tend to the shrubbery. She knows from experience, where there's one lie there are bound to be more. She keeps walking until the Mustang comes into view. It's there at the corner, parked beside a stop sign, still covered with red dust. All along the hood the seeds of strangler figs are embedded in the paint; nothing will ever get rid of them. Lucy grabs the door handle and gets inside. The car smells like french fries, and she has to swing her legs over the empty Coke cans that litter the floor. She doesn't turn to look at him until she's locked her door, and when she does Julian Cash takes off his sunglasses.

"Let me guess," he says. "You think you found yourself a murderer."

Chapter Eight

THE meanest boy in Verity knows the difference between right and wrong, though not everyone would agree with the choices he makes. Since the night when he discovered he couldn't run away he's been breaking a rule, not out of spite but because he knows in his heart it would be wrong not to break it. That's what happens when someone comes to depend on you. You begin to consider feelings other than your own. You know what it must be like to be caged as the darkness falls and the owls call from the trees. That is why every evening, after Arrow has eaten his dinner and been given a bowl of fresh, cool water, the boy unlocks the chain-link gate and carefully swings it open. The first time he did this, the dog looked at him, puzzled. He wouldn't move until the boy crouched down and softly clapped his hands. Arrow tilted his head, then slowly walked out of the kennel. He looked out at the woods, where the scent of cypress and pine was thick and the darkness settled quickly, covering the air plants that grew wild, and then he stopped and sat down beside the boy.

The boy clapped a hand against his thigh and began to walk through Julian's yard, toward the woods. Still the dog sat where he was, watching. The boy nodded and clapped his hands again, and after a moment the dog took off. He passed right by the boy, and kept going. At first the boy could hear him running through the undergrowth, and he followed, but then there was nothing, not a sound. The boy sat down on a tree stump, realizing that he might have gotten himself lost. He could hear things moving in the woods, bats in the treetops, the soft, padding steps of opossums and cotton rats. He sat there in the dark, wondering how he could ever explain himself to Julian if the dog didn't come back, but when he looked up, the dog was suddenly beside him. He'd been running, hard, and his body was trembling. In his mouth was a large stick, an old root or a fallen mangrove limb. He carefully laid the stick at the boy's feet before backing away. The boy took the stick, lifted it over his head and threw it, as far and as high as he could.

Since then, they have played this game every night, walking farther and farther into the woods each time. Tonight, the boy made certain to coat himself with bug spray before leaving Miss Giles's house, and he's brought along a flashlight, even though his night vision is rapidly improving. He jogs all the way to Julian's, and when he gets there the dog is waiting at the gate. Arrow yelps happily when he sees the boy; his tail starts to wave, slowly at first, then faster and faster. As soon as he's let out, the dog races for the woods, but he waits every now and then for the boy to catch up. There's some moonlight tonight, and the boy feels that he never in his life has seen a creature more beautiful than Arrow; he's grateful that the dog has the decency to wait while he lumbers through the underbrush. When they are deep within the woods, in a place where no one has gone since Bobby and Julian Cash were children, the boy finds a good stick and lets it fly. Squirrels and yellow bats scatter in the trees. Dark swirls of mosquitoes rise to the highest branches. He throws the stick again and again, until his arm aches. When he stops and sits down on a log, the dog trots over and lays his huge head in the boy's lap.

Since losing his voice, the boy has realized that he never did have all that much to say. The panic he felt at first when he opened his mouth and nothing came out is gone. He's said enough nasty words to last a lifetime; the absence of sound makes him feel a kind of peace. He thinks of all the people in his life who thought they knew him. They didn't know him, they just listened to what he said. No one has ever known him the way this dog does. He knows when the boy's about to rise to his feet before he does; he knows exactly how fast the boy can travel through the woods back to Julian's house, and that the boy will return the following evening to set him free once again.

Running away is no longer a possibility. That's just the way it is. Some people understand this when they first look into their newborn baby's eyes, or when they fall in love; the boy knows it from the way the dog waits for him in the woods. They walk side by side toward the kennel, until the boy real- izes that the dog has stopped at the edge of the yard. The ruff of fur around his neck seems thicker, his ears are straight up, as though he is listening to something only he can hear. His legs shudder slightly as he considers whether or not he should run. The boy walks back toward Arrow, looking past him. There is nothing out there, just some old owls and the merlins nesting in the trees. The sound of a branch breaking perhaps, or the low crooning sound of the wind.

The boy reaches down and pets the dog's head, and Arrow startles; he has a wild look in his eyes. The boy keeps stroking his head, comforting him, until whatever disturbance the dog has sensed fades. Now the dog can follow the boy to the kennel; dust rises whenever he sets his feet down. Dogs can gauge disaster long before it strikes; they can smell a person's truest nature. Arrow steps back inside the kennel with the full knowledge that the boy who closes the gate behind him doesn't have a mean bone in his body. But something out there does. Something in the woods, disguised as the wind, has been watching them, and that is why when the boy double-locks the gate and heads off toward the road, the dog puts his head back and howls, and by then the moon has disappeared into a band of dark blue clouds, so that you couldn't see a man's shadow in the woods even if you tried.

Julian Cash spends the night in the car again, but he doesn't fall asleep until dawn. In the middle of the night he thought briefly of climbing up the trellis, then through the guest room window, but he didn't do it. Instead, he folded himself up in the driver's seat and rested his head against the window. When he wakes it's nearly eleven and all his muscles feel twisted. Evan's car is gone, so Julian walks Loretta, then grabs his suitcase and uses his MasterCard to enter the house. He can hear Lucy in the kitchen, but after thinking about her all night, he's not ready to see her. He lets Loretta off her leash, then goes upstairs, to the guest bathroom, where he takes a shower in the largest bathtub he's ever seen. There are dials and jets and all sorts of Jacuzzi things he stays away from, and he also stays away from the shampoo, which smells like coconut and lemon grass, and washes his hair with Dial soap instead. It gives him some pleasure to discover that even in a bathtub like this you can run out of hot water too soon. When he's through he puts on his old jeans and a clean shirt, which is a relief, since he hasn't changed his clothes since leaving Florida. There's still some red dust on his jeans, and when it falls onto the white-tiled floor Julian has to get on his hands and knees and clean it up with a washcloth, although all that seems to do is spread the sand around.

He shaves quickly, without looking in the mirror. He's done this so often he never nicks himself; he figures he can shave better than most blind men. He's got to be crazy to be here. He doesn't even like New York tap water: it's too soft, and it has a metallic taste that you never get with well water. He's left Loretta downstairs, because the truth is he doesn't want Lucy to be alone. That's the reason he hasn't checked into a motel, not that he could afford one around here. He has the feeling that someone is about to snap real soon.

Julian tosses his dirty clothes into his suitcase, hangs his towel up to dry, then brings his suitcase downstairs. He's already taken a look in all the bedrooms; he did it even though he felt like a peeping tom. He's got to lock himself back up, and he has to do it soon. They're not going to talk about it, that much is clear. They're not going to let it happen again. If that means staying on opposite sides of a room, fine. If it means they're not supposed to look at each other, Julian figures he can do that, too. He's run out of cigarettes and he needs some. But before he heads out in search of a 7-Eleven, he goes into the kitchen and finds Lucy has already poured him a cup of coffee. He cannot remember anyone ever doing that before, not just setting the coffee out, but assuming he'd want it, figuring that he'd even be there to drink it. He guesses he can have coffee without making too much of a fool of himself.

"This is him," Lucy says. She's got an old yearbook open in front of her, and she slides the book across the table to Julian.

In the parking lot of the country club, all Julian had been able to see was Randy's back, but in that he saw everything. It comes as no surprise that the boy in this black-and-white photograph taken more than twenty years ago got whatever he wanted, even back then, and that he knew it. Randy Scott Lee. There is a list of awards below his picture: the boy most likely to just about everything.

"What does this mean?" Julian asks. " 'Biff'?"

"*Death of a Salesman*," Lucy says. "He was in the drama club."

"Well, he may have killed a salesman," Julian says, leafing through the yearbook, "but he didn't kill his wife."

"He sat there and told me his wife and child were in Holland, when I had seen the receipt for a rocking horse she ordered."

Julian shrugs. He's found what he's looking for in the yearbook, on page 52. A photograph of Lucy.

"You can tell he didn't do it, just by looking at him?" Lucy says. "In a twenty-year-old photograph?"

At seventeen, Lucy had a more distant look, as if she hadn't even been in the room when the school photographer took her picture.

"He doesn't have the nerve," Julian says, closing the yearbook. He takes a sip of coffee; it's not steaming hot, but it's good, richer than what he usually drinks. "He thinks too much of himself."

"You think a lot of yourself," Lucy counters.

Julian laughs. "That just goes to show how easily fooled you are."

"You think you're smarter than other people," Lucy says stubbornly.

"Suspicious doesn't mean smart," Julian insists. "It just means you're harder to bullshit. A guy like this, he doesn't have to kill his wife. If he wants to get rid of her, all he has to do is divorce her. He's got the money, he's got the lawyers, he's ready to go on to the next one."

"I don't care what you say. He's the reason she's dead," Lucy insists.

She can't even sit at the table with him, because if she does she's going to think about things she promised herself she'd forget. She gets up and goes to the refrigerator and takes several ice cubes, which she drops into her coffee mug. Lucy's face is flushed, and she's got this strange, hot feeling she gets whenever she sees him. It's insanity to think they could have anything together. They both know that. Even here, so far from Verity, where the heat doesn't confound you and make you do things you'll later regret.

"I'm going to find out whatever it is he knows," Lucy says.

"All right," Julian says. He won't be able to talk her out of it; he wouldn't even try.

Julian leaves her in the kitchen, and takes Loretta out to the backyard. He watches from the patio as the dog chases a tennis ball Julian found in the front hall closet. He's got a funny feeling that he doesn't want to step on the grass, it's too well tended. Better to stay on the stone patio, beneath the latticework arbor. Whether or not it's right, he hates Randy Lee, hates his ability to have whatever he's wanted. Loretta comes and lays the tennis ball at Julian's feet, then she backs up and waits eagerly. Julian throws it too hard, so that it topples a wooden birdhouse out of a magnolia tree. As he crosses the lawn, Julian remembers that Bobby Cash could climb a tree in seconds flat. He'd wrap his arms around the trunk and hoist himself up into the branches and disappear before you could count to three. He could imitate an owl so well that the owls would answer his call from miles around, one after another. Before the age of ten, Julian couldn't climb a tree worth a damn. He'd have to stand down at the bottom and wave his arms around, reaching upward, so Bobby could grab hold of his wrists and swing him aloft, toward the sky.

The birdhouse is cracked in two. Julian crouches down on the lawn, holding both pieces in his hands. The boy made this, he can tell, with plenty of help from his father. It's highly unlikely that any birds ever set up house; the roof wasn't matched evenly and rainwater has seeped inside. There are no signs of inhabitants, past or present, no feathers, no bits of straw or string. Julian isn't surprised that the one thing he's touched here has fallen apart. It's clear he was never meant to have what other men receive so easily.

He can think about Bobby all he wants or erase his memories completely, he can black out in the parking lot of the Burger King, or drive a thousand miles, and it's still not going to change what happened. He can't alter those last few seconds, the strangler figs split open on the road, the darkness, the sound of the tires, the knife through his heart. He can't stop Bobby from reaching for the steering wheel, turning it in one smooth motion, the way he used to swing Julian up into the branches.

Julian whistles for Loretta and goes back inside, holding the broken birdhouse. He carefully puts the birdhouse down on an oak table in the front hallway, and he's there staring at the pieces when Evan walks through the front door carrying two white bags of take-out food for lunch. Loretta stands close to Julian and makes a low growling sound in the back of her throat. Evan stays where he is in the doorway; he looks at Loretta and at Julian, then at the number on his front door.

"Is this my house?" Evan says.

"This is your house," Julian says.

"I know this isn't my dog," Evan says.

Julian grins and tells Loretta it's okay, and she trots over and sniffs Evan, who stands perfectly still as the dog checks him out, then retreats.

"I broke the birdhouse," Julian says, nodding to the hall table. He goes to Evan and takes one of the bags of take-out food. "I'm a friend of the family," he explains.

"That's good," Evan says. He quickly looks away from the scar across Julian's forehead. "That's a relief."

They go into the kitchen, where Evan sets the food down on a butcher-block counter.

"Plates?" Julian says.

"Top cabinet," Evan tells him.

Evan goes to the refrigerator and gets two beers.

"Have you known Lucy long?" he asks.

"Since the first of the month." Julian accepts the beer Evan offers him and sits down.

"A close family friend," Evan says dryly. He gets some forks from the silverware drawer. "You're not going to rob me or something like that?"

"I'm delivering Lucy's car," Julian says, which is not exactly a lie.

"You know Keith?" Evan asks.

"Well enough," Julian says.

"He'd be happier here."

"Maybe." Julian's not getting involved in this.

"If you're really a friend, you could talk to Lucy about it," Evan says. "Convince her to let him move back."

Julian drinks his beer and eyes the food in the containers as Evan opens each one. He's never had Chinese food before, and it doesn't much look like something he'd enjoy. You can't tell what any of the ingredients are, for one thing, and Julian doesn't like to be surprised.

"That's her decision," Julian says. "Isn't it?"

He puts his feet up on a kitchen chair and watches Evan set the table. Even when Julian's not moving he seems dangerous, much more so than the dog, who lies in the kitchen doorway.

"Well, if we're going to be honest," Evan says as he places napkins on the table, "I'm a little uncomfortable with people wandering into my house uninvited." He stands facing Julian. "No offense."

"You don't have to worry," Julian says. "I'm sleeping in the car. I just came in to take a shower."

"I have the feeling something's going on here," Evan says.

"Do you have any Special K or anything like that?" Julian asks as he eyes the Chinese food. "No offense."

By the time Lucy comes downstairs, both Julian and the dog are eating cold cereal with milk and Evan has started his second beer. Lucy feels almost weightless. Nothing she's wearing belongs to her: the white blouse was taken from her neighbor's closet; the short yellow skirt, obviously Melissa's, she found in Evan's bedroom. Seeing Evan and Julian Cash in the same room, let alone the same universe, doesn't do her stomach any good.

"You've met," Lucy says flatly.

"I'm starting to feel like I'm running a bed and breakfast," Evan says. "No offense," he tells Julian.

"He's been sleeping in the car," Lucy says. She sits down at the table, although she won't be able to eat. Before she came downstairs she went into Keith's room, and placed the plush dragon in the center of his pillow, even though she knows that when he comes home he'll toss it somewhere out of sight, the top shelf of his closet or behind the comic books on his bookshelf.

"So I hear." Evan nods.

Lucy looks down at the plate of Chinese food Evan's set out for her. Julian's watching her, she can feel it, just the way she feels the pulse at the base of her throat.

"Do you want to tell me what's going on here?" Evan says.

Lucy looks up and blinks her large gray eyes. "Nothing's going on."

Julian concentrates on his cereal so he won't laugh out loud.

"Did you say something?" Lucy asks Julian. She could have sworn that he did.

Julian carefully places his spoon on the tabletop. "Did you want me to say something?"

"No," Lucy says. "Since this is none of your business."

"What's none of his business?" Evan leans toward Lucy. "If this has anything to do with Keith, I need to know."

Julian watches as Lucy begins to tie knots in the truth.

"There is nothing going on," Lucy says.

If she's not careful, she's going to get caught in those knots, so Julian sits back in his chair and reaches for his beer. "You know the amazing thing?" he says. Lucy and Evan both turn toward him, startled. "I've never seen snow."

"Does that mean you're staying until November?" Evan says. "I'm joking," he adds. "That's a joke."

"It seems to me that people must view the world entirely differently depending on whether or not they've ever seen snow. Think of what it's like for dogs." Julian puts his empty beer bottle on the table. He has no idea if he'll ever shut up. "What do they think? Do they think the sky is falling?"

By now he knows that he's not going to let Lucy walk into Randy Lee's house alone. She's staring at him as he babbles on about snow; he's talking so much his mouth hurts. He still thinks she's wrong about Randy; he knows nothing about his wife's death. Maybe he wanted to impress Lucy with an exotic past, maybe he just likes to lie, or maybe Lucy's so desperate to get her boy off the hook that she's ready to believe anything. But Julian still has the feeling that someone's about to snap, it might even be him. He's not going to sit in the parked car tonight. He'll wait until she's gone inside the house, and then he'll follow her. His boots will leave imprints in the grass; he'll be so close to the window his breath will fog up the glass. There's not a chance on earth that he's going to come close to losing her tonight.

The Angel is perched on the end of a branch. Since he's fallen in love, the birds have been able to make out his shape; they've begun to avoid the gumbo-limbo tree. He misses the song of the oriole and the chattering of wild parakeets. If he stays in love much longer he'll grow heavier, he'll start to leave footprints in the ground. Once that happens he'll be nineteen forever. Time and space have already become so real that it's now possible for him to get a sunburn if he doesn't stay in the shade.

A long time ago, when he and his cousin spent whole

afternoons in the marshes, he'd come home with red patches on his back and shoulders that would ache all night long. His mother would put white vinegar on him, to cool the burn, and he'd lie on clean sheets and listen to the mocking-birds outside his window. His mother worried about him constantly; she could never look when he climbed trees. He'd scramble into a live oak, and when he peered down he'd see her with one hand over her eyes and the other clutching her breast. Sometimes he'd pretend not to hear her when she called him down. Crouched among the leaves, he'd watch carefully as each bird took flight. It seemed to him terribly unfair that he should be trapped by his heavy limbs when even the silliest birds, the bobwhites and the flickers, could do so easily what he could not.

At night, after he'd thrown stones at his cousin's window to wake him, they'd go deep into the woods, where they should not have gone, not caring about scorpions and ticks. His cousin would plant himself on the ground and watch as Bobby climbed the tallest tree he could find. Once his cousin had urged Bobby to flap his arms and take a running start off the highest branch. Bobby beat his arms against the air and he ran: for one moment he was higher than he ever thought possible, up where the hawks flew, weightless, moving through blue sky until he began to drop, so suddenly he didn't feel it happening to him until he landed in the dirt with a thud.

The wind was knocked out of him, all at once. His cousin ran to him and shook him hard and told him he couldn't just lie there, he had to get up. His cousin was only seven, but his voice was so stern and commanding that Bobby had no choice but to rise to his feet. He stood, doubled over, until the air came back to him and he could breathe. Bobby's cousin was crying by then, and it was the oddest thing: instead of tears, little rocks fell from his eyes, and they kept on falling until there was a pile of stones at his feet.

No matter what Bobby said, his cousin wouldn't let go of the idea that he was to blame for the fall.

"I made you do that," the little cousin cried, but of course he hadn't, not any more than the birds had forced Bobby to make that dangerous leap. He had wanted to know what would happen when he was in the air. He'd wanted to feel what it was like to have the air push him upward, toward the stars.

Now he wants to know what would happen if he could kiss Shannon. Would he have that falling feeling all over again? Would he be enveloped in the same endless blue space? Would the flesh reappear on his bones, or would he evaporate into nothingness? He starts to shiver when he sees her walking through the parking lot. She's wearing blue jeans and a red blouse, and there's a vinyl purse hooked over her shoulder. All the black tint has been washed out of her hair, and the real color, a rich chestnut brown, is beautiful; it nearly brings Bobby to tears.

She stops before she reaches the tree and shades her eyes with her hand. It's almost as if she can see him, so Bobby shrinks back. He scrambles into a low branch and when Shannon narrows her eyes all she can make out is a faint outline of a dove. She walks right up to the tree, and as she begins to cry, Bobby drops down and sits beside her in the grass, his chest throbbing in the place where his heart used to be.

Shannon has to go away and she knows it. No matter how much she might want to change her mind, she won't. It's too late for that. Bobby can see all the years she'll have, he can see the orange moons and the cold winters. When she's an old woman, her chestnut-colored hair will turn white and she'll cover her shoulders with thick woolen sweaters. He can feel her entire life, from start to end, uninterrupted; it's already flowing right past him. As Shannon wipes her eyes with the back of her hand, Bobby leans his head against the tree and studies the arc of her neck. No matter what, she will always be the same for him.

Shannon has heard that when a gumbo-limbo tree is cut down, the sap that rushes out is the color of blood. If it's allowed to soak into the earth, a dozen saplings will rise in the place of the fallen tree. Shannon leans close and puts her mouth against the bark. Bobby Cash is right there, and that is why he is, for those few instants, blessed with the ability to be human. He kisses her back for as long as he dares.

He knows she won't miss this place the way she thinks she will. She'll fall in love, she'll live in a house on the edge of a lake that begins to freeze early in October. For years to come, she'll avoid returning to Verity during the month of May. And tonight, when she finally tells her mother and grandmother about her acceptance to Mount Holyoke and they take her out to celebrate at the Post Café, she'll hold her breath when they come to the intersection of Long Boat and West Main, right where the Burger King stands, the way some people do when they drive past graveyards.

He has dinner waiting for her, out in the sunroom with its wall of glass, and he's already dismissed whoever's so carefully set the table and lit the candles. The sky outside is

211

still light; there are thin pink clouds and the lightning bugs have yet to settle in the bushes. When he comes up behind her, Lucy can feel her palms start to sweat, and she hopes he won't reach for her hand. She's used to her work in obituaries, where she's given all the facts and merely has to list them in chronological order. Now she wants to know the smallest details of Bethany Lee's life. She wants to run upstairs and open all the doors to see where Bethany slept at night, where she washed her hair, where she sat rocking her baby to sleep.

"This is better than any restaurant," Randy says. He goes to the table and pulls out a chair for her. There is asparagus and cold trout on white china plates rimmed with gold that Bethany probably spent hours choosing.

When Lucy sits down, he puts one hand on the back of her neck.

"It looks fantastic," Lucy says, as she shrugs away from his touch. She can barely glance at the fish on her plate.

She's here to question him, but right away he's the one asking questions. He wants to know if she came up just for the reunion, and if she already has her return ticket to Florida.

"You sound like you're trying to get rid of me," Lucy says.

"Oh, no," Randy says. "I think we should have done this twenty years ago."

"Meaning?" Lucy says. She's eating asparagus like a starving woman, even though it tastes like paper.

"You were such an ice princess," Randy says, leaning back in his chair to study her. "Those are the girls who are always the hottest."

"Was your wife an ice princess?" Lucy asks. She actually manages to smile.

Randy tosses his napkin on the table. "We keep coming back to that."

"Well, was she?" Lucy asks.

"No," Randy says, as he pours the wine. "She was just a pretty girl."

"From Holland," Lucy says.

Randy leans back in his chair. He's not smiling now. "I think you're onto me," he says.

Lucy would like to take a sip of water, but she doesn't dare move.

"Maybe I should have been more honest with you," Randy says. "But it's not easy to admit that your wife just walked out on you, and you have no idea why, and you haven't seen her since. My life hasn't exactly turned out the way I thought it would." He breaks apart a piece of French bread, then places the crusts on his plate. "She was from Ohio, and her name was Bethany, and I still can't figure out what went wrong."

"You haven't seen her since . . ."

"October," Randy says. "That's the truth."

Lucy sees now that his eyes are really green. Julian was right: Randy could never kill anyone. He's not the one who was down in the laundry room, he didn't find the rings and bury them. That was someone else, someone with a history of bad judgment and thievery. Someone who might have made an earth-shattering mistake if he'd been caught in the act.

"Look, I have something awful to tell you," Lucy says. "Bethany's dead."

Randy looks up at her and frowns. "That's not funny, Lucy."

"No," Lucy says. "It isn't."

"You're serious," Randy says. He gets up from his chair

213

and goes to the window. "You're really serious." He puts his head down, as if he were dizzy.

Lucy pushes her chair back and goes to him. "I'm sorry," she says. "She was my neighbor. I was looking for the person who killed her, and I thought that might be you. I'm sorry that I had to be the one to tell you."

"Oh, Jesus." Randy stares at Lucy. They are inches away from each other. "I can't believe it," he says as he takes her hand and draws her to him.

Lucy remembers how much she hated to be touched after she was told about her parents.

"I can't believe she's gone," he whispers, and he pulls Lucy even closer.

As he does, Lucy feels chilled, right down to her bones. He hasn't once asked about his daughter.

"Maybe we need some fresh air," Lucy whispers.

It should have been his first question. He should be beside himself with worry. He should be reaching for the telephone, making reservations for a flight down to Florida tonight.

"I just need to hold you," Randy says.

Out in the backyard it is growing dark; there is a high cedar fence, and in all probability no one could see them if they did go outside for some air, no one could hear her even if she cried out loud.

"Randy," Lucy says.

"I just need to think," he says.

When the window breaks he pulls her close beneath the shower of glass that bursts above them like stars. Lucy kicks him hard, and when he lets go of her, she's propelled backward, across the shards of glass. Julian has already reached in through the broken pane of glass and unlatched the French door. At his signal, Loretta follows him inside. Her hair

214

stands on end, making her look twice her size, and Randy
scrambles up on a chair.

"Oh, Christ," he says. His hair is dusted with bits of glass.
"Jesus."

Julian holds Loretta's lead loosely, he gives her enough
slack so that when she snaps her jaws open and shut Randy
can get a good look at her teeth.

"Call the dog off," Randy shouts.

Julian reels in the lead, but he lets Loretta go on barking.
He can smell how afraid Randy is, and he knows that Loretta
can smell it, too.

"Who the hell are you?" Randy says.

"I'm the guy who doesn't believe a fucking word you say,"
Julian tells him. Turning to Lucy, Julian says, "It looks like
you're right." What he wouldn't give for a cigarette. "Let's
talk about the way you killed your wife," he says to Randy.

"Lucy?" Randy says, panicked.

Julian steps forward. He takes up a lot of space. "Why
are you talking to her?" he asks. "I'm the one asking you
the fucking question."

"Lucy," Randy says. "You know I would never do anything like that."

Lucy is standing with her back against the table. The
tablecloth probably belonged to Bethany's mother; it's white
linen with pink dogwood blossoms carefully stitched along
the border. Julian comes up next to Lucy. He takes out his
gun and lays it on the tablecloth.

"All right," Randy says, terrified when he sees the gun.
"I saw that she had Bethany's photograph. I figured I'd get
some information out of her, that's not a crime. My wife's
been missing since October. I think I have a right to know
what happened to her."

He still has not asked about the child. Lucy stares out at the yard. If you set up a swing set out there you could easily watch your child at play from every window. You could close the cedar gates and know she was safe.

"He did it," Lucy says flatly.

Julian lurches forward. He grabs Randy and drags him off the chair and onto the floor.

"I didn't do it!" Randy says.

"Then you know who did," Julian says.

"It wasn't the way it was supposed to happen," Randy cries.

Julian's got Randy by the throat now. If he didn't know how to stop himself, he could snap his neck in two right now.

"He wasn't supposed to kill her?" Julian asks.

Behind Julian, Loretta is growling, though she doesn't break the stay command.

"No," Randy says. He struggles to get up, but Julian tightens his grip. "He was just supposed to take Rachel, but she walked in on him."

Julian realizes that the sound he hears is his own pulse; he's gasping for air, but so is the boy who had everything.

"And he killed her," Julian says.

"He killed her," Randy says.

When Julian lets go, Randy's head hits hard against the floor. He stays where he is, still gasping, as Julian stands and backs away.

"Are you all right?" Julian asks Lucy.

"I'm fine," Lucy says. A lie, and they both know it.

"Did you pay him up front?" Julian asks Randy.

Randy is sitting up now, his eye on Loretta. "Half."

"That's good," Julian tells Lucy. "He might come back for what he's owed. Even if he did botch the job."

Julian sits down and tilts his chair back, so that it scrapes against the highly polished floor. "What'd you do?" he asks

216

Randy. "Put an ad in *The New York Times* for a kidnapper, or meet the sleazebag in a bar?"

"In a bar," Randy says.

"That's original," Julian says. "That's the place to find someone you can trust."

He notices that Lucy hasn't moved. She should be relieved that her son has been cleared, but instead she has a fevered look.

"He's not telling us everything," Lucy says.

From the look on Randy's face, Julian knows that she's right, but he keeps his mouth shut. Lucy picks up the gun. Julian watches her do it, and he doesn't stop her. He wants to see how far she'll go.

"There's something you're not telling us," Lucy says.

She's waving the gun around, and she's not kidding. Julian and Randy can both see that.

"I didn't start this," Randy says. "I told her she'd never win if she was going to fight my parents on custody."

Lucy points the gun at Randy's head. She has never held a gun before in her life; she has no idea of what a safety catch is, or whether or not it's clicked into place. Julian knows now that she would actually do it; to protect someone, she wouldn't think twice.

"She never let that baby into the pool without water wings," Lucy says. Her voice is uneven, a breakable thing. "She never once slept through the night, not since the baby was born."

"Do you think I wanted this?" Randy cries. "He keeps calling me, asking me for more money. He has to stay down there and he won't leave, no matter what I say. There's a witness he wants to get rid of and I can't do a damn thing about it."

That witness is asleep in borrowed pajamas a thousand

miles away, and although he cannot say a word, he's seen more than a boy his age ever should.

It takes only a few seconds to race through the house, to run down the driveway where the bluestone is carefully set in gravel, to get into the car that has been parked out of sight. They leave behind shards of glass and footprints in the flower beds. They don't have to discuss their destination, because they know exactly where they're going. If they started now and drove all night, it would still take them thirty-six hours to get home, and that is why Julian Cash finds himself breaking the speed limit all the way to La Guardia and why he finds himself thrown into the black night as, for the first time in his life, he leaves the ground.

"A long time ago," Miss Giles tells the boy while they sit on the porch after supper, "I received a sign that my life was about to change, right here on this porch, when I was peeling lemons."

Even though the crickets have begun to call, the sky is still blue. Miss Giles has a colander full of lemons on her lap, and every once in a while she hands some of the shavings to the baby, who sits near her feet. The baby sucks on the bits of lemon peel with a funny puckered look on her face, but she continues to reach for them greedily. The meanest boy in Verity does just what Miss Giles expects him to when she begins her story: he rolls his eyes, then turns his back to her and slumps against the porch steps.

"Don't think I'm crazy," Miss Giles says. "Don't be too quick to judge," she warns him.

The baby comes up behind the boy and hands him a piece

of lemon peel, which he places between his teeth, though he'd much rather have a cigarette.

"It was a hot day," Miss Giles says. "And it was May. People around here are known to have sunstroke under conditions like that, but I was wearing a big straw hat, so that wasn't the case. My life was somewhat messed up, not that I would tell you about it, since it's none of your business, but that day when I was peeling lemons a circle of light appeared right over there."

In spite of himself, the boy raises his head and squints. He sees nothing but a porch railing badly in need of paint. He spits out the lemon peel, but he still feels the sharp taste in his mouth.

"It wasn't what you're thinking," Miss Giles says. She dumps the peeled lemons into her lap and gives the baby the colander so she can gather up all the rinds. "It wasn't a religious situation at all. You hear these people on *Oprah* saying they've seen this and they've seen that—well, this wasn't anything that would ever get you on TV."

When the baby brings Miss Giles the colander, Miss Giles lifts her onto her lap and gives her a hug, but it's the back of the boy's head she's watching. She catches the boy as he looks at her, then quickly looks away. It's been so hot today that the blue sky seems white in the center, not unlike a circle of light, if you were stupid enough to believe in such things.

"I knew something was going to happen," Miss Giles goes on. "And of course I was right. That same night I heard someone screaming in the woods."

The boy has turned, just a bit, so he can see Miss Giles from the corner of his eye. He has chopped so much wood for her in the past few days that there are calluses on the

219

palms of his hands. Not far from here, everyone else in seventh grade is settling down to study for final exams. The boy will either have to go to summer school or be left back to repeat a grade he found boring enough the first time around.

"The screaming was real bad," Miss Giles says.

The boy can feel the hair rise up on the back of his neck.

"It was the kind that makes you jump out of bed and not bother with a bathrobe or slippers or anything like that."

Miss Giles pauses to take a bite out of a lemon. She almost has him now, she can feel it.

"I was half asleep, but I knew what was about to happen. And here's the thing: It was pitch-black outside, but I could hear bees buzzing, and that's never a good sign. It means they're real disturbed about something, and when bees can't sleep, nobody can. I suppose I could have stayed in bed, pulled the covers up, and put my hands over my ears, but by that time the screaming creature was at my front door."

The boy casually swings his legs up from the steps onto the porch, twisting slightly, so that he almost faces her.

"I was fairly certain that it was the devil at my door," Miss Giles informs him.

The baby on Miss Giles's lap is humming to herself; all she wears in this heat is a diaper and a white T-shirt dozens of babies have worn before her. Miss Giles takes one unpeeled lemon and slips it into her apron pocket. She'll use it later as a rinse for the baby's hair, since lemon juice has been known to keep ticks away.

"I knew it from the way the doorknob was shaking, and the way those bees came out at night and then the wind came up suddenly, even though it was May and there shouldn't have been any wind. Whether it was foolish or not, I opened the door. And there she was. She had dark hair all in knots, and her clothes were all torn up, and I could see, even in the dark, there was blood all over her skirt."

The boy's breathing has quickened; he's holding on to the old wooden banister.

"I could have sent her away right then. But my father had told me that if the devil ever appeared at my door, I should invite it in and act polite, even if I wasn't feeling much like it. So I invited her in, and when she came inside, a swarm of bees came in with her, and they knocked over all my tables and chairs. I turned on the light and those bees just flew out my window, all in a rush. I saw then that I knew the woman, she'd been a neighbor of mine for years and years, but never a friend. I hadn't recognized her because she looked so wild, like something was after her or she was after something. And she couldn't talk, she just kept screaming, and that's when I saw she was covered with bee bites. Some of the stingers had been left in her, and there was more than that. There was blood on her skirt because she'd just delivered a baby, all by herself, in the woods, and worse than that, the baby she was holding had already turned blue.

"I took that baby from her since she was dangling it so carelessly, almost like it was a pumpkin, and I wrapped it up in my bathrobe, and then in some towels, but it was even bluer than before. It was so cold you'd think she'd carved that baby out of ice. I asked her questions about what had happened and what had gone wrong, but she couldn't hear me over her own screaming, so I stopped asking. I went into the kitchen and lit the woodstove, and I put that baby right inside the oven, because I knew, all of a sudden, that he was already dead and he might have been dead even when I first grabbed hold of him."

The boy has inched over, closer to Miss Giles.

221

"I brought a wooden chair over to the stove—it may have been this one I'm sitting on—and I sat there and watched the baby, and while I was doing that I heard the front door slam, and I knew that she was gone, but I still didn't get up from my chair. The bees came into my house again, but I didn't pay any attention to them, they weren't going to scare me. The air got thick and heavy. That kind of air can put you to sleep in an instant, but I just ignored it. I kept on watching that baby, and after a while the bees flew out my window and the bad air slipped through the cracks in the wall that I'd meant to fix, and the baby's color started to change. I grabbed him out of the oven as quickly as I could, and then I heard the sound of birds and I realized it was morning.

"Every night after that I heard her out in my yard. She never came any closer than the willow trees I used to have right there, but I could hear her, even when she didn't make a sound. I kept waiting for her to knock on my door again, but she didn't. She kept circling out there and she didn't stop. Sometimes I'd see her during the day, at the general store or walking down the road. She'd just ignore me, like she'd never seen me before in her life. But then at night she'd be there again, and she came closer and closer, and then she took to looking in the window. That was when I realized what it was she wanted."

Miss Giles puts the baby down on the porch, then stands up. "I'm talking myself silly," she says.

Miss Giles takes her colander of lemons to the back door, then calls to the baby, who follows her inside. When the screen door slams shut behind her, the meanest boy in Verity sits alone on the porch, feeling very cold in spite of today's record temperature. When darkness falls it will still be over

a hundred; the leaves will drop from the trees and turn dusty
and dry. From where the boy sits he can see the rabbits in
their cages, stretched out on their beds of cedar chips, limp
from the heat. The boy gets up, walks to the house, then
slowly pushes the screen door open. Miss Giles has taken
her dough out of the refrigerator; she's given the baby a little
ball of dough all her own to roll out on the wooden tabletop.
When she hears the squeak of the screen door as it closes,
Miss Giles turns, as if she were surprised to see the boy in
her kitchen.

"Would you like a cold glass of milk?" she asks him.

The boy shakes his head. He's got chills all down his arms
and legs; what would he want with milk?

"I suppose I can tell you just about anything," Miss Giles
says, considering. "Since you're not about to go and repeat
it. I'm right about that, aren't I?"

The boy shrugs, and then, when he sees that's not good
enough, he nods.

"She wanted to make certain he was alive," Miss Giles
says. "That's why she kept coming back. I had no idea what
happened in those woods, or what happened before that,
but I saw then that people leave their children for all sorts
of reasons they're never going to tell you or me. So one night
I took the baby out of his crib, at around the time she used
to come, and I held him right up to the window."

Miss Giles has come to sit down at the table. It's no longer
possible for the boy to pretend he isn't listening. He's getting
more and more uncomfortable; he's not sure he wants to
hear this story anymore, especially not the end.

"She looked inside when she came that night, and she
saw him. She saw that he wasn't blue, and that he was a
real live baby who was crying for his bottle of milk, and I

could tell she was satisfied. She must have been, because she never came back, except for one time, and then I didn't see her. One morning, a few weeks later, I found a piece of notepaper on my front porch, with a rock set on top of it, so it wouldn't blow away."

The boy stays where he is at the table, in spite of the heat and the scent of lemons and the terrible feeling in his stomach.

"She wrote for me to name him Julian," Miss Giles says. "And that's exactly what I did."

Miss Giles's voice sounds funny, as if the edges were broken. "I've told Julian every bit of that story. Except for one thing. I didn't remember this for the longest time, and when I did it seemed too late to tell him. As I wrapped him up to warm him, I noticed he didn't have a single bee sting on him, which was unusual, considering his mother's condition. I don't know how she did it, but she didn't let those bees get anywhere close to him, not one."

The boy doesn't know what's happening, but whatever it is, it's what he's desperately tried to avoid. When he looks down at the tabletop there's a pool of water in front of him. Miss Giles hands him the dishtowel she's kept over her piecrust dough, and he uses it to wipe his eyes. It's been so long since he cried he believed he was no longer capable of it. And although he's not sure why, by the time he's finished he's extremely hungry. He doesn't leave Miss Giles's kitchen until the pie is out of the oven, and has been cooled in the freezer, then cut into wedges, to be served on the good blue-and-white plates Miss Giles likes to use for pie, the ones with the willow pattern, which her father left to her, since he knew she would always be certain to take good care of whatever came into her possession.

Chapter Nine

L ATE in the afternoon, the plane circles Hartford Beach three
times before beginning its descent. For the past half
hour they have been flying through heavy turbulence,
and in his aisle seat, Julian Cash curses to himself, repeatedly
and silently. This trip has been pure misery; they had to
change planes twice—in Raleigh and again in Atlanta. Each
time Julian had to argue with the security guards in order to
bring Loretta on board; in Raleigh, two police officers were
called to the boarding gate before Julian was allowed on with
his gun. Now Julian wonders if he was ever meant to fly at
all. None of the other passengers seems to be bothered by
all the bumps, by the club soda spilling onto the floor, or
the flight attendants buckling themselves in tight. Julian tells
himself that if they don't crash in the next ten minutes,
everything will be all right. Verity is, after all, only a few
miles away.

"In case we die, there's something you should know,"
Lucy says.

225

She is hunched over, clutching a plastic glass of ginger ale. At their feet, Loretta stretches out as best she can, yawning each time there's a loss in altitude.

"What are you saying?" Julian asks. "Are you saying this isn't a normal flight?"

Sitting next to each other, surrounded only by air, they don't need to talk above a whisper, but Lucy leans closer. All through this flight she's been panicked. She can't close her eyes, because when she does all she sees is Keith, at some killer's mercy. Now that the plane has begun to drop from the sky, she finally turns to Julian. He looks calm, but he's holding on to the armrests so tightly his fingers are white.

"It's not important, but I want you to know I would have never spent the night with Randy, no matter what," Lucy says.

In spite of himself, Julian laughs. "I know that."

"How do you know that?"

Julian figures they are careening to earth right this second; what he says or doesn't say can't matter a whole lot.

"Because you spent the night with me," he says.

"Kitty Bass told me to stay away from you," Lucy tells him.

"You should have listened to her," Julian says.

They can see the lights of Hartford Beach below them, as if the dusty earth were littered with stars.

"Well, I didn't," Lucy says.

Julian Cash believes that's what she says, although he's not positive. The engines are straining and they seem much too loud.

"Nothing will happen to Keith," Lucy says.

"That's right," Julian agrees.

"I mean it," Lucy says. She closes her eyes now; she wills it to be true. "Nothing can happen to him."

The plane touches down, hard, on the runway, then skids to a stop. Although they are the first ones off the plane and Julian has called ahead so that there's a rental car waiting at the terminal, it's close to dinnertime when they finally get on the road. What Julian's not prepared for is the scent of lemons in the air, and a fog so thick he has to switch the windshield wipers on. Since the night of the accident he's been a fairly cautious driver, but now he speeds with his hand on the horn and his foot so heavy on the gas that Loretta slides off the backseat. Julian doesn't speak as they travel along the Interstate; he's not going to allow himself to think he might have a chance at something, he's just not going to think that way. He concentrates on the road, for when they pull off at the Verity exit it is even foggier, and the asphalt is slick with the pulp of strangler figs. Every now and then they drive right through a cluster of white moths that beat their wings against the windshield and then are held on the glass until the wipers clean them away.

A long time ago, Julian used to sit by his window, trying to figure out what he'd done wrong. But that wasn't the only reason he stayed up late. He was waiting to see if his mother would come back for him, even after it became clear that she never would. With every night he spent at the window, his heart closed up a little more, and it would have stayed that way if Bobby hadn't come looking for him. He remembers exactly the way he felt, sitting on the porch with his bucket of toads, blinking in the sunlight, not quite believing that someone had actually found him. He knew, even at the age of seven, how dangerous it was for someone like him to have hope. He knows how to have no expectations. He can completely control not just what he wants but what he needs.

As they turn into Miss Giles's driveway, Lucy unhooks her seat belt. Julian throws the car into neutral before it comes to a full stop, then opens his door and jumps out. Lucy gets out just as quickly, but she stumbles over what's left of the willow roots, and for that one moment she panics completely. It is so foggy out here at Miss Giles's, anything can happen. As Lucy runs across the yard she can see that Julian has already reached the front door and is banging on it with his fist. She can see the old woman who swings the door open, and just by watching them Lucy knows something is not right. The old woman is tiny, but she stands on her tiptoes so she can reach up. She touches Julian's forehead, as if for fever, in the place where he has his scar. Lucy has done the same thing a thousand times herself, with her own child, since it is so much easier to cure a fever than all the other horrible things that can go wrong. And something has certainly gone wrong now; her son isn't here, she can feel that without being told.

When she meets Julian halfway across the yard, he's illuminated by the porch light the old woman has switched on. He's had to make his way through the mosquitoes and the moths. Lucy's mouth is completely dry; all up and down her legs she can feel tiny pinpricks of fear. She felt this way for weeks after her parents died; she thought she had MS or arthritis, because it got so bad she could hardly walk. If she had made a fuss, and refused to stay home alone at night, maybe both her parents wouldn't have been in the car. If only they hadn't kissed each other for so long, if only there had been a full moon.

"He's gone to feed the dog," Julian says.

Lucy stares at him blankly.

"Go ahead," Julian tells her. "Scream at me. Tell me it's my fault."

The scar on his forehead looks terrible tonight, and Lucy finds herself backing away from him.

"I shouldn't have let him go," Julian says. "Tell me that."

"I don't care what you did!" Lucy says. "I just want my son."

When they get in the car and Julian speeds down the rutted driveway, Lucy could swear the earth was turning to water beneath them. The car veers sharply when they reach the road, and Lucy is propelled forward; she has to stop herself by putting both hands on the dashboard.

"Put your seat belt on," Julian tells her.

Everything that has ever gone wrong around him has been his fault, and now it's about to happen again. He can feel it. If you don't have anything, you can't lose it. If you don't give a damn, what difference does it make?

"Don't tell me what to do," Lucy says. She's looking straight at him, her face drawn and white. "Don't give me orders."

Julian Cash knows what can happen when a road is slick with strangler figs, he knows exactly what a windshield sounds like when it shatters into a thousand pieces.

"Please," Julian says. "Put it on."

Lucy reaches and pulls her seat belt over her shoulder; her hands are shaking so badly she can barely manage, but finally it clicks into place, and when it does Julian is certain of one thing: He's not going to let it happen again.

In the middle of the clearing, the boy finds the perfect stick, a slightly bent length of live oak smooth enough to seem polished by human hands. It is so hot this evening that even the owls stay roosted in their nests; it's so damp that when the boy tries to light a cigarette the match disintegrates. Thin strands of fog twist around the tree roots and the air plants.

The boy runs his fingers over the satiny piece of wood. Not long ago he stole eight dollars from a classmate's locker; now he realizes that there's nothing he wants to buy. He was like the greedy squirrels and the crows, hoarding things for the sake of it, wanting whatever he couldn't have, especially when it belonged to someone else. If he happened to meet up with Laddy Stern now, on a street corner or in the parking lot of the Burger King, they'd have nothing in common, except that brief, hazy time spent in front of the TV drinking Kahlúa and beer, that, and the fact that everything in the universe once caused them both equal amounts of dissatisfaction and agony.

The boy is not the same person he was before. It's nothing to question or be afraid of; it's a simple fact. He can practically see in the dark, he can tell the difference between a merlin and a red-tailed hawk, he can throw a stick farther than he'd ever imagined. Arrow has come to sit before him, his legs quivering as he anticipates running. It's dark tonight, and the sky is filled with clouds, but that means nothing to the dog. He nudges the boy's knee with his nose, just to remind him that they are in these woods for a reason, and the boy reaches down instinctively and strokes the dog's head between his ears. The dog's fur smells sweet now; the boy brushed him just after feeding him, then filled the kennel with clean hay. Hay is far better than the wood chips and marsh grass Julian has always used; it's softer for sleeping, and it won't get soggy in the rain. The dog looks from the boy's face to the stick and then back again to the boy's face, so that the boy will be sure to understand what he wants.

When the boy sees himself reflected in the dog's eyes he knows exactly who he is. He is the boy with the fair hair, who wears a borrowed white T-shirt and old jeans and knows how to throw a stick with such a good spin on it that it sails above the trees. He is the boy who can sleep through the night without one bad dream, who can find his way over the twisted roots of the mangroves without stepping on a spider. Now he bends his arm back and lets the stick fly. Before the stick has even left his hand, the dog is running. At first the boy can hear him, leaping through the undergrowth, then he is so far that there's no sound at all. The boy doesn't hear anything until he bends down to tie the lace of his sneaker, and then he hears a branch crack, which is odd since the dog is so light-footed. It is odder still that the merlins in the cypress trees have begun to call and beat their wings at this late hour, when they're usually asleep.

The man grabs him from the rear before he has time to sort out all the sounds; he twists him around so hard the boy's back makes a snapping sound. The man is tall, or maybe he just seems that way since he's standing while he pushes the boy down to the ground.

"You should have kept your eyes closed," the man is whispering to him, as he edges his hands around the boy's throat. "You just looked for trouble."

The boy realizes that every breath he's taking is painful; every time he manages to get in any air his throat hurts under the pressure.

"Now I'll close them for you," the man is telling him, and that's when the boy feels the sharp thing poised against his throat, some kind of metal. He can hear the frantic beating of cricket wings and the fire ants moving through the dead leaves as he is pushed on top of them. The tree trunks twisted on the ground are alive with fire ants, he sees that now, whole universes he's never noticed before. The ground is shaking, probably because he's kicking his legs and flailing his arms upward, trying to get away from the metal, but then he hears something else, a thud like a tree falling, and that's when he sees that he's not the only one on the ground. Even though he's having trouble breathing, even though he can't move, no one's holding him down anymore.

The dog has charged into the clearing, and as soon as he has the man down on the ground a tornado of dust rises around them. The boy pushes himself backward, then forces himself onto his side in spite of the pain near his back, which has suddenly become as hot as fire. He can hear the dog now, like a hundred branches breaking, his growl so furious it's shaking leaves out of the trees. The dog took the man down by the thigh, just as he'd take down a deer, but now he's after the throat. The man's pants are shredded and blood is seeping into the dirt and the man screams and curses so horribly, as the dog shakes him by the throat then drops him on the ground, that the boy moves to cover his ears. And then something happens, it must be something with the knife, because the dog's coat is red and wet.

The boy's whole body is heaving, he can barely see straight, and somehow everything seems speeded up. The dog stands poised above the man with his red, bloody coat, his teeth bared, thunder coming out of his throat. It shakes the earth, it spirals and slams into the sky, you can hear it all through the woods and up along the driveway, where Julian Cash throws open the door of the rental car. Right away he sees that the kennel is empty. The gate swings back and forth on its hinges, and all that golden hay, so carefully spread with a pitchfork, has not yet been slept on.

"Oh, fuck," Julian says. He leans in the passenger door, reaching over Lucy, and gets his gun from the glove compartment. "Stay here," he tells Lucy, but she's out of the car before Julian swings open the back door for Loretta.

He can hear Lucy's ragged breathing behind him as he crashes through the woods, following Loretta, and he's thankful that Lucy doesn't know these woods. She'll lag behind no matter how hard she tries to keep up, and maybe that will keep her from seeing something no one should have to see. The growl from the woods rises higher, like a fever that won't stop, and then, all of a sudden, there is silence, and because of that Julian runs faster than he's ever run before. He nearly trips over Loretta. When they get to the clearing, Julian sees that Arrow has the man by the throat. He is shaking him so fiercely that this full-grown man looks like a toy stuffed with straw. Loretta immediately begins to growl; she charges toward the man, then looks back.

"Stay," Julian shouts, and Loretta holds herself back, barking and circling as the dust rises up even more.

The boy scrambles to his feet. Something in his side has been broken, a rib, maybe two, and it's still hard for him to breathe, but he doesn't give a damn about that. All he cares about is Arrow's red coat. Nothing else in the world matters.

"Stay back," Julian calls to the boy. "Arrow, off!" he screams. But the dog doesn't hear him; commands are meaningless. Julian runs toward the dog and tries to grab him, but all his strength is worthless. The dog's jaws are clamped so tightly nothing could separate them.

There are bubbles of spit coming out of the man's mouth, and a scream so high-pitched it's terrible to hear. From where she is in the woods, lost in a grid of branches and leaves, Lucy hears that scream and knows this night will never end for any of them; they will be in this together for the rest of their lives.

"Get off," Julian is begging the dog. But it's too late for that. Arrow doesn't hear him anymore. He couldn't if he tried.

Loretta shows her teeth and circles closer, as if she's about to charge. "Stay," Julian warns her, and she does. Julian is down on his knees, wrenching on Arrow's collar. "Get off!" he cries.

The man is reaching into the air, clutching at nothing as he slips away. In the center of the clearing, surrounded by blood, Julian Cash finally lets go of the dog and backs away before he reaches for his gun. He shoots quickly, before the dog has time to turn and recognize him, before the boy can get in his way.

"No," the boy screams.

The dog falls to the ground slowly, letting go of the man's throat at last. Julian can see that the man is no longer moving. He can see Arrow leaning into the earth as the boy races to him, doubled over, weeping, coated with blood as soon as he throws himself across the dog.

"You killed him!" the boy screams. "Why did you have to kill him?"

The boy's T-shirt has turned a dark red. He's hunched on his knees, weeping, his face buried in the dog's coat.

"Why did you?" the boy wails, as he rocks back and forth, his arms around the dog's neck.

Julian signals for Loretta to come to him, but for an instant she hesitates. She points her head toward the sky and then she howls, far back in her throat, before walking to Julian and lying at his feet. All Julian can do is stand and be a witness; he hasn't the right to intrude, since Arrow isn't really his to mourn. But standing there he feels as if he's just shot a hole in himself; it's the kind of emptiness the wind can sweep right through. He takes off his shirt and finally walks back to the clearing so he can place it over the dead man's face. How could he ever explain why to this boy, who is

234

soaked in blood and grief? Does Julian tell him that some things are right and some things are wrong, even if it tears you apart? Since it will never be possible to explain that, Julian goes to the boy and puts a hand on his shoulder. The boy rises to his feet, wailing, and Julian lets the boy hit him again and again, cursing and moaning, until he gives up and lets Julian put his arms around him.

And that is what Lucy sees when she gets to the edge of the clearing. She sees her son step aside so that Julian can lift the dog and carry him back through the woods. She sees Keith turn away from her as she runs to embrace him. He is safe, he's alive in this clearing, but he doesn't look at her or anything else. He follows far behind as they all make their way through the woods; he doesn't care if anyone sees that he's crying and he doesn't give a damn about his cracked ribs. As he stumbles over tree roots, he makes a high-pitched sound that won't go away. The sound is what he feels inside, and it's already changing him. When they reach Julian's yard, and Lucy checks to see if he's kept up with them, she has to blink to make certain she's seeing right. He no longer looks like a boy.

Lucy goes into Julian's house and turns on all the lights. She takes the blanket from the bed, then goes back outside. It's over now, she can feel that inside her, and there's not one thing she can do about it. Maybe she should have guarded him more carefully. Maybe she should never have let him out of her sight.

"Keith," she says, when she goes outside with the blanket.

Standing beneath the black sky, he doesn't answer her. She could swear that he hasn't even heard her.

The dog's body is already stiffening when Julian kneels

235

to wrap him in the blanket, but the wound in Arrow's side continues to bleed. Julian quickly passes his hands over the gash. He won't wash the blood off until morning, and even then he'll find blood beneath his fingernails for days afterward.

All that time Arrow spent pacing in his kennel he was dead, and whether or not the boy will ever believe it, he's the one who's set Arrow free. It's their duty to do this together, no matter how much the boy hates Julian. They get two shovels from the back shed, and they bury the dog beneath the cypress trees, and after that Julian can't get the scent of cypress out of his throat, and it just about breaks what's left of his heart. Keith stands beside him in the dark, shivering. There will never be another dog like Arrow, they both know that. Not if they search for a million years. And it seems somehow terrible that as they stand there, the center of the black sky is cleared of clouds, and a white moon rises to remind them that they are both still alive.

Twelve hours later, Walt Hannen is standing over the body of the dead man. Unfortunately for Walt, he quit smoking last night and his wife will kill him if he starts up again after spending two hundred dollars on acupuncture down in West Palm Beach. He hates it when people die inside the Verity town limits; he takes it personally. Julian is standing right next to him as they study the body.

"He's definitely dead," Walt Hannen says.

There are masses of flies on the body already, and it says a lot that Julian has so quickly buried that killer dog of his and left this man out in the hot sun.

"There's no ID," Julian says. "I checked."

"Of course, you didn't bother to wait for me before you searched him."

In spite of all the visualization techniques Walt has learned from the acupuncturist, what he wants is a cigarette. He and Julian have walked down from the house with mugs of coffee, which Julian pretty much ruined by adding Cremora, and they're both careful not to get too close to the body, because of the flies.

"So what do we have here?" Walt asks. He sits down on a tree stump and sips his coffee. He knows this is going to be good.

"I figure he was a vagrant. He killed our lady on Long Boat Street, then swiped the daughter, thinking she was worth something to somebody." Julian crouches down. "I've got the little girl. Over at Miss Giles's. Did I tell you that?"

"You mentioned something about that," Walt says. "What's interesting is that the dead man wound up on your property. Don't you think so?"

"I don't own this," Julian tells him. "State conservation land." Julian takes a deep breath, then shakes his head. "This heat is really doing something to that guy. Maybe I'd better call Richie."

"And what are we planning to do with the little girl without some next-of-kin?"

"Leave her with Miss Giles," Julian said. "I've taken care of all that."

"You sure have," Walt says. "Give me a cigarette," he adds.

"I can't," Julian says.

"What the hell is that supposed to mean?"

"I quit," Julian says.

"Just like that?" Walt says. "Jesus." He narrows his eyes. "Are you sure Rose didn't call you and put you up to this?"

"She didn't call." Julian notices that Walt has shifted his gaze back to the body. "How is Rose?" he asks.

The dead body stinks like hell and the flies are now buzzing over their heads, too.

"You want to talk about Rose?" Walt asks.

"Well, no," Julian admits.

"So is this the story you expect me to believe?" Walt asks.

Julian gulps down what's left of his coffee, even though it's now cold.

"We just forget that our lady from Long Boat Street had a false identity, and we don't try to find out who the hell she was? And the kid who was missing? We forget about him, too?"

"I already told you," Julian says. He's extremely careful now, since this is the moment when he's more than likely to screw up. He knows the boy will never forgive him; he doesn't expect that. The truth is, he'll never be able to forgive himself. He'll never know if he did what he had to do or only what he thought he had to do, and it doesn't make much of a difference since the result is the same. He killed a dog the like of whom he'll never see again, because of a worthless man whose name he doesn't even know. It was the right thing, he knows that; you have a dog who makes the decision to attack all on his own, and he'll probably do it again. But doing the right thing doesn't mean you can sleep at night. It doesn't mean you won't regret it for the rest of your life.

"The kid took off after some trouble in school. Miss Giles found him hiding out in the woods and took him in. She figured he needed some time before going back home. You know how Miss Giles is."

"That's all of it?" Walt asks.

"That's what went on," Julian says.

They stare at each other, and neither one blinks. Walt Hannen has a real good stare; he's been perfecting it for nearly twenty years.

"It's not a bad story," Walt says thoughtfully. "I just wish it were true."

Those brown buzzards that some people mistake for red-tailed hawks have begun to circle above them; they're already fighting over the feast laid out below.

"Well, yeah," Julian says finally. "That would be nice."

"I've got forty-three weeks left," Walt Hannen says. "Not that I'm counting."

"I think my story would look great on your record," Julian says. "It doesn't have any loose ends."

"No one's going to come looking for that baby?"

"Nope," Julian says. "Not in my lifetime."

"Well, the fact that it all ends up on your property is kind of a question mark," Walt tells him.

Walt's fairly certain he'll never know what happened here, he's not even sure he'd want to. But whatever it was, it's changed Julian Cash and probably a lot of other things, too. If Walt was just a little different, more like Roy Hadley, the chief over in Hartford Beach, he'd get to the bottom of all this; he wouldn't let the fate of a twelve-year-old boy or one of his men get in the way.

"I already told you," Julian says. "This property doesn't belong to me."

Walt Hannen looks up at the sky. As far as he can tell, Julian's still got good instincts. If anything, he's too unrelenting in his appraisal of what's right and what's wrong, and it's a good thing he isn't a judge, since most of the trespassers who came up before him would certainly hang.

"I hate buzzards." Walt sighs. When he retires he'll spend some time up near Lake Okeechobee. He'll finally be able to take Rose up to Atlantic City; he'll just surprise her one day and walk through the door with the plane tickets and the hotel reservations and maybe even a new dress to wear, since she's never liked to spend much money on herself. "Goddamned worthless creatures," he says of the buzzards.

Walt rises to his feet, and when he does Julian knows he's going to look the other way. He's going to let Julian write up his story just as if he believed it.

"Let's call Richie and get this guy out of here," Walt says.

They go back the way they've come, where the earth is so damp in spite of the heat that Arrow's pawprints can still be seen. Julian knows that most people believe a dog is worth less than a human, but they've never looked into a dog's eyes. They've never stood beside a dog when the moon rises and fills up the night.

"You know the only thing that could possibly bother me?" Walt says as they reach Julian's yard. "It's the thought that someone who's guilty is getting off easy. I'd hate that."

"No one who's guilty gets off easy," Julian tells him.

"Karma?" Walt says. His acupuncturist has mentioned it once or twice. When Julian looks at him, Walt explains, "You reap what you sow."

Julian nods. He believes in that. They have reached the cypress trees, and above them the merlins are unnaturally quiet. He will never be able to pass this place and not think of Arrow.

"I'm sorry about your dog," Walt Hannen says.

Julian manages to look away from the cypress trees. "Yeah, well, he never thought he was my dog," he says.

"I told you to get yourself a good Labrador retriever,"

Walt reminds him. "They can track anything a shepherd can."

"It wouldn't be the same," Julian says.

"You're goddamned right it wouldn't be." Walt grins. "A Lab would listen to you."

"Arrow listened to me. He just didn't give a crap about what I had to say."

Walt avoids the dog's grave as he goes to his car. He calls in for Richie to head over with an ambulance, so they can get the corpse in the woods to the morgue. Then he takes out some of the Juicy Fruit gum Rose has stocked in his glove compartment. Since he's in charge, at least for now, no one will question his decision to forgo an autopsy, no one will even know whether or not he contacts the state police about an ID check. Walt has always been social by nature: he plays poker with several guys on the Hartford Beach police force, he's got quite a few buddies he grew up with, and he and Rose often get together with some of the other Labrador retriever breeders they've gotten to know over the years. But he supposes that if he had to pick someone to stand by him, someone to trust, he'd choose Julian. He's not even sure of the reason why—maybe it's only because he happened to be on duty the night of the accident, or maybe he's just a good judge of character.

"I've got a new batch of puppies right now," Walt tells Julian as they lean on the porch railing, waiting for Richie. "Four yellow and two black. I'd give you a good deal."

"Do you ever get the feeling that your life isn't really your own, and you've just sort of let things happen to you?" Julian asks.

Walt looks at him, to make sure it's Julian Cash who's just strung so many words together.

"No," Walt admits. "Although I've felt something like that when I've gone to the mall in Hartford Beach with Rose."

Julian laughs out loud, but the laugh cracks midway and turns into something else. A gasp maybe, a tearing sound.

"Are you going to keep on talking like this, or is this just some sort of spell you're under?" Walt asks.

"I hate people who talk a lot," Julian says. "Now I'm one of them."

They can hear Richie's siren and Julian can gauge that he's just passed by Chuck and Karl's diner. Most likely, the people sitting in the booths by the window are craning their necks to see what's going on outside. Well, they can look all they want, they're never going to know the truth: that a hundred-pound dog could tear a man apart yet love a boy so much he wouldn't notice his own wounds, that a man like Julian could feel something after all this time.

"You're not cracking up on me or something like that?" Walt asks softly as Richie's car and the ambulance pull into the driveway and those damned merlins start to jabber.

Julian is staring at the place in the earth where the dog is buried, now and forever, beneath those cypress trees. Inside his house, Loretta is probably sleeping on the bed, though she knows she's not allowed. Twenty years ago, Julian could have wound up anywhere, but instead he found himself here, not four miles from where he was born. On that night, all the bees rose out of their hives in the woods, startled by his mother's cry. If she hadn't covered him with her dress, he might have been the one who was stung. If she hadn't run all the way to Miss Giles's house, he would never have been alive. Maybe he can remember it if he tries: the folds of her skirt, the bees so confused by the darkness they followed all the way to Miss Giles's front yard.

"Maybe you're the one who's cracking up," Julian tells Walt. "Maybe it's nicotine withdrawal. Ever think of that?"

"I never thought of that," Walt says, surprised to find he's actually relieved to hear Julian talking again.

Walt won't miss this job. He's getting out while his blood pressure's still in the high-normal range and his ulcer is under control. Richie Platt isn't ready to take on the job, and so Walt will probably have to look outside Verity when it comes to finding his replacement. It's not that he hasn't considered Julian. He has, in spite of the reaction he knows he'd get from the city council; he just couldn't do that to Julian. When Walt packs up his desk that will be the end of it, he won't look back, although there's the possibility that he will drive out here to Julian's every once in a while, when he's got nothing better to do, or when he just wants someone to talk to.

When Keith packs his suitcase two weeks later, he discovers that there's really not much he wants to take with him. A sweatshirt, his favorite jeans, his jar of pennies, and at the last minute, the tennis racket his father gave him last summer, even though he hasn't touched it since they moved and probably won't have time to use it this year, since he's signed up for summer school at Great Neck North. His father doesn't know everything, but he knows there's been trouble. He's already phoned to advise Keith that he'll have a curfew, ten o'clock, even on weekend nights, and Keith didn't argue with him. He's not going to bother to call Laddy Stern to say good-bye, since he probably won't be coming back. He's been given the option to stay in New York when the summer ends, if that's what he wants. But of course, the only thing he truly wants is his dog back, and he can't have that.

Since his voice returned, he hasn't used it much. He's talked to his father twice on the telephone, and to the super once, when the dishwasher overflowed and had to be fixed, and once to say thank you to Kitty Bass, who brought over a huge box of jelly doughnuts. What he's dreading most is the drive to the airport. He's managed to avoid his mother at home, but when they drive to the airport they'll be trapped together, just the two of them.

This morning, Keith woke up long before dawn, when there was still a moon in the sky. He'd been dreaming about the dog again, and when he woke his heart was racing. His broken ribs have been taped twice, but they still ache whenever he gets out of bed. He went through the darkened living room and out onto the balcony in his underwear, shivering. It was low tide and the scent of seaweed was bitter and sharp. Around this time the baby always startled in her sleep and had to be rocked for a while. Miss Giles might be a little deaf, but she always managed to hear when someone had trouble sleeping. If Keith was in her house, she'd come out of her bedroom in her robe and slippers and fix him some hot chocolate or tea, in spite of the hour.

He went out to say good-bye last evening. He took a taxi, which he paid for with his own money, and he brought with him a bundle of the clothes he'd borrowed from Miss Giles, all washed and folded. The baby was out by the rabbit cages; she'd been given a pan full of leaf lettuce and alfalfa sprouts. She'd gotten a little bit taller, she must have, because she could now push the rabbits' lettuce inside their cages. Since nobody knows her birthday, Miss Giles has let Keith pick, and he's chosen March first. On that day he'll always make certain to send her a present, no matter where he is, even if she forgets him completely.

Last evening he told the taxi to wait for him, since he knew he wasn't staying long. He got out and walked over to the rabbit cages, and as soon as the baby saw him she reached up her arms and said, "Uppy." It was a brand-new word, one he'd never heard her say before. He picked her up and held her near her favorite rabbit's cage and told himself it was a good thing that babies had such short memories. Already she was so crazy about these real live bunnies that she often forgot her stuffed toy on the floor of Miss Giles's kitchen, and she never used to let go of it, not for an instant; if anyone had tried to lift it out of her crib while she was sleeping she would have woken immediately and begun to cry.

He had never called her by her name or spoken to her, and he probably never would. When he put her down on the ground he could still feel how heavy she was that night when he ran along the drainage ditch carrying her. By next spring she wouldn't need any help feeding the rabbits; she'd drag an old wooden chair over and climb up all by herself to unlatch the highest cages. Keith let the taxi idle in the driveway, and as the meter ran, he bent down on one knee so the baby could hook her arms around his neck. She smelled like lemon juice and graham crackers. Miss Giles was watching from her kitchen window, she always did that, let you think you were on your own, when really she was watching over you all the time. Keith stood and carried the baby up to the porch, then put her down on the steps and nodded for her to go inside. After next March, when she

245

turned two, she might put her hands on her hips and shout "No," but now she went right inside and Keith knew she'd probably head for the kitchen table, where Miss Giles always doled out cookies and milk before bedtime, whether you were good or not.

All the wood Keith had chopped was neatly stacked beside the porch, and he was surprised to see just how much of it there was. Seeing that wood, he almost burst into tears, but instead he walked to the taxi and told the driver to take him back to Long Boat Street. And now, as he stands out on the balcony, looking at the beach below him, he realizes that he no longer remembers what summertime smells like in New York, but he will never forget the scent of cypress and seaweed and lemons. He could be in an airtight air-conditioned room on the other side of the planet, and he'd still remember.

He goes to his room, gets dressed, and finishes packing right then. By the time Lucy gets up at six, he's already in the kitchen having a glass of orange juice. Keith can tell she's upset, because she doesn't fix the yogurt and granola she has every morning; she just makes herself a cup of instant coffee, not even that drip stuff she prefers. She would never believe it, but none of what he has done or is about to do has anything to do with her. Keith thinks that Julian Cash might understand this; he would know that sometimes your life leads you to places where no one can follow, except, if you're lucky, a dog who for however brief a time might offer you complete devotion, no matter who you are.

He wishes he could stay with his mother and be who she wants him to be, but he can't do that. He's not angry or anything; it's just who he is. So he brushes his teeth, and washes his face, and gets his suitcase. The sun is breaking through the sky as they walk across the parking lot. In a matter of hours, heat waves will rise above the asphalt, and all the best shells left at low tide will be picked off the beach. Lucy fumbles with her keys, then finally unlocks the trunk of the Mustang so Keith can lift his suitcase inside.

"I just want you to know one thing," Lucy says, when they are both in the car, making sure not to look at each other. "You can always come back."

"Thanks." Keith nods.

"You don't have to thank me." Lucy's voice sounds strange, even to herself.

"I know I can come back," Keith says.

"Fine," Lucy says as she turns the key in the ignition.

The most jealous moments Lucy has ever had came when she watched other mothers in the park, whose toddlers clutched on to them. She remembers exactly how she felt whenever she saw a little boy reach for his mother's hand before crossing the street. She has heard, down in the laundry room, that some of the children get hysterical when summer vacation comes and a visit to their father means a separation from their mother. They can't sleep, they get the hiccups, they refuse to eat anything but toast and water, they cry all the way to the airport, then worry the flight attendants with bouts of nausea and red rashes that appear at the moment of takeoff. But as they near the airport in Hartford Beach, Keith opens his window and sticks his head out, scanning the sky for planes headed north.

Lucy parks in the short-term lot, gets out and unlocks the trunk, then starts to haul out the suitcase.

"I can take that," Keith says.

The early-morning sky is the color of a bluebird's egg.

"Really," Keith says when she won't let go of the suitcase. "I'll get it."

Lucy backs off and lets Keith carry the suitcase. With every step he takes, the jar of pennies inside rattles. By this afternoon he'll be where the lilacs grow taller than a man, where lawns are green and the nights so cool you rarely need air-conditioning.

"The plane stops once, in Atlanta," Lucy says. "But you don't have to get off. Just stay in your seat."

"Right," Keith says.

Inside the terminal, he goes to the check-in line and lifts the suitcase up to be tagged.

"I'm going to La Guardia," he tells the ticket agent. "Via Atlanta."

Hearing him say this as he fills out the luggage tag with his New York address, Lucy knows he's never really coming back, no matter what happens.

"All set?" Lucy asks.

Keith runs a hand through his hair and nods, but for a minute he looks slightly baffled. Lucy hugs him quickly, then, before he can pull away from her, she lets him go. Just yesterday, Lucy ran into Kitty and Janey Bass at the K Mart, where they were picking out new outfits with Shannon for her to take to Mount Holyoke. Lucy noticed that although all three of them were laughing, their eyes were as pink as rabbits'; they'd already spent days crying over Shannon's departure at the end of the week.

"Oh God, I'm such a baby," Janey had said. "I feel like I'm losing my little girl."

But Janey would never lose Shannon, that much was clear to Lucy from the way they were hugging each other in the sweater department. When it came time for Janey to take Shannon to the airport, Janey wouldn't have to swallow her tears, she wouldn't have this burning feeling in her throat.

248

"Well," Keith says, backing away from Lucy, "I guess it's time."

Lucy watches him walk past the metal detectors. She lowers her eyes, so she won't actually have to see him go through the boarding area, and then, after only a moment, he's gone. He has disappeared so completely it's as if he never existed at all, except that Lucy suddenly recalls the exact moment he was born. She remembers the fierce surge of pain, like a brand of devotion, and that last instant, when he was both separate from her and still a part of her own body.

She goes to the water fountain, and bends so she can drink deeply, but the water doesn't help the way she feels inside. When she turns to face the row of windows, she sees Julian at the far end of the terminal. He's arguing with a security guard.

"I'm just saying this is against policy," the security guard is telling him. But Julian's not listening; he's watching Lucy walk toward him.

"There's no turbulence today," Julian tells Lucy. "I checked."

Lucy looks past him so she can see the runway. The light outside is blinding; just one look and your eyes begin to sting.

"I guess I'm always going to hate airports," Julian says. He takes out his wallet, then flips it open to show the security guard his ID. The guard backs off, though he doesn't look happy. "All right?" Julian says to him.

Julian reaches down for a wooden crate, and when he shoves it toward the guard, Lucy hears a peculiar sound.

"What's in there?" she asks.

"I wouldn't be surprised if I never get on a plane again,"

Julian says. "Considering my last experience." He shifts his gaze to the security guard. "Want to do me that favor? Or do you want me to tail you every time you get in your car?"

Lucy watches the security guard carry the crate to the boarding gate. The terminal is supposed to be air-conditioned, but it's unbelievably hot.

"What makes you think he'll want that puppy?" Lucy asks.

"People want all sorts of things they never thought they would," Julian says. "You know that."

When the plane leaves the ground, Lucy and Julian both watch the sky. After the boy opens the wooden crate, somewhere above them, maybe he'll find a way to live with what's happened to him, and maybe Julian will too. It's amazing how many losses a person can bear. If Lucy walks away now, Julian will survive. He knows that as well as he knows that by noon the temperature will be in the high nineties. He can look at the long, thin clouds dissolve over the runway and be certain of what the weather holds. And, since it's the end of May, he can live with the heat too. People in Verity get used to it; it's no longer so daunting once May has passed. It's simply what you have to get through every day until the end of summer.

At around this time of the year, when Julian was a boy, Miss Giles used to take out her mosquito netting to hang over the beds. He remembers that when he used to sneak out at night, the mosquitoes zeroed in on Bobby and left him alone. He always wondered about that, whether he had some special sort of protection, or whether even mosquitoes didn't dare come too close to him. He has plucked a bee right out of the air and had it sit in the palm of his hand, too shocked to sting. He has had fire ants run away from his

shadow, so what can he expect from Lucy? The best he can
do is to keep his mouth shut as the plane taxis out on the
runway. When the plane has disappeared and he asks Lucy
if she needs a ride home, he knows she'll back away from
him. It is, after all, nearly the end of the month, the time
when people begin to snap out of whatever sort of spell
they've been under and realize just how close they came to
ruining their lives.

Lucy goes back to work the last Friday in May, and when
she gets to her desk she discovers that two women have died
the night before, of natural causes, over at the retirement
home on West Main. One of the women had been a school-
teacher in New Jersey, the other a homemaker for fifty-eight
years. They both left loved ones scattered all over the Eastern seaboard, children and grandchildren and great-grand-
children, all of whom owned woolen afghans that had been
knitted during hot afternoons on the porch of the retirement
home.

As she types, Lucy thinks of the obituary that will never
be written for Bethany Lee. She keeps Bethany's photograph
in her wallet, wedged between her driver's license and her
MasterCard, and it will still be there long after 8C is cleared
out and resold. For a while, Lucy wondered if Randy had
gotten off too easily; now she sees his punishment as just,
whether he knows it or not. He will never know how quickly
his child will learn her colors and numbers. He won't know
that when her hair is washed with lemon juice it will turn a
shade of gold you can't find anywhere else.

If she wrote the obituary for Bethany, there wouldn't be

space to list everything: the look on Bethany's face when she heard the cry on the intercom, the way she held her baby in the pool so she could kick her feet and pretend to swim, the way her heart beat, so fast it seemed like the heart of a dove, when she crossed the New York State line. Lucy would have to stick to the simple facts, and they don't even begin to tell the story of someone's life. She's tired of that. And so after Lucy finishes her last two obituaries, she packs up her desk. She intends to resign on Monday; there's no reason to drag it out. If she's learned one thing from this job, it's that every second she wastes becomes morning, afternoon, long cool evening.

She leaves at exactly five o'clock, and as it turns out, it is still the hour she dreads, only now it's because she no longer has Keith to argue with. She can do whatever she wants, but that's just it. She ties a scarf around her head before going out to her car. The Mustang is driving much better; Evan had the radiator replaced before sending it back from New York. Lucy stops at the 7-Eleven for yogurt and soda and a small package of chicken wings, then drives home. But when she gets to Long Boat Street, she pulls over to the side of the road instead of making the turn into the parking lot. It is the time when you can sense evening falling, even though the sky is still filled with light. You can almost tell what it used to be like here, before there were condominiums and paved streets. Right here, in the parking lot of 27 Long Boat, there was a small pond where alligators slept, submerged beneath the murky water, called to the surface by the yellow light in May.

Lucy puts her car in reverse and backs up, then heads out toward the marshes. She turns off her air conditioner and opens all the windows, in spite of the gnats and the sticky air. When she gets there the merlins dive at her car, then retreat to the tops of the trees. Every nest they make is wound out of cypress leaves and willow branches; not one has ever toppled to the ground. Julian's car isn't in the driveway, but Lucy gets out anyway. The piles of hay in the empty kennel are a rich, golden color. They haven't been touched, and they'll stay exactly as they are until a heavy rain mats them down. But out in the woods, the dog's last pawprints have already disappeared; they've been covered by leaves and a layer of sand.

There are no parakeets here, so Lucy reaches up and takes off her scarf. She's glad she cut her hair. She lives in Florida now, after all. She can't help but stare at the vines that grow along Julian's porch; they're so old no one can remember who planted them. Surely not Charles Verity, who never gave a damn about gardens, but he did have a daughter, and it's quite possible that she was as different from her father as most children are from their parents. It's possible that she stood outside this house at exactly this time of day, at this exact time of year, to watch what she planted grow.

Lucy knows she should start home. It's nearly dinnertime and she's got a sack of groceries in the backseat of her car, but instead she goes up to the porch that hasn't been painted for years. All along the porch steps there are spider webs and stones, but Lucy sits down anyway. The fact is, it's too hot to cook and the sky is filled with light and she's driven all the way out here, she might just as well stay. If they get used to her, if she comes here often enough, those merlins in the trees might begin to recognize her. They might come right up to the porch railing if she leaves out breadcrumbs and rice.

253

During the dinner hour the parking lot is always crowded. Gas fumes rise into the orange sky as cars idle; clouds turn crimson. If the Angel cranes his neck he can see through the plate-glass window to where teenage boys in uniforms work behind the counter. There are the customers, waiting for their supper. There are the children, held by the hand. The gumbo-limbo tree is completely empty now. No birds nest here anymore. Even the fire ants have fled. The Angel feels as if he's been coated with glue; it's not easy to lift his feet and he hasn't tried to climb into the higher branches for quite a while. Sometimes he paces out the radius of the circle he has to stay in, other times he just stands there, not moving, for hours or days.

He knows what he'll feel at the moment of his release: the cold blue reaches of the sky above him, the weightless flight, uncharted, even by birds. The Angel waits for that moment, growing paler in these last few hours of the month. He is standing there, beneath the tree, when Julian Cash pulls into the parking lot. Julian should be on his way home, he wants to go home, he's dead tired and he has to feed Loretta, but instead he finds a space near the drive-in window. He sits in his car for a while, then locks his gun in the glove compartment and tells Loretta to stay. Twenty years ago he never would have imagined they'd actually go ahead and cut down all those gumbo-limbos to make room for a fast-food restaurant. Not that he's against fast food; it serves its purpose, he'd be the first to agree to that. He just figures you can never get those gumbo-limbos to grow as tall again. You'd have to wait about five hundred years. Those trees used to be filled with birds, especially in the early evening. The sound could spook you if you weren't used to it. You'd swear the trees had a voice of their own.

Julian gets out of the car and slams the door shut behind him, then starts walking toward the last tree. He thinks about all the stupid, senseless things he's done in his life; he thinks about the trees he and Bobby climbed together so long ago. Before the Interstate, before the beach was anything more than a tangled mass of sea grape and sand, there were thousands of stars in the sky; they could make you dizzy if you stared up for too long. For as far back as he can remember, Julian has heard the sound of bees. He hears them now, even though it's twilight, or maybe the sound is inside him. Maybe it's always been that way.

Twenty years ago, beneath this tree, everything changed forever, except for Bobby. He is so young, and the white shirt he wore that night is still just as clean. He rises to his feet and walks through the grass, and his grin grows wider when he sees his cousin, just as it always did when he'd throw stones at Julian's window, then wait for him to tag along. Past the mangroves and the air plants, past the twisted live oaks. They never needed flashlights because they knew the way back home. They still do.

Julian has never seen anything more brilliant than the light above him. A light like this could blind a man, but that doesn't stop him from looking at the sky. He will always remember this color blue, and he'll go on remembering it for the rest of his life. For a long time the gumbo-limbo tree will seem to shudder once a year, on the third day of May, but it will be nothing more than the songbirds in the tallest branches, and Julian Cash will probably be the only one to notice, since he's the only one who cares.